# ADAM'S
## SECRET

Text copyright © 2011 by Guillermo Ferrara

English translation copyright © 2012 by Diane Stockwell

*Adam's Secret* was first published in 2011 by Santillana Ediciones Generales, S. L. Translated from Spanish by Diane Stockwell. Published in English by AmazonCrossing in 2012.

Published by AmazonCrossing
P.O. Box 400818
Las Vegas, NV 89140

ISBN-13: 9781612185613
ISBN-10: 1612185614
Library of Congress Control Number: 2012940299

# ADAM'S
## SECRET

### GUILLERMO FERRARA

Translated by Diane Stockwell

**amazon**crossing 🌐

For my mother, Maria del Carmen Fritz, who carried me inside her body for nine months.

In honor of the goddess inside of you and all women.

And to my father, Julio Ferrara, of generous Italian blood, and to our ancestors.

To Barry Gibb of the Bee Gees: your voice and melodies are my spiritual inspiration. And the memories of Andy, Maurice, and Robin.

To Demis Roussos and Vangelis: your music can vibrate my soul too.

Now the serpent was more subtle than any other wild creature that the Lord God had made. He said to the woman, "Did God say, 'You shall not eat of any tree of the garden'?" And the woman said to the serpent, "We may eat of the fruit of the trees of the garden, but God said, 'You shall not eat of the fruit of the tree which is in the midst of the garden, neither shall you touch it, lest you die.'" But the serpent said to the woman, "You will not die. For God knows that when you eat of it your eyes will be opened, and you will be like God, knowing good and evil."

Genesis 3:1–5

Our world of hatred and materialism will end on December 21, 2012. On that date, humanity must choose between disappearing as an intelligent species that threatens to destroy the planet, or evolving toward harmonic integration with the whole universe, understanding that everything is alive and conscious, that we are part of everything, and that we can exist in a new age of light.

Fernando Malkun, excerpt from *Infinite: The Masters of Time*

# Author's Note

Highly respected scientists and archeologists from around the world have studied the Mayan prophecies, and six out of seven prophecies from the wise Mayan astronomers and mathematicians have come to pass. The seventh reveals a critical, transcendent change for all of humanity that will take place in 2012.

All of the information found in this novel—from details on the human genetic code to Atlantis to information about the ancient Mayans, Egyptians, Gnostics, Greeks, and mystical sexual practices—has been researched and documented through careful studies and through my own explorations. The diverse institutions, books, and projects that appear in this book all really exist.

All of the names of the characters in this book are fictitious. But the names of famous archeologists, researchers, organizations, historical people, and events are real, as are the monuments, dates, symbols, and works of art that figure in these pages.

# New York, July 18, 2012

dam Roussos snapped awake when the phone next to his bed rang. The digital clock on the nightstand said it was five in the morning in the city that never sleeps. The loud, insistent ringing brought an abrupt end to his deep sleep, ripping him out of a vivid dream of a warm, tropical beach. Groggy and disoriented, he rolled his six-foot frame over the white satin sheets and fumbled for the receiver. It took some effort to speak.

"Mmmm. Hello," he mumbled.

"Adam! My dear friend, it's me, Aquiles. I'm in Greece."

"Aquiles? Aquiles Vangelis?" Adam pushed himself up to a sitting position at the sound of his friend's voice. "How wonderful to hear from you. But do you know what time it is over here?"

"I know, I know," the older man said, almost in a whisper, "but believe me, it can't wait. Don't worry, it's not bad news. Just the opposite, in fact."

Adam took in a deep breath. "I understand, but couldn't it wait until the morning?" He rubbed his half-shut brown eyes to convince himself he wasn't still dreaming. "What's this all about? What's so important?"

"I can't tell you much over the phone." Aquiles sounded agitated. "But I've discovered something that could change everything. Adam, please, I need you here in Greece!"

Adam was fully awake now. "But…"

"It's very important that you come," Aquiles insisted. "I have to see *you*. You're the only one who can help me with what I've discovered; you're a sexologist and an expert in religions," he argued. "My discovery is not only about sexuality, but also Christianity and the ancient city of Atlantis. If this miraculous finding is what I have a feeling it is, I swear to you we're going to be a huge headache for Christianity and all the other religions."

Adam was reluctant to be too swayed by Aquiles's enthusiasm, especially at such an early hour. "I understand," he said, "but I have to look at my calendar. I have conferences, patients—"

"Find someone on your staff to cover for you, Adam," Aquiles cut him off. "None of that matters, not when what I have waiting for you here could be the most important adventure of your life."

Adam tried to think clearly. Aquiles was known for his passionate nature, but the plea in his voice was strong even for him. "Okay, whatever you've discovered is obviously remarkable, Aquiles. I'll figure out how to manage it later today."

"I'm counting on you, my friend. What I've found…" He paused, holding his breath. "It will shock you. And not just you, but the whole world." With that, he hung up.

An abrupt silence, quickly followed by a whirlwind of thoughts—like a wild swarm of buzzing bees—ran through

Adam Roussos's mind. He got out of bed and went into the kitchen to make some coffee. Through the large window in his bedroom, the lead-gray sky barely hinted at daybreak in New York. A shudder ran the length of Adam's spine as his bare feet left the warmth of the parquet floors in his living room and settled on the cold marble in the kitchen. He had to get his thoughts in order.

Aquiles Vangelis—an eccentric, vigorous, powerful man, in spite of his lean frame—was very dedicated and a man of his word. He'd worked for two decades as a consultant on scientific archeology and educational paleontology for UNESCO, which had earned him considerable political and social influence. For the last twenty-five years he had also been on a tireless personal quest to find the ruins of Atlantis, undertaking more than fifty unofficial expeditions to search for any physical manifestations of the ancient civilization that the Greek philosopher Plato had written about thousands of years before in his dialogues *Critias* and *Timaeus*.

With those projects conducted well outside of the establishment, Professor Vangelis endangered not only his life but also his career as an archeologist and paleontologist. Serious scientists, it was understood, viewed Atlantis as a myth and a legend, not as an actual place.

Aquiles had spoken with conviction and confidence, Adam reflected. He knew he'd be able to persuade Adam to drop everything and join him; after all, Aquiles had been instrumental in getting Adam his current job at the Sexuality Institute. At only forty, Adam had been named director, a job that, aside from his professional skills, he had won in no small part because of Professor Vangelis's personal intervention.

Adam sipped his coffee, absently running a hand through his thick hair, trying to get a handle on this latest development. Whenever he needed to think, Adam did two things: ran his fingers through his curls and then rested his index finger along the side of his Greek nose. Finally he stood up and paced while glints of light reflected off a crystal statue on his mantle and danced along the walls.

Adam Roussos was known in New York as Doctor Love. Television shows and magazines often interviewed him about his revolutionary sexual healing practices. The release of his book *Metaphysical Mysteries of Human Sexuality* had rocked the publishing world, and some universities made the text part of their curricula. Reviewers had credited the book with opening a door to understanding sexuality that centuries of religious and moralistic societies had kept firmly closed.

Adam enjoyed an excellent reputation, considerable financial resources, and a very comfortable lifestyle. He threw himself into his work, obtaining excellent results for his long list of patients. He loved his life, but he also had a restless spirit. He craved adventure and discovery, and he was tempted by archeology's siren song. He was also tempted by his beloved Greece, the land he had left behind a decade earlier. He missed its customs, food, dance, and people. He missed its sun. He hadn't been back since his father's death some years before. Before that, he used to go back every summer to visit his parents and friends and to enjoy the bright Mediterranean sun on the islands.

If he accepted Aquiles's request, he would just have to move his vacation forward by a month, which he had been planning on taking in August. He needed to put his thoughts and feelings in order.

He jumped into the shower, letting his mind go blank for a moment under the cascade of warm water. When he left the bathroom, the clock on the wall read six thirty in the morning, and he pushed aside all his uncertainty. With a determined stride, he walked to his desk, a towel loosely wrapped around his waist and his hair still dripping wet. He turned on his laptop and bought a seat on the next flight to Athens, scheduled to depart the following day.

Adam's friendship with Aquiles Vangelis stretched back almost twenty years, when Nikos Roussos, Adam's father, had gone to live on the island of Thira, now known as Santorini. Aquiles kept his scientific and archeological labs there, and it was where he spent most of his time feverishly researching everything that had to do with the mysterious civilization of Atlantis.

Nikos Roussos had also spent years chasing after Atlantis—named for the mythical hero Atlas, son of Poseidon—and its technological, mystical, and spiritual advances. A mutual colleague introduced the two men at one of the many UNESCO events they both attended, and they'd become constant collaborators. Within the scientific community, anyone who was actually searching for Atlantis was labeled as "incurably insane," but Nikos and Aquiles turned a deaf ear to the insults and jokes. The archeologists shared a mutual love of Plato, who'd written of Atlantis in some of his works. But Aquiles and Nikos had more than just a shared professional and philosophical passion in common; they were also both divorced—almost at the same time—because they were unable to balance the demands of a marriage with their relentless research pursuits.

Nikos Roussos had been on a submarine mission examining archeological remains in Santorini when a vicious, unpredicted storm unleashed its fury in the Aegean Sea. Nikos went missing. Though his body was never recovered, he was officially declared dead. The other members of the research team had better luck that day, and Nikos was the only casualty.

An extroverted, rebellious, challenging man, throughout his life Nikos moved wildly between passionate emotion and analytical thought. Adam was much more even-keeled and liked to believe, as Aristotle did, that "virtue lies in the middle."

Nikos was known around the globe for his work defending the natural world and the relics of ancient Greeks. One of his campaigns had been to convince the British Museum to return Greek sculptures and tapestries to their rightful home. He had a voice within the highest circles of political power and had helped people understand the urgency of global warming years before Al Gore became the issue's poster child.

Adam had inherited his father's research documents. But it was Aquiles who continued to search for Atlantis.

Since Nikos's body was never recovered, it was especially hard for Adam to bring any sort of closure to his grieving. He had a nagging sense that the calm exterior he exuded belied something very unclear, and very raw, underneath.

Though Adam hadn't been back to Greece in several years, he had been planning to take a vacation there over the summer—just not quite as soon as Aquiles wanted him to. He'd been looking forward to the trip—to enjoying the sun, sand, and food, to relaxing after a long year of hard work. Now, however, he didn't know what was in store. *Knowing Aquiles, it could be anything*, he thought. His old friend had sounded so urgent on the phone, as if his very life depended on Adam flying to Greece.

And as it would turn out, it did.

# 3

# ATHENS, JULY 20, 2012

**K**alimera!" said the attractive young woman in the information booth at Eleftherios Venizelos Airport in the Greek capital.

"*Kalimera*," Adam responded in his native Greek.

It was a sunny day, a very "good morning" indeed, with a light breeze and not a cloud in the sky, typical weather for the summer months in Athens.

"Can I help you with anything?"

"No, thank you, I'm fine," he said politely. "I'm waiting for a friend; he's probably just running late."

Adam smiled warmly at the young woman before continuing on to the waiting area. He took off his black jacket, as the lightweight, dark-blue button-down shirt he had on underneath was all the weather required.

People came and went; taxi drivers and greeters stood with signs indicating whom they were meeting. As in all major airports, the shops, bright lights, loud colors, and sounds bombarded newcomers as they tried to adjust and navigate the new territory. Adam was better off than most; he knew the place like the back of his hand. He had passed through that airport countless times since he was a boy traveling with his father.

Just a few minutes after disembarking, Adam remembered to turn his BlackBerry back on. It immediately alerted him that he had received two text messages. The first read, "Welcome to Greece. The Cosmote Company will bring you the wireless service you need throughout our country. Enjoy your stay."

When he opened the second, he found a chilling message:

MY FATHER HAS DISAPPEARED.

ADAM, CALL ME RIGHT AWAY.

I'M SCARED.

ALEXIA

Adam's face drained of all color. A chill ran up his spine as he instantly relived the years of grief he had experienced after his own father had disappeared. Instinctively he swiveled his head around, searching the crowd in vain for a familiar face. His heart began to pound, his breath grew shallow, and his veins swelled, like a thoroughbred just before a race. He didn't see a soul he knew. He was disoriented and confused. *How could Aquiles just disappear?*

A thousand questions whirled through his head like a carousel. He sat down in the first empty seat he could find. His body temperature continued to rise, and beads of sweat began to run down his face.

Alexia Vangelis was Aquiles's daughter. When they first met, Adam was twenty-two and she was only fifteen. They were together frequently, not only because of their fathers' work, but because they lived on the same small island. With his thumb, Adam quickly dialed Alexia.

"*Parakalo*," a woman's voice answered.

"Alexia? Is that you? What happened?"

"Adam, I don't know, it's all so confusing…My father's disappeared!"

"But, where? When? I just talked to him two days ago." Adam took a deep breath to try to calm himself.

"Listen," Alexia said calmly, "we need to meet. It's very important that we talk. Make sure no one follows you."

"That no one follows me? Alexia, what's going on?"

"No one knows you're coming, but be careful. Something extraordinarily important is at stake. Let's meet in an hour at the Five Brothers bar. It's on Aiolou Street, close to the Greek National Bank, at the foot of the Acropolis."

"Yes, I know it. I'll be there in an hour."

Adam stared at his BlackBerry, grave-faced, his mind in a blur. He left his black suitcase at a luggage check. He kept his wallet, cell phone, notebook, and a pen and quickly left to catch a taxi.

# 4

Viktor Sopenski's bulging eyes seemed ready to burst from their sockets. The obese police officer looked every bit of his fifty years. His gleaming bald spot was just as prominent as his humongous belly, which was the result of his addictions to beer and fast food.

He'd been born in Albania and raised in the United States after his family immigrated. Shunned by the American kids, he'd been a loner through high school. Somehow he'd made his way through high school and college, and after graduation he'd joined the investigative unit of the New York City Police Department. But the damage of a lifetime spent alone or fighting had been done.

As the years passed, he became cozy with the more renegade, corrupt elements of the department; he ended up working as a strongman for the powerful international organization known as the Secret Government. He was considered a captain, and they called him the Vulture because of his cunning, his animal instinct, and his merciless approach when it came time to devour his prey.

The Secret Government was a wide-reaching organization, a complex, inscrutable web with members in the highest ranks of power within the US, Russian, and European governments. It was also connected to a powerful global financial entity, the Bilderberg Club, which operated secretly under the cover of the Freemason fraternity.

Supported by a turbulent, dominant hierarchy within the Catholic Church, the Secret Government aimed to develop and consolidate economic, social, psychological, and religious power. They had scientists, high-ranking military officers, and representatives of global pharmaceutical interests on their payroll. The Secret Government not only kept its structure a secret, it was practically impossible to figure it out. To ensure this, lower-ranking members of the organization were not allowed to know the identities of everyone within the group. They knew who their immediate superiors were and not much else.

That morning Viktor Sopenski wore a light-blue shirt dotted with sweat marks under a tightly fitting brown suit and a loosened dark-blue necktie. His bad taste in clothing—which did nothing to conceal the poor state of his body—was compensated for by his single-minded, unyielding pursuit of those who, as he put it, "tried to violate the system."

Aquiles sat on a chair with his hands and feet tightly bound, in the middle of a dark, dank, smoke-filled room. Sopenski's right-hand man, Claude Villamitre, a skinny, hunched-over Frenchman of almost forty-five with an ever-present cigarette in hand, was clearly experiencing the grim toll nicotine and tobacco had on his weary lungs. He would do anything Captain Sopenski asked. Countless times the ungraceful Villamitre had proven his steadfast loyalty to the captain, performing the dirtiest of jobs without hesitation. They both drew two salaries: their New York City police officer wages—of relatively modest proportions—and a very generous monthly payment from the Secret Government. The latter quickly silenced whatever faint voice of ethical doubt their consciences were capable of producing.

Though the men lived in New York, they were in Greece for "an extremely high-priority, confidential job," as Sopenski's boss had explained over the phone. His direct superior, whom he had never met in person, was called the Magician. He was always very demanding when he delivered the orders for a job and very generous when it came to paying for every bit of "extra work."

A third man was in the room with the kidnapped archeologist. He was known as the Owl because of his very large, round, light-blue eyes, and he stood partially hidden in the shadows. His face obscured in darkness, all that was visible was his fine, jet-black Italian shoes under an expensive, well-tailored black suit. He seemed to emanate a fine mist of cologne, giving off an intense scent of patchouli.

Sopenski addressed Aquiles coldly. "As you might have already guessed, Professor Vangelis, we don't treat people with the classic Greek hospitality," he said dryly as he glanced over at Villamitre.

Blinded by a bright light shining directly into his eyes, Aquiles didn't move. He kept his eyes closed so as not to be subjected to the glare, and remained absolutely silent.

"I see that you want to protect your name, Aquiles," the Frenchman said ironically, pronouncing his name slowly, with a look of disdain.

Aquiles broke into a sweat under the harsh light.

Villamitre poured some vodka into a plastic cup and brought it to the man observing the scene from the shadows, motionless and attentive. The Owl refused the offering with a brusque gesture with his left hand, a fine Rolex around his wrist. The Frenchman sneezed after inhaling the strong cologne wafting from the mysterious man he'd only recently met. Claude Villamitre did not trust the man, and he hated the strong patchouli smell he gave off.

Sopenski gripped Aquiles's wrists so tightly the blood flow to his hands was cut off. Aquiles let out a moan from the pain.

"Let's get right to the point, Professor Vangelis," Sopenski growled. "Don't waste our time, and we won't hurt you. Just tell us what we need to know, and everyone's happy."

Aquiles gasped as the pain in his arms intensified. His stomach turned over and over like a rugby ball in the middle of a match.

"I won't tell you anything." Unable to defend himself, the only thing Aquiles had left was the integrity of his spirit.

"Fine," Viktor Sopenski said curtly. "I get the picture. You want all the fame and glory so you can show off to your little professor friends, right? I don't know what it is with you Greeks and personal glory. I'll never understand it."

"I guess you wouldn't know anything about it. Glory is only for the brave."

"Oh, right," Sopenski said sarcastically. "I suppose you must be very brave indeed, Professor. I'll tell you what you are." His voice rose. "Another ass-kisser, *desperate* to be recognized for your discoveries. You're nothing more than a senile old man with delusions of grandeur." He pronounced his words slowly, spitting them into Aquiles's face.

Blinded by the light, Aquiles couldn't see well, but he sensed the man was mere inches from him by the onslaught of his putrid breath.

"If they are just an old man's delusions," he replied, "I don't see why you're so interested in getting information out of me."

"My superiors believe you're a threat."

"Then your superiors are the delusional ones."

"I am running out of patience!" Sopenski shouted. "I'm not here to have some kind of dialogue with you. I am *a soldier*," he emphasized. "I'm required to act, Professor Vangelis."

Aquiles felt suffocated. Little air circulated through the windowless room, and his three inquisitors seemed to be breathing all of it.

Sopenski saw the man in the shadows move his right hand. He nodded.

"Proceed," he ordered Villamitre.

The Frenchman put his cigarette in his mouth and stooped to pick something up from the floor. He plugged the apparatus into an outlet, and it started to hum. When it touched Aquiles's body, it unleashed an electrical shock designed to simulate a hundred bees stinging at the same time.

Vangelis controlled himself in the face of the pain, although he felt like screaming, more out of a sense of powerlessness than actual physical agony.

"You should know that my assistant enjoys this, but we don't like to waste time. We need results," Sopenski snarled.

The Frenchman threw a powerful punch that connected with Aquiles's cheek. Aquiles felt one of his incisors fly out of his mouth onto the floor, and a stream of blood gushed out.

"Look, Professor Vangelis," Sopenski said, excited by the sight of blood like a predator moving in for the kill, "I will be very clear. If you do not want to suffer the same fate as your colleague—what was his name? Oh, yes! Professor Nikos Roussos—then I would ask you to be smart and tell us what you know."

Aquiles turned his head, furious. "I knew Nikos didn't die a natural death. You sons of bitches!" he yelled, spitting out blood.

Sopenski and Villamitre laughed.

"Killers!" Aquiles shouted, enraged, his voice a dark clap of thunder.

Aquiles knew Nikos had been threatened on a few occasions, but neither one of them had taken the threats very seriously. Threats were common in the world of off-the-record research; most independent scientists who poked around in controversial areas received them sooner or later. There were certain discoveries that people did not want made public, whatever their motivations. But even though his friend's disappearance had always unsettled Aquiles, he hadn't gone so far as to truly believe foul play. Now he knew better.

"Do you think I'm afraid of death at my age?" There was no response. "People searching for truth, working in the light, have been persecuted ever since the Inquisition. Honest scientists have always been persecuted by the powerful!" Aquiles shouted furiously. "Your methods have not changed since the Middle Ages."

Aquiles forced himself to try to get his bearings. All he could see was a shiny chain with a crucifix resting against Villamitre's chest, the mark of a blind faith that the crooked man might one day call on to straighten out the disastrous course of his life.

"Professor," Sopenski said, as if he were addressing a disobedient child who refused to leave the playground, "people like you and your friend Nikos have gone out of style. You have no place in *our world*. You want to go beyond what our establishment allows. Now, what's it going to be? Cooperate with the establishment or meet the same end as your friend?"

Once again Villamitre delivered a painful shock to the middle of Aquiles's back.

This time, Aquiles let out a piercing wail.

"Talk! What did you find in Santorini? What were you doing there?" Sopenski screamed at the top of his lungs.

Silence and smoke.

The mysterious man in the shadows turned and opened the only door in the little room, letting in a bit of fresh air as he left. His mission had been to see the archeologist. His work was done.

*I know that scent*, Aquiles thought as he breathed in the man's cologne, the strong smell of patchouli sparking a foggy memory.

Just then Sopenski's cell phone rang.

"Yes?"

The voice on the other ended sounded clipped and authoritative.

"He hasn't talked yet, sir, but he will soon."

The voice on the line replied, prompting Sopenski to crack a malicious smile.

"Excellent idea. I'll do just as you say, sir," he said, nodding. "I'll call you as soon as I have news to report."

For the next two minutes, Viktor Sopenski was silent as he slowly paced around Aquiles, a shark circling his victim before the attack.

The obese captain whispered something to Villamitre, who smiled diabolically, exposing his gray, nicotine-stained teeth.

"I know just what we'll do, brave professor," Sopenski said deliberately. He paused before continuing. "We'll ask your daughter instead. How does that sound?"

Aquiles felt an enormous weight come crashing down on him. He didn't have the strength to even try to escape. He drew in as deep a breath as he could in that airless room. *My daughter is worth much more than my secret*. He could withstand any attack on himself, but with her, it was different.

Aquiles adored his daughter—she was his pride and joy. He'd sent Alexia to the very best private schools in Athens and had always been very involved in her life. Despite his consuming work, he'd made time for her. He taught her about the ancient gods and instilled her with a love and appreciation for nature while shielding her from the rituals of guilt and remorse that he felt marked their community; more pointedly, he protected her from the influence of the Catholic Church.

Aquiles strongly rejected everything related to the Catholic Church. He was an old-fashioned Greek and thought that the invasion of the church into Hellenistic lands had destroyed the younger generation's appreciation of beauty, pleasure, and human perfection, as well as their love of wisdom and respect for the ancient gods. Aquiles believed the church trivialized the individual and made people dependent on bizarre moralities and scornful, unnatural ideas.

"Ever since they came to Greece, there's been no more Socrates or Plato or Aristotle or the Acropolis—just existential mediocrity," he frequently argued. In part, Aquiles's goal was to vindicate the ancient Greeks and, going back even further in time, the Minoics and people of Atlantis.

But now, all that mattered was the safety of his daughter. He thought quickly, trying to see a way out.

*I hope Alexia realizes what's happened and acts accordingly.* He knew the chances were good—she was smart, independent, and free-spirited.

"All right," Aquiles finally said. "I'll tell you what I've found, but leave my daughter out of it." He sounded tired and beaten.

Sopenski brought his face a mere ten inches from Aquiles's. "I'm pleased you're being reasonable." He took a small digital recorder out of his pocket. "I knew you'd be more intelligent than brave in the end, Professor Vangelis. After all," he added, a triumphant smile playing on his lips, "every man has a weak spot."

# 5

The Mercedes-Benz C-270 Adam rode in sped along at ninety miles an hour over the warm asphalt. It took the yellow taxi over thirty-five minutes to reach downtown Athens since the airport was located well outside the metro area. Then they headed for the south side of the historic city, down Adakimias Street toward Kolonaki Square, the posh neighborhood that was home to many traditional cafés and upscale Greek restaurants. Adam could see his beloved Mount Likavitos from there. The highest point in the city, it afforded the best views of the Acropolis and the Parthenon.

In less than ten minutes, they continued toward the National Garden, first passing by the Parliament building, where a changing of the Greek National Guard happened to be taking place, in honor of the Unknown Soldier. A hundred tourists were gathered around to watch the spectacle of the two impressive soldiers, called *epsones*, who had to march back and forth over ninety yards. They wore a highly unusual uniform including a man's skirt with four hundred pleats, symbolizing all the years the Turks had occupied Greece, and most fascinating of all, they wore shoes that weighed six pounds each. The whole uniform was made up of fifty pieces. That ritual, which Adam could see from his taxi—and which he had watched many times as a boy—came right before their entrance into Sintagma Plaza, the nerve center of Athens. People freely came and went on foot, in cars and buses careening by at a breakneck pace typical of the fast rhythm of any world capital.

A jumble of thoughts ran through Adam's mind at the same rapid, chaotic rate as the traffic. He was confused and very worried. His meditation practice was the only thing that would allow him to stay calm and think clearly. He had been taking classes with his meditation and yoga teacher for three years at the Meditation Center in New York. She liked to tell her students that to solve a problem, sometimes you had to *stop thinking* to arrive at the solution. Even Einstein had written that problems are not solved in the same mental state that created them.

The Mercedes slowed down as they drove through the narrow streets of the Plaka neighborhood—the oldest part of the city—under the Acropolis. It took little effort to imagine the neighborhood as it had been in ancient times, to envision Plato or Pericles among the pedestrians. Socrates himself used to walk around the neighborhood thousands of years before.

Even now, there were archeologists hard at work right in the middle of the city, excavating and discovering vases and bowls, ancient dwellings and columns, while curious tourists surrounded them, hoping for a photo op.

"I have to leave you here," the driver explained. "This area is for pedestrians only."

"That's fine—I need to stretch my legs."

"*Parakalo.*"

Since he had no luggage to carry, he just put on his black jacket, in spite of the heat, and his blue Ray-Bans.

The outer walls along Plaka were over six thousand years old and gave the impression that time had stopped, even though Monastiraki Plaza had been renovated and updated.

Greek *sirtaki* music wafted out of some bars and shops, forming a backdrop for the throngs of tourists and others relaxing in the outdoor cafés, drinking their frappés. As tourism was one of the largest sectors of the economy, the area was packed with shops selling local crafts, jewelry, keepsakes, miniature statues of gods and mythical heroes, and models of ancient helmets worn by soldiers in the infamous battles of Troy and Sparta.

But Adam barely noticed any of it as he walked briskly through the crowds to meet Alexia. He sat down at a table in the shade next to the street.

"*Kalispera*," said a waiter.

"*Kalispera*," Adam answered, although this particular afternoon was anything but good. "I'd just like some very cold mineral water, please."

Although the waiter had understood Adam's flawless Greek pronunciation, he frowned impatiently. The restaurant's owners wanted tourists to order as much to eat and drink as possible instead of soaking up the spectacular view of the Parthenon from a comfortable table that was worth much more than the cost of a soda.

Adam glanced at his watch—it was already four forty in the afternoon. The temperature had reached ninety degrees that day, and it was still very warm. Adam closed his eyes behind his sunglasses, trying to relax for a moment, but opened them quickly when he heard his name.

"Hey, Adam!"

He looked over his right shoulder to see the woman who called him from inside a black Citroën C4. She gazed at him from behind a pair of large brown sunglasses, with a silk scarf tied around her head. She looked like a movie star right out of Hollywood's golden years; she could have been a stand-in for the legendary Ava Gardner.

The young woman, who a month before had just turned thirty-four, took the blue scarf off her head, letting a cascade of dark hair fall in waves down her back. She took off her sunglasses, and her almond eyes were like warm rays of sunlight shining on Adam.

Alexia wore a white dress of crisp Italian linen, along with an accessory that immediately caught Adam's attention: a necklace with an unusual white gemstone. Adam felt a sense of peace settle over him as he looked at her. He'd always believed that the reason some religious traditions required women to cover their faces, the reason these traditions forbade women from assuming power, was that they feared their allure would unravel men's abilities to think rationally. "When men take the time to really take in a woman's beauty, they see visions of paradise," he often said at his conferences.

Alexia was not only attractive, she was sensual—much more so than the last time he'd seen her, years before. She looked as though she'd been plucked from a lush garden of ancient Babylonia, Sparta, or Persia. Her beauty was not of this century. Hers was an exquisite, ancestral beauty of the old empires, of queens and empresses.

"Let's go, Adam. We have to hurry."

He left a two-euro coin on the table and headed for the waiting car.

"*Teia gou!*" she said in greeting, in a tone that conveyed warmth and urgency all at once.

"Alexia? Is it really you? I'm sorry, I wouldn't have even recognized you. It's been years."

"Get in. We have to get out of here," she said tensely, and hit the gas.

"How did you manage to drive in this area? They don't allow cars here."

She pointed to a card on the dashboard: "AUTHORIZED. EXCLUSIVE ACCESS."

"Don't forget my father is a very influential man."

Alexia drove like a professional, exiting the historic district within minutes. She sped down two more blocks on Nikodimou, turned and headed up Amalias, took a zigzag route up two smaller streets, and then finally came out on Pindarou right under the famous Likavitos monument.

Seeing a green light ahead, Alexia accelerated. The burst of speed made Adam lean back even farther in his seat.

"What's going on with your father?" he asked, cutting straight to the point.

Aquiles's daughter gave him a sidelong glance as she deftly maneuvered past cars and taxis. "This morning we were supposed to meet at his house and then go to the airport together to pick you up. He was thrilled to have finally found what he'd been searching for all those years, as you can imagine. He wanted to wait to tell you in person about what he'd discovered and to be certain his findings could be verified. You know he wouldn't announce any finding unless it had been tested scientifically first. He said it would have a real global impact, that it could spark a worldwide revolution."

"Why do you think he disappeared? He couldn't have just lost track of time?"

"No. Today when I went by his house to pick him up, it had been ransacked. All the drawers had been dumped on the floor, the mattress on his bed was turned over, and his library was a disaster, with books scattered everywhere. That's when I knew he'd been kidnapped."

"Kidnapped!"

"He'd received anonymous threats 'suggesting' that he abandon his research. But as you know, he's the most obstinate, stubborn man on the planet."

Adam nodded, trying to make sense of it all. "But what's it about? What has he discovered?"

"You need to hear the whole story." Alexia put the windows down, and a light breeze brushed across her face as she accelerated even more. They were both upset. "I need fresh air to think."

"Good, I'm ready to hear it all," Adam said. "But first, what can we do?"

Alexia glanced at Adam. "I suppose he didn't tell you anything, right?"

"He called me up at five in the morning, really excited, and he told me he had discovered something related to Atlantis and sexuality, and that his discovery could completely unhinge Christianity and the other religions."

"That's just one part of it," she replied, watching a black car that was driving very close to them.

"Just one part? Why did he say he needed my help to interpret something?"

Alexia hit the accelerator hard and went through a red light. "Once there were incredible human beings, people who possessed amazing scientific and metaphysical knowledge—the Atlanteans. You may know this already, but Plato suggested that a catastrophe of colossal proportions virtually wiped them off of the face of the earth." She was silent for a moment before continuing. "The scariest part of all is that now we might meet the same fate. Do you know about the Mayan prophecies?"

"That's what my father was researching," Adam murmured. "I've read his book almost a dozen times." The prophecies predicted eclipses, wars, plagues, geological events, earthquakes, and changes in governments. "He was working on it when he disappeared," Adam said quietly.

"That's the work my father was trying to finish, picking up right where yours left off. Those predictions are immensely important, Adam. Especially the seventh Mayan prophecy."

Adam tried to remember the seventh prophecy, but the travel and chaos clouded his memory.

"The prophecies talk about 'the end of an era,'" Alexia said, filling in for him, "a vitally important, hopeful transformation for humanity on December 21, 2012."

*Just five months away.*

"The six previous prophecies all came true," Alexia said. "There's no reason to believe that the seventh one won't. Adam, I think my father found out something life-changing about the seventh prophecy."

# 6

Raul Tous was the youngest cardinal among the twenty likely candidates who could be elected the next pope of the Catholic Church. He'd been born in Lisbon, Portugal's capital. To many Portuguese, he personified the fervent hope of having one of their own occupy the church's highest office one day. And he was one of the few possibilities who still cut a more-or-less dashing figure. At fifty-three, his back was still straight and strong—he wasn't hunched over like most of the high-ranking priests. The belief that the weight of the cross had to be borne on the inside made a deep impression on clerics. They tended to internalize the concept, resulting in a pronounced, painful curvature of the spine from the sacrum up to the nape of the neck. Raul did not have this pain inside of him.

Cardinal Tous's posture was due in part to regular workouts at the gym and lap swims at the pool, but his greatest motivator for standing straight and tall was his voracious hunger for power. He'd learned he could strike a much more effective blow by using words and acts than by getting down on his knees to pray. Calculating and fiercely intelligent, he devoted more time to making useful political connections and advancing his own interests than to relating to people. He was accustomed to being in control and giving orders. He had grown up with four older sisters, and as the youngest child, he'd received the least attention from his parents. Not only did they ignore him in favor of his sisters, but as devout Catholics, his parents were primarily interested in the Bible and what their parish priest had to say. In a desperate attempt to get their attention, Raul Tous decided to enter the priesthood himself.

Raul's parents believed he had been truly called to serve and welcomed his decision. Their relationship with their son changed, as having a priest in the family was the highest honor his mother and father could hope for. And the young seminary student quickly demonstrated a steadfast dedication and impressive discipline that served him well on the challenging path of training for the priesthood. Over time, his hunger for power and his need for recognition and respect paid off. With hard work, he had finally come out on top as a high-profile cardinal firmly entrenched in the highest ranks of power.

He had thick gray hair, which he frequently touched to make sure nothing was out of place. When someone talked to him, he could stare for minutes without blinking, as if his mind were continually calculating and ranking a selection of possible responses that would best serve his own interests. Within the Secret Government, Tous was known as the Magician, an unusual alias since he'd come from the highest ranks of a religion that had persecuted anyone who practiced magic.

Earlier, while attending an important meeting, he'd gotten the phone call from Viktor Sopenski in Athens.

"Professor Vangelis has confessed. I have the audio recording," Sopenski said proudly.

The cardinal had decided to travel to the Greek capital on the first flight out the following morning. He wanted to get his hands on the archeologist's discoveries immediately and make very sure that nothing he'd found would come to light. While many people around the globe viewed it as more myth than reality, affirming that the very first man was named Adam and had been made of earth, while Eve, the first woman, had been made from Adam's rib, was a basic tenet of the Catholic faith, and Professor Vangelis's discovery might call the story into question. Cardinal Tous could not let that happen.

## 7

While there are many civilizations that seemed to have vanished without a trace, the most famous and elusive of them all is without doubt Atlantis. The most important evidence pointing to its existence can be found in Plato's dialogues *Critias* and *Timaeus*, written around 355 BC when the wise Greek philosopher was about seventy years old.

The beautiful, imposing Atlantis Plato described represented a golden age for the human race: a virtual earthly paradise before the fall, to put it in Biblical terms. The description of the Garden of Eden had been so rich and influential that speculation surrounding that place and time had continued, more or less uninterrupted, ever since the philosopher first touched on the subject.

In his impassioned dialogue, Plato wrote that Timaeus heard Solon, one of the seven Greek wise men, tell these stories, and he in turn had heard them from an Egyptian high priest.

In that time, beyond the Pillars of Hercules, there was an island the size of a continent, more extensive than Libya and Asia Minor combined, which was called "Atlantis" in honor of its first king and founder: Atlas, the son of Poseidon.

From the overall context, it was revealed that the place was in the middle of the Atlantic Ocean, and it was an archipelago, since it was possible to go from one continent to another by hopping from one island to the next.

When the gods divided up the world among themselves, the island fell under the domain of Poseidon, lord of the seas. A man named Eveneor, who had been born on Earth, lived there, together with the mortal Leucida. They had a daughter named Clito, who was extraordinarily beautiful. After her parents died, Poseidon desired Clito for himself. He had several children by her, and they would in turn populate the island under the reign of the eldest son: Atlas.

To protect his children and shield his beloved from the rest of the mortals, Poseidon decided to fortify the territory with a canal a hundred yards wide and a hundred yards deep, ten miles long, which connected to another interior canal that also could serve as a port, allowing the largest ships of the day to anchor there. Then locks were opened to cross the other two belts of land that surrounded the citadel, located on the central islet, so that only one ship could pass through at a time. The canals were covered, so the boats navigated them below the surface.

The first trench was five hundred yards wide, the same width as the stretch of land that surrounded it like an atoll. The second was somewhat smaller, 320 yards, the same as the second ring of land. Finally, there was a third canal, 150 yards wide, which surrounded the citadel or acropolis, with a diameter of seventy miles. This central islet was completely walled, with guard towers constructed of remarkably beautiful colored stones—black, white, and red—that had been laid in intricately designed patterns, putting man's highest creative talents on display.

The defensive wall around the first islet was completely coated in copper, and the second in tin. One very important thing that characterized the city of Atlantis was that it had a wall covered in a metal unknown to us: it was called orichalcum, which means "copper of the mountains." It was extremely valuable, second only to gold in its worth.

A temple dedicated to Poseidon and Clito stood at the center of the acropolis in Atlantis, surrounded by a gold fence. Its exterior was covered in silver, except for the corners of the roof, which were covered in gold. The temple's interior was of orichalcum, adorned with artwork of carved ivory with silver and gold accents. An imposing statue of Poseidon was the center of attention, made of solid gold, surrounded by water nymphs astride dolphins.

Since Plato's was the only known written reference to the strange metal, the exact composition of orichalcum has been widely speculated upon. One popular theory, and the most likely, holds that it was a mixture of gold and platinum. The Atlanteans inscribed their metaphysical, astronomical, bio-chemical, and spiritual knowledge on the surface of tablets made of this metal.

The riches of Atlantis accumulated and multiplied in such abundance that no other civilization could ever equal it. Atlanteans enjoyed all the resources that cities and entire countries were capable of producing, and because of the great power and glory of the empire, they were able to rely on themselves to produce most of life's necessities.

Their forests supplied all manner of materials needed for carpentry, and the island produced generous amounts of aromatic plants and grains and seemingly endless supplies of fruit. Thanks to their strong agriculture, the Atlanteans began to prosper in industry, constructing countless bridges and ports, ornate palaces, and temples.

Atlantis was rugged, its cliff-lined coastline extremely difficult to penetrate. Combined with its man-made defenses, Atlantis was practically invincible. Still, the Atlanteans were a highly advanced, peaceful, and spiritual people, deeply connected to the laws of the cosmos, although they maintained defenses against aggressive, savage cultures who had not yet reached the Atlanteans' highly evolved level of consciousness. The Atlanteans were prepared. It's believed the Atlantean army was composed of over a million men, a very considerable number for the time.

The Atlanteans were very powerful on many fronts. Above all, they derived their power from the sun, and they were able to condense that power in large and small crystals of white quartz. A quartz could store energy and later emanate it, providing whole cities with light. But mostly, Atlanteans used the quartz crystals to store metaphysical information, secrets, and existential knowledge. The Atlanteans' most precious information was stored in the quartz stones so that others could later "read" it through telepathy, letting the knowledge from the quartz penetrate the deepest recesses of their minds.

# 8

After parking their car on Alopekis Street, Adam and Alexia briskly walked two blocks north toward Kapsali Street, in the heart of the upscale Kolonaki neighborhood.

The graceful streets of Kolonaki were lined with welcoming sidewalk cafés where people sat enjoying a leisurely drink, while others strolled, pausing to gaze in the windows of some of the world's finest luxury stores.

"We're here," Alexia said tightly. "Try to see if anyone followed us."

Adam looked all around but didn't see anyone suspicious.

They went through a narrow door painted dark blue. A small staircase took them up to the second floor. Alexia used her keys to open up two locks on the door, and then they were inside her father's secret laboratory.

"Listen," Adam said, trying to think rationally, "shouldn't we call the police?"

Alexia looked at him incredulously. "My father doesn't trust the police," she said dryly.

Adam was taken aback. "But we're dealing with a possible kidnapping here."

"We'll find out for ourselves. I'm sure we'll find him."

"I'm glad you're so confident." Adam wasn't nearly as sure as Alexia that they could handle what was coming, but he knew better than to argue with her. "Was your father working with anyone?" he asked, changing focus. "Would anyone else have known about his discovery?"

"He's usually a loner, but he did work with an assistant."

"Where is he? Let's talk to him and see if he knows anything."

"I already did," Alexia quickly replied. "He's in Santorini."

"So what did he tell you?"

"That two nights ago, he left my father in the lab in Santorini, and that yesterday my father didn't show up in the lab at all, and he didn't get in touch with him all day either."

"Who is this assistant?"

"His name's Eduard Cassas. He's a young man from the Catalan region in Spain. He started helping out in the lab a little over a year ago. I don't know him very well, to tell you the truth. He's a little, shall we say..." She paused, searching for the right words. "He's kind of distant, a little reserved. Not very Greek, if you know what I mean."

They continued looking around the main room of the floor that had been converted into a research laboratory. The decor was minimalist and functional; there was just a table, a computer, a floor lamp, and two pictures on the wall. What stood out the most was a large floor-to-ceiling bookshelf filled with hundreds of volumes that Aquiles had carefully organized into sections, with neat labels on the shelves: "Mythology," "Mysticism," "Architecture," "History," "Geography," "Ecology," "Religions."

"I could spend a whole month in here," said Adam, who had always been a passionate reader.

"My father is extremely well-read. Wait, you haven't seen the most important part."

She took a large painting off the wall. An artist friend of theirs named Apostol had done the oil painting of a beautiful sunrise on one of the Greek islands.

"It's Santorini," she said, cradling the work. "A friend of my father's painted it; he lived there, too."

On the wall behind where the painting had been was a silver lever that, when raised, opened a hidden door into a second room. It was a secret library with shelves holding an array of disorganized books and files that read "Atlantis," "Mayan Prophesies," "Sexuality," and "Secret Government." Alexia took a step closer to examine the documents. A small label written in blue ballpoint pen affixed to a paper on the shelf read, "*The Origins of Man: Adam's Secret*."

"We have to find clues, data, anything that can tell us what the kidnappers were looking for." Alexia paused, slowly turned around, and then stood perfectly still. She was beginning to feel the impact of what was actually happening. A well of emotion began to rise to the surface, but she returned to her train of thought. "If we want to know everything my father had to tell us, we have to read through *all* of this."

Then she went to the kitchen to find a bottle of ouzo. She returned with two small glasses full of the strong Greek anise liquor.

"All right, where should we start?" Adam asked, putting his jacket down on the chair.

Alexia's dancing brown eyes studied the shelves full of papers and books.

"Let's start with this," she said, picking up a book with a blue cover, "even though you know it very well already."

"My father's book?" Adam said, surprised.

"Yes. First I want to understand the relationship our fathers had better. And I want to know what exactly the connection is between Atlantis and the last Mayan prophecy."

"All right, we have to start somewhere—I'll read to you out loud the most important parts that Aquiles underlined."

Adam sat down on a small loveseat while Alexia nervously gathered up papers and put them in a gray leather satchel. Adam looked down at the book he held in his hands, written by his father before he disappeared several years ago.

He read the personal dedication his father had written by hand inside the front cover: "To my great friend and colleague Aquiles, who works alongside me to discover the secret of man. *Nikos Roussos, Athens, April 18, 2005.*"

Tears welled in his eyes as he read the words that had flowed right out of his father's heart and onto the page.

"Go ahead, Adam. We don't have much time."

He nodded and turned to page nine. The chapter heading read, "The Seven Mayan Prophecies and the Atlantis Connection."

## 9

Less than three hours after it had taken off, the Boeing 747 passenger jet carrying Cardinal Tous touched down on Greek soil. Captain Sopenski awaited him in a rented blue BMW 320. Tous had told him he would be wearing a white Caribbean-style hat, a gray jacket, and black pants. The password would be, "The Vulture welcomes the Magician," to which Tous had to answer, "The Magician greets the Vulture."

Though the Vulture had assured him the situation was under control, Cardinal Tous needed to find out for himself what information had been revealed, and he wanted to see the archeologist in person. The cardinal only traveled on rare occasions; it had to be an issue of utmost importance for him to leave the Vatican. This was. He wanted to interrogate Aquiles himself, to find out if he'd divulged his "secret" to anyone.

Almost ten years earlier, Aquiles Vangelis had met Cardinal Tous at a conference at the UN. At the time Tous had been a bishop. Tous had been rather irritated by the tone the archeologist had taken with him, especially in front of so many high-ranking ambassadors.

"Your religion has destroyed all of the great scientists through the ages," Professor Vangelis had accused. "Galileo,

Copernicus, Newton, Kepler...you can't continue to obstruct our research and keep us from discovering hidden truths. We have a right, and you cannot censor us."

"You have lost your faith, Professor Vangelis, and what you speak of is in the past. We need to let it go," Bishop Tous had timidly replied. Pope John Paul II had issued an apology in the name of the church 359 years after Galileo was sentenced to life in prison for asserting that the earth revolved around the sun and not the other way around, as the church maintained. The stains of blood and repression marked the pages of history, although the church would go to any lengths to minimize and conceal it. The encounter established a tension between them, and to Tous, Aquiles Vangelis belonged in the same category as other nonconforming, renegade scientists, including Adam's father, all of whom were blacklisted. *The time will come,* thought Tous, *when an invisible hand of justice will make absolutely certain that all of their work has been in vain.*

The ambitious Portuguese bishop had risen swiftly up the Vatican chain of command, like the steep ascent of an eagle, becoming one of the most popular cardinals in the ecclesiastic hierarchy. Several years after that distasteful encounter at the United Nations, he wanted to see if that pretentious archeologist would be so arrogant this time around.

## 10

We have to hurry," Alexia said, anguished. "My father's life is at stake!"

Adam did what he could to put the array of folders strewn across Aquiles's simple but disheveled laboratory in some kind of order. There were two desks, a wooden chair, and two paintings of Greek landscapes adorning the whitewashed walls. Adam tried to keep his head from spinning as he looked over all those numbered folders, which were labeled with various headings: "The Sun," "Activation of the 64 Codons," "The End of Time," "Kybalion," "The World's Fate," and "Atlantis and Its Capital," among many others. There were also articles cut out of newspapers from around the globe, whose headlines read, "Russian Scientists Discover New Properties of DNA," "Chemtrails: Chemical Contrails of Military Aircraft," "HAARP Accused of Causing Earthquakes," along with scholarly papers on various subjects.

"I think I found something your father wrote that could help us."

"Read it," she said. "I'll keep looking around here for his laptop, but I'm listening."

"I'll read what's been underlined on each page."

*"The seventh Mayan prophecy describes the moment in which the solar system, in its 5,125-year rotation cycle, leaves the 'galactic night' to enter into the 'dawn of the galaxy.' On December 21, 2012, the light emitted from the center of the galaxy will synchronize with the sun and all living things. The energy of the cosmic rain transmitted by Hunab-Ku, the Supreme Being, will progressively activate the vital spiritual functions of a divine origin in all beings that are vibrating at high frequency. This could raise the consciousness of all men, giving rise to a new individual, collective, and universal reality. Human beings will connect with one another, as One, and will give birth to a new galactic order."*

And below that, Aquiles had noted:

*"If this prophecy comes to pass, one predictable consequence is that we will be able to consciously access an internal transformation capable of invoking new realities of a previously entirely unknown nature. People will have the opportunity to make a radical change and surpass their limitations, which will result in an entirely new sense: direct communication through thought.*

*"What the Mayans predicted is now being supported by NASA. In 2012 the solar system will pass through a quadrant of the galaxy known as the Photon Belt, which will impact the movements*

*of the planets. As a result of this phenomenon, I predict that humans will absorb a strong stream of photons, which will make possible a new awakening of consciousness, allowing us to fully comprehend that we are all part of one enormous organism. This is what is referred to in quantum physics as a 'unified field.'*

*"Through this cosmic passage, all humans who possess the vital life energy and have a high interior vibrational frequency, transforming fear into love, will be able to feel the universal connection and inner peace and will be able to express themselves telepathically. In this way the sixth sense, the heightened internal perception that the Atlanteans and Mayans exercised, will thrive once again.*

*"It is believed that in order to achieve this, the Mayans affixed a small piece of resin to their children's foreheads from a very young age. The scent of the resin forced them to turn their attention to their 'third eye,' the eye of consciousness, our ability to see and perceive beyond the superficial physical world. They also tied a type of tablet around their heads so that they grew into an oval shape at the back, toward the rear of the cerebellum, and in that way completely activated their extrasensory abilities."*

Adam's voice grew louder, with greater conviction, and Alexia stopped what she was doing to look at him.

*"The end of this cycle, terminating on December 21, 2012, according to the Mayan calendar, suggests that we will experience changes of tremendous magnitude. The Mayans knew that solar activity impacts Earth's functioning and that any variations would affect everything that occurs on Earth. To complete their calculations on sunspots and the exact nature of the relationship between those spots and rises in temperature on Earth, the Mayans observed the cycle of Venus, a planet easily viewed from Earth, as they noted in their well-known Dresden Codex. Every 117th orbit of Venus, the sun experiences notable changes: eruptions occur on its surface, solar winds are much more active, and sunspots are visible.*

*"NASA has also confirmed their calculations about Earth, the sun, the stars, and the rest of the planets. I would suppose that the realization of this prophecy would transform the individual, and as a consequence of genetics, would present the possibility of humanity's expansion throughout the galaxy. I am reminded of my dear friend Carl Sagan, who commented that if the library in ancient Alexandria had not been destroyed, we would be traveling to the stars right now.*

*"Those who harmoniously absorb this 'stream of photons' or 'cosmic rain' will enter into a new age of spiritual unity and knowledge, where telepathic communication will mean that individual*

*experiences, memories, and learning will be freely available to everyone, just as it is believed it was in Atlantis. It will be like a holistic mental web, a kind of 'Internet of consciousness' that will greatly advance the speed of discovery and forge connections never before imagined.*

*"We will be able to deeply understand that we are all an integral part of a single limitless organism, and we will connect with the earth, our sun, and the entire galaxy.*

*"Following the cosmic event of December 21, 2012, we can predict that relationships will be founded on spiritual unity since man will feel that other men are a part of himself, a concept the Mayans called In Lakesh, 'I am another you.' The day will mark the discovery of our common cosmic origin.*

*"In order for the shift in consciousness to be viable, I believe we will live for artistic and spiritual pursuits and contact with other realities. This will fully occupy the human mind, erasing the effects of thousands of years of belief in duality and man's separation from his fellow man, years when mankind worshipped a distant God who judged and punished them.*

*"Spiritual growth and excellence will spread from those people who have already expanded their existential awareness. Although I imagine that this*

change will not be easy, first a global movement will take place, order will emerge from chaos and confusion, and the earth will be intensely shaken by a series of seismic events.

"My research also indicates in all likelihood the sun will turn red because of the impact the cosmic rain will have on it, producing what astrophysicists refer to as solar storms. There will also be a reversal in Earth's magnetic poles. On the other hand, ancient writings of various religious traditions and the Bible itself suggest the possibility that once again, as it is believed happened thousands of years ago, there will be three days of complete darkness during the planetary transition. I believe these changes will initiate a process whose outcome will depend on the individual's transmutation, in order to effect collective change on a global scale.

"I fear that, unfortunately, not everyone will be able to successfully ascend to this new reality. If the solar storms are even stronger than expected, they could affect Earth's electromagnetic fields, impacting all of our systems that interact with it: the financial world, computers and the Internet, radars, and planes. Even our bodies' physical systems could be affected: our immune and nervous systems, emotional health, etc.

"We need to be more alert than ever before. These changes could bring ecstasy, or they could bring *unimaginable suffering. Humanity must choose between continuing on as a new race, forming a whole new cosmic order, or face the consequences of not doing so."*

When Adam finished reading, the two sat still in silence for a long time.

"What do you think?" Alexia finally asked.

Adam took a sip of ouzo. "I don't know. It's hopeful and yet very alarming. But what do you think the connection is with Atlantis?"

Alexia was quiet a moment. "I think my father found proof that the ancient Mayans were survivors of the lost city of Atlantis," she said. "Think about it. Both the Atlanteans and the Mayans lived in a state of expanded consciousness. And remember, too, that there's an ancient Aztec city called Aztlan." Adam knew exactly what she was talking about. The city was now called Mexcaltitlan, which meant circular island. In fact, the word *aztecatl* meant "coming from Aztlan," possibly the *Atlanteans*. "Evolutionary cycles repeat themselves..." Alexia murmured.

Adam didn't respond. He was thinking about the famous clairvoyant Edgar Cayce, a man on par with Nostradamus, who had predicted that Atlantis would one day return. There was another prediction, too—a much darker one that Adam's father had spoken of frequently. Alexia knew it, too, and the look in her intelligent brown eyes made clear it was on her mind every bit as much as it was on Adam's.

"Are you thinking about the meteorite?" Adam asked, and Alexia nodded. Biblical prophecy suggested that a stellar body could collide with Earth; it was called *Ajenjo*. The prophecies of Nostradamus warned of a meteorite that could strike Earth around the same time.

Alexia stood, leaned over, and took off her high heels. Then she pulled a chair over next to the bookcase and stepped on top of it to pull some papers off of the highest shelves. Even though it wasn't exactly appropriate at that moment, Adam could not help but admire his friend's graceful curves, his gaze running slowly from her feet all the way up to her luxurious mane of thick brown hair.

Alexia didn't notice Adam's gaze. She was preoccupied with the idea of the meteorite but tried to shake the thought. "The sheer chaos that will break out could be a catastrophe in itself," she said. "Imagine how confused a very religious, orthodox person would be if his beliefs were shaken down to the very core."

"I think we're getting ahead of ourselves," Adam replied. "Let's go step by step, Alexia," he said. "If we want to find your father, we have to gather together all the pieces of the puzzle."

## 11

Cardinal Tous was dying from the heat. "Turn the air-conditioning on, please."

Captain Sopenski was not the most skilled driver, as it turned out, even though he was driving a beautiful BMW. "Uhhh...I'm not sure what all these buttons do."

The Magician was forced to roll down his window to get some air. As they zipped along at over eighty miles per hour, the strong breeze that blasted him left his carefully coiffed helmet of hair looking as if he had just rolled out bed. After a few minutes, he decided he'd rather swelter than ruin his hairstyle even more.

"Are we almost there?"

"We'll be there in ten minutes."

"Do you have the audio recording?"

"It's in a very safe place, sir; don't worry."

Much could be said about Captain Sopenski, Tous reflected, but one thing was certain: he was a faithful watchdog. And Tous liked that his arrival had made Sopenski nervous. Clearly, the Vulture knew his place with the Magician.

Less than ten minutes later, Sopenski parked the rental car in Kotzia Plaza, not far from Hermou Street. The dark room where the kidnappers were holding Aquiles was just one block away from the car, and—though no one knew it—a mere six blocks from Aquiles's secret laboratory.

Cardinal Raul Tous stepped into the dank room to see the archeologist for himself. The rancid stench of the small chamber assaulted him. He felt a wave of nausea, but he kept it at bay by discreetly holding a small handkerchief perfumed with violet essence to his face.

"Well, what do we have here?" he asked haughtily. Still, the cardinal could not help feeling the faintest glimmer of compassion when he saw Aquiles. He remembered him as energetic, outgoing, and quick-witted—nothing like the defeated man slumped in his chair. Tous inhaled deeply, pausing to regain his composure before continuing. "If it's not the great archeologist Aquiles Vangelis! It looks as if you're not very comfortable, Professor, and I offer my sincere apologies."

The Magician whispered in Captain Sopenski's ear, telling him to shine the bright spotlight directly in their prisoner's eyes. He did not want to risk being recognized.

"I'm pleased that we were able to find our dear Professor Aquiles's vulnerability. You have shown, just like the Achilles of myth, that every strong man has his weak point," the cardinal laughed. "Believe me, no matter what, we would have found your weak point. Our men are very effective."

The cardinal shot a look at his underlings. Sopenski and Villamitre watched from a corner. With his back to the archeologist, Cardinal Tous looked like an all-powerful specter, casting a long shadow on the wall. The scene mesmerized the morbidly curious Villamitre, while Viktor Sopenski casually poured himself a glass of vodka.

"The reason I'm here," Cardinal Tous continued, "is not to conduct a seminar on our methods of extraction, Professor. I'm here for something much more important."

Aquiles coughed. His throat was dry; he'd been in the same position without a drink for hours, and he was hot and dehydrated.

"I have listened to your confession," Tous said. "Very well done, Professor, well done."

Though Aquiles had convinced Captain Sopenski and Villamitre that he'd actually confessed, the claims on the tape recording had not been what Cardinal Tous expected.

"I suppose you know we don't have much time. My interest is not only to ensure that curious people keep their noses out of things that do not concern them, but also to make sure that certain things never come to light." He uttered these last words directly into Aquiles's ear. "Another one of my informants told me that you have an extremely valuable, shall we say…'instrument of power' in your possession that is of great interest to me."

Aquiles swallowed hard. The Magician continued, backing him into a corner.

"It's come to my attention that there is a ridiculous rumor circulating about a prophecy that is about to be fulfilled."

The Vatican was very nervous about the predictions of the sacred Mayan calendar and the Mayans' predictions for the human race. Ever since the time of Nostradamus, the church had tried with all its might to prevent the general public from learning of the prophecies. In the sixteenth century, under Spanish Archbishop Diego de Landa, the church mutilated great discoveries and documents of supreme value when the Spanish invaded Mexico. Followers of the Roman patriarch

Cirilo had burned the grand library in Alexandria in order to ensure the Bible became the only sacred book in the eyes of God. The church had even altered important texts during the first Council of Nicea in the year 325, when Constantine the Great changed sacred texts, replacing words like "reincarnation" with "resurrection."

Tous turned to face Aquiles. The cardinal knew full well that he could never let Aquiles go free, but he had to convince Aquiles otherwise. "If you ever want to see the light of day again, Professor, you should cooperate."

Aquiles Vangelis tried to think clearly. Alexia must have figured out what had happened by now. *I have to stall them,* he thought. *Alexia will waste no time in finding Adam. They'll know what to do.* Though he'd left Alexia all the information she'd need, he began to worry it would take her too long to find it.

"Tell me exactly where we can find your discovery, or we will take your daughter's life," said the Magician. "It's very simple. Take careful measure of the situation you're in. I did not come all this way only to leave empty-handed. What do you think?"

Silence.

Villamitre was eager to spring into action. The professor's back was torn up and bloody from the earlier punishment Villamitre had meted out, and Villamitre was eager to break him. "He's a tough guy," Villamitre said.

The cardinal shot him a sharp look of disapproval that seemed to suck the little air there was out of the room. Tous didn't like others sticking their noses in when he was in charge.

"I know you're not afraid. I know you're very stoic in withstanding my assistants' punishments, but understand very well that with one order from me, we will go after your daughter. It seems that's what you want, to bring her back here." His voice rose to a thunderous bellow. "Do you want to see her suffer?"

"My daughter can take care of herself. You'll never find her."

"Is that a dare? Tied up and on the verge of death, you have the nerve to challenge me? We can find anyone anywhere on the planet. There's no hiding place that can keep her from us."

From the first, Aquiles suspected that the Secret Government was behind his kidnapping, but hearing those words, he was sure. All he could do was trust that the divine spirit would inspire his daughter and Adam, and show them the way.

## 12

*hat did Aquiles want from me? Why did he say I would be so useful to his discovery?* Adam wondered. He kept turning it over and over but couldn't see any point of connection between the archeologist's mysterious discovery and his own profession as a sexologist.

"I don't remember it ever being this hot in Athens," Adam said.

"Do you want a bottle of water?" Alexia asked.

"Yes, thanks." He held out his hands and caught the bottled water Alexia tossed his way. "Did you find anything interesting?"

"Same as you, just information, and more information…" She ducked under the desk.

"I'm looking for his laptop and calendar. I'll go see if they're in the other room."

Adam kept grasping at a glimmer of comprehension. Among a pile of file folders, he found two sheets of paper that seemed to have been written in Aquiles's hand. They were titled, "United Nations Talk. Invitation for October 28, 2012."

*What's this? Aquiles was planning on giving this talk just three months from now?* Adam wondered. He got settled on the sofa and read to himself:

*We are crossing a frontier of new awareness. Time is short. So everything accelerates and intensifies. Societies around the world are plagued by chaos and confusion, where suffering and evil reign over the human race. Time is ending. We need to change.*

*Most people are full of fears, and we have reached a limit of egotism, conflict, and separation. There is no respect for life, or for the planet, or for others. We are motivated by money. Negativity and consumerism rule the day. Ancient civilizations lived according to divine laws: Atlantis, ancient Greece, Mexico, Australia, and India. What has happened to us? Why have we forgotten that wisdom?*

*I have here today, ready to reveal to the whole world, confirmation that the work of my friend and colleague Nikos Roussos, along with the Mayan prophecies, and my own recent discoveries, prove the truth of our origins and offer us the key to changing the individual and the world.*

*Now everything is moving very quickly. Can we not change? We have shown that we cannot do it alone. From antiquity, men have confronted one another in wars; have generated pestilence and pandemics; and have certainly run the risk of running themselves into extinction. But never before now has humanity had stockpiles of nuclear weapons sufficient to turn the planet to dust, not just once, but fifty times over.*

*Never before has man faced such extreme threats as severe climate change and the potential annihilation of all life. On the other hand, phenomenal advances in communication have facilitated globalization like never before, and never before have humans been pushed out of their protagonist role in the sense that the monster they have created could devour or annihilate them. With globalization, never before now has individual liberty been so limited and censured. No one can escape the system because with its laws of apparent freedom, the system will destroy you, labeling you as a radical, crazy person or as a pathologically antisocial individual.*

*We have forgotten how to venerate life, and we have lost all respect for ancient civilizations; young people today are more in touch with the pop icon of the moment than they are with the divine. We have forgotten where we came from, above all because of the blinders and filters imposed on individual consciousness.*

*For those of us who have made it to the ripe old age of seventy, we realized long ago that the urgent desire we've had from adolescence to change things has not resulted in changing much of anything, in the greater world or in ourselves. Many scientists have been censured and silenced.*

*Today I will not be.*

*I am at the United Nations to tell you about my discovery.*

*We cannot resign ourselves since the greatest battle of all, the change in humanity, has been out of our hands for some time; it lies in the hands of powers far superior to us.*

*I have found these higher powers.*

*Now more than ever we will see that being consciously aware and persistent has its rewards. In the present-day world, the brutal, the ignorant, and the criminal occupy high positions in government, society, and the financial world. It has been a very long time since the wise man led the people.*

*The ancient, wise people were taught by messengers and prophets, but we have not followed their teachings. We have progressed on the material plane at an astonishing rate, but not on the spiritual or humanistic plane.*

*We know from the ancient and wise Mayan civilization that our solar system is moving toward the cosmic center. Everything is being compacted and unified. There is hope there since within man's collective subconscious something is not right, something has to change. Religions have failed, and the hope of finding a moral, ethical, or spiritual way out has been lost. If we could take a reading on the*

*collective mood of our modern societies, hopeless-
ness has given way to a shared feeling of resignation, loneliness, and apathy. Psychological illnesses
such as depression and suicide are rising at an
alarming rate.*

*I am a spiritual scientist who has found his life's
quest. The world of Atlantis could be right in front
of our eyes right now, and what's even more important, its wisdom and the answers to the existential
questions we have always asked ourselves: Who am
I? Where did I come from? Who was the first man?*

*The development of all civilizations has been based
on the observation of the universe and the stars:
lunar cycles, solstices and solar equinoxes, the study
of the planets closest to us, Mars and Venus.*

*I cannot deny the natural tendency to look up and
gaze at the stars after the sun has set.*

*Millions and millions of suns all shining at the same
time leads me to wonder why, with so many stars in
the heavens, humans do not lie down and surrender
before so much beauty. I think it is because we have
been programmed and brainwashed into forgetting
our true origins.*

*If we bear in mind that just the Milky Way is made
up of twenty million suns, I cannot even conceive
of how many there would be if we added up all*

*of the galaxies. I have come to the conclusion that there has to be a principle that is the opposite of light, something that inhibits it, a kind of ether that extinguishes life.*

*The Mayan calendar, which measured time with amazing precision, tells us that since 1999, we began living in the "time of no time." We are about to live through the close of a 5,125-year cycle. Exactly in this year of 2012, we will cross over into a new age, and the human race will come face to face with itself and with a new era of energy.*

*We know that we carry extraordinary potential within us in our DNA, but it lies dormant. If we can let the new energy affect us and not resist, we will reach a new dawn of genetics, and our vibration will increase to a higher frequency. The human race could evolve, or on the other hand, if we don't we will perish.*

*The Mayans revealed that every 25,625 years we complete an evolutionary cycle. During that time, we travel through an elliptical path that brings us farther away from, and then draws us closer to, the cosmic center, from which the one true Life Force emanates. And after December 21, 2012, we will be given the chance to start down a new path that will gradually lead us to an age of hope and progress for all of humanity, a golden age like the one Atlantis had.*

*For the Mayans, those thirteen years between 1999 and 2012 are tremendously important. According to their calendar, we are in the last* katun, *or period, of the age.*

*The Mayans left us, the current inhabitants of Earth, written messages, symbolism etched into stone, and a metaphysical language that contained seven prophecies, in part warning us of danger and to adapt, and in part encouraging us to change. The warning of danger prophesized about what was going to happen during the times we are living through, and the positive message talked about the changes we need to make within ourselves to propel humanity forward toward evolution and change.*

*We are faced with the possibility that this new age will be the age of woman, the age of the mother, the age of sensitivity, the age of the goddess.*

*In one way or another, all of us feel as if the age of the Apocalypse is upon us. We feel the battle: the battle over oil, battles for land, battles for peace.*

*Every day there are more volcanic eruptions, and the pollution caused by our own technological advancements has reached alarming levels. We have damaged the ozone in the atmosphere that protects us from solar radiation, and we have contaminated our home planet with industrial waste and garbage. The environmental devastation we have caused has contaminated the water we drink and the air we breathe; the climate has changed, and the temperature has risen dramatically. All of this was predicted many years ago.*

*We are paralyzed, growing accustomed to what we see around us: glaciers and polar ice caps melting, devastating floods happening all over the world, deadly tornadoes and hurricanes springing up with greater frequency. We could even experience a kind of information gridlock and paralysis; poverty and the crisis caused by the chaos of the global financial markets is more pronounced and widespread by the day in almost every country in the world. We are all grasping for answers, trying to find the best path to follow for the times we live in. These problems are a sure sign that we are not living in harmony.*

*We should not just pay attention to what statistics and science are telling us. Many religious traditions have also prophesized about what is happening now. The Bible said that when all of these things begin to happen at the same time, the times of the Apocalypse and the revelation of the Truth would begin.*

*If there is any truth in the wisdom of the ancients, we will begin to see that we are at the beginning of a cycle in which people of good faith and those who have already attained a higher level of consciousness will draw together in unity, as all bod-*

*ies and energy are undeniably one. The light that is intrinsic in all things will fuse and become stronger: planets with planets, galaxies with galaxies, spirits with spirits, bodies with bodies—everything will be unified as one entity.*

*Respected representatives of all nations, what does not defeat us makes us stronger. After years of searching, I have something to share with you. And today I am pleased to tell you what I have found.*

*What I have to present to you today are two groundbreaking, never-before-seen discoveries. I have scientific proof of the origin of humans and of what could happen to us as a species very soon, and I would like you all to take this knowledge back and share it with your home countries. It's paradoxical to think that now that we understand where we really come from, we are also threatened with complete extinction as a species, which could take place within a matter of months.*

*My own work, along with that of my disappeared colleague and dear friend Nikos Roussos, will confirm tonight that humanity is about to confront a life-or-death change, and that what had been thought of as a myth or literary illusion is really the divine truth.*

*Aquiles Vangelis,*
*United Nations Talk, October 28, 2012*

"Hey, Alexia," Adam called. "I've found a talk your father was planning on giving at the United Nations three months from now."

"I've found something too," Alexia said from the next room, "on his laptop."

Adam went into the other room and found her staring into the computer screen, watching her father speak on a video. Her pupils glowed like two flames.

"What's that?" Adam asked, taken aback by the sight of Aquiles's image. He looked so enthusiastic and energetic.

Alexia turned the computer so Adam had a good view.

"I don't know if this is the same talk that you found. For security, he usually recorded a version on video."

"This says he was going to give this speech at the UN in October." Adam showed her the papers he'd just read.

Alexia's eyes opened wide. "On this video he says he's going to give the talk in London."

"In London? Why?" Adam didn't see any obvious reason for choosing the capital of Great Britain to unveil his findings.

Alexia smiled knowingly, her bright face lighting up the room. "My father wanted the whole world to know about what he'd found." Now her voice sounded powerful and sure. "My dear Adam, the next Olympic Games will take place in London."

# 13

They searched for more files on Aquiles's computer together.

"Your father planned on announcing his discovery at the UN and at the Olympics in London. If he managed to do that, the news would spread like wildfire. There couldn't have been any better publicity than that."

Alexia stared at the screen in intense concentration. She opened folders that were labeled "The Hall of Mirrors," "Three Days of Darkness," "The Red Sun," "The Origins of Man," "The Island of the Snake," and "Adam's Secret."

"The Olympic Games will open in London in less than a week from now. They start on July 27 and end on August 12. We have only a few days."

Alexia knew from living in London herself how monumental a task the preparations for the Olympics were. She was constantly being reminded of them because, for the past year, the country's publicity machine did nothing other than promote the international mega-event.

"One week!" Adam exclaimed. "Your father hoped to resolve everything by that date. What should we do? Just show the video? We're not doing anything to actually find him."

Alexia fixed him with a resigned gaze from her expressive almond eyes. Adam couldn't tell what she was thinking.

"I still think we should call the police," he added.

"Don't even think about it!" she snapped back.

"They could help us."

"They would just be another headache, more than anything," she argued.

Adam raised an eyebrow. "But we haven't been able to find out what *the key* is. We're trying to figure out what he discovered, exactly, to help lead us to his kidnappers, but…"

"If he was calling on you for your expertise in sexuality, what's missing must have something to do with sexuality and religion."

"Alexia, what is there about sex that hasn't already been said? We already know that religions are deeply suspicious of the body and sex. That is what they have emphasized the most in order to repress people."

"Maybe that's exactly why. My father told me several times about Atlantean sexual rituals that included the sexual act, meditation, and special breathing techniques. Through these practices, he said, they increased their power and were able to awaken extraordinary paranormal and creative powers, expanding their consciousness."

Adam nodded slowly, acknowledging and considering what he had heard.

"What do you mean? Do you think your father discovered something with respect to sexuality that he didn't understand?"

"And what would happen if he found some kind of irrefutable evidence that sex is not what we've always been told it was? He was researching Atlantis and the secrets of humanity's origins. And all human beings came into this world as a consequence of a sexual act."

"That's obvious," he said, "but do you believe he may have discovered another way of coming into the world?" He mumbled these last words with the uncertainty of a child, as if all of his professional accomplishments and accolades did not count for anything.

She shook her head silently. She absently touched the quartz stone at her neck; it gave off an otherworldly color.

Alexia looked away from the computer screen, abruptly turned around in the swivel chair, and faced Adam directly, her expression determined.

"No, Adam," her tone conveyed intelligence and sharp insight, "I believe the fundamental point here did not have anything to do with the prophecy or Atlantis. What my father discovered, and what had him so excited, is something to do with sex. It has to do with how the *very first man* came into the world."

# 14

As Adam and Alexia worked in the confines of Aquiles's secret laboratory, they were unaware of the larger story unfolding around them. Every single international news service, television channel, newspaper, radio show, and journalist was frantically delivering the same enormous news.

The sun—the star worshipped by all cultures since the ancient Egyptians, Hindus, Greeks, Atlanteans, Mayans, and indigenous tribes throughout the Americas, Africa, and Asia—had mysteriously and inexplicably turned completely red.

The headlines screamed that it was as if the magnificent celestial body had suddenly been bathed in blood. The incandescent orb, like a volcano erupting, had turned an intense shade of crimson with yellow-and-red flames. Meteorologists and scientists were thoroughly baffled.

On the BBC, a commentator warned viewers, "Don't look at the sun at all; the risk of ocular burns is extremely high." CNN sounded the alarm with segments explaining the risk of being exposed to any sunlight and recommending that people drink plenty of water. The story quickly spread around the world like sand slipping through an open hand. And all over the world, people began to panic.

Engrossed in his labor, Cardinal Tous was starting to lose his composure. He wanted to command respect even though Professor Vangelis had no earthly idea who he was. Tous stood behind the archeologist and rested his hands on his shoulders.

"This is the last time I'm going to ask, Professor."

*I have to buy some time,* Aquiles thought. He was now completely dehydrated, and his hands were grotesquely swollen from the ropes at his wrists.

Villamitre stepped from the shadows, ready to use his electric prod. Tous had already given specific instructions: "I don't want any torture to take place in my presence." In spite of his zeal for power, the cardinal had an ideology he believed in—a Christianity "of his own design," where brute force was not necessary to convince anyone, just well-reasoned arguments. The arguments could be threatening, of course, but he did not want to witness any physical suffering.

"I will give you five minutes to think it over, Professor. When I return, you will have to give me an answer."

The cardinal went into the bathroom while Sopenski and Villamitre kept watch over Aquiles. He took out one of the two cellular phones he always carried with him, one exclusively for Vatican business and the other for his work with the Secret Government.

He closed the door behind him and stepped to the farthest corner of the room to dial the Owl. "Where are you?" Tous demanded.

The voice at the other end of the line sounded nervous and upset. "I'm at the hotel bar. I was just about to call you."

"What's going on? Why do you sound so upset?"

"Something's going on out here," the Owl answered, his voice shaking.

"Calm down—tell me what's going on."

"It's the sun," said the Owl.

"What do you mean? What about the sun?" The cardinal could feel his heart rate speed up.

"It's surreal—it's all over the news. The sun's turned red! Everything looks red, as if the world is sepia-toned."

Tous took it in, comprehension slowly dawning. Sweat broke out on his brow.

"Since when?"

"I'm not sure. I had a headache, so I took a nap. When I woke up and opened the curtains, everything looked reddish, and I watched all these people on the streets running home in a panic. It's the only thing on television—everyone around the world is talking about it. Governments everywhere are telling their citizens not to leave their homes..."

*This can't be happening, especially not now*, Tous thought. *It can't be true.*

Tous and many others within the Vatican viewed the Mayan prophecies as some kind of savage, uncivilized cult, but they still had a certain amount of respect for them. The prophecies stated that before the seventh prophecy was fulfilled, the sun would display unusual activity. It would cause electrical storms in the early phases and then bring about serious catastrophes.

With his characteristic rationality, Tous knew that trying to struggle against the designs of nature would be an exercise in futility. "We must remain calm. I'll come to see you at the hotel soon. Don't worry, everything is going to be all right."

## 15

Adam took a long drink of water. He was feeling the heat, and he unfastened another button on his shirt. Suddenly one of the window panes shattered, with glass falling all over the floor, letting in a blast of very hot air from outside.

They both turned around fast, startled.

"What was that?" Alexia asked. She jumped up from her chair and started to walk toward the window. But as soon as she got up, she fainted.

"Alexia!" Adam ran over to her but couldn't keep her from collapsing onto the floor.

From outside he heard shouts and screams, horns honking and tires squealing. It wasn't at all normal to hear that kind of noise in that upscale Athens neighborhood, which was always so peaceful.

"Alexia, are you all right?" He lightly tapped her cheek with his palm, trying to revive her.

"Yes," she murmured, confused. "What happened?"

"You fainted. You were about to walk over to the window when your legs buckled beneath you."

"It's so hot...I got dizzy."

"Drink." Adam brought her a glass of water.

She slowly drank, then got to her feet and sat on the sofa.

"What's going on out there? It's so noisy."

Adam went over to the window and took in a spectacle reminiscent of Dante. The few pedestrians still on the streets were frantically trying to find some shade—under an awning, in a bar, or anywhere at all. Cars were driving around willy-nilly, ignoring traffic rules.

"Oh God!" Adam brought his hands to his face. "Don't look up at the sky!"

He grabbed Alexia, who had stepped behind him, and pushed her back.

"But…what's going on?"

"Everything looks red! The sun!" They both had the same thought. The prophecy.

Adam covered the window with a piece of wood that was sometimes used as a shelf. The heat was overwhelming, and all the noise and chaos from outside made it very hard to concentrate.

"What should we do?" Alexia asked.

Adam looked at her calmly. "If this is about the sun and the changes…if…the seventh prophecy has begun, then the only thing we can do is be peaceful and calm," he said almost in a whisper. His regular meditation practice always helped him overcome his more rash impulses.

"You're right," Alexia answered, somewhat calmer but still unnerved.

As Adam looked at Alexia, he noticed something. "What is that?" he asked, gesturing toward Alexia's chest.

"What's what?"

He stepped closer to her and examined her upper chest closely. There was a small red mark where the stone from her necklace, now askew, had lain.

"You have a burn."

Alexia raised her hands to her chest and looked down. She saw a red circle there, but she didn't feel as if she'd been burned.

"The quartz!" she exclaimed, fingering the necklace with the white stone. It had been a gift from her father. "Touch it; it's very hot."

Adam lightly touched the chain and stone. "You're right."

Alexia closed her eyes. "Wait…" She drew in a deep breath. Alexia felt a strange lucidity come over her. She was tremendously alert. Since she'd recovered from fainting, her mind seemed to be functioning at twice the rate as before.

Alexia closed her eyes again. Thoughts raced through her mind like a quick succession of cars speeding down the highway.

"My father—and your father, for that matter, Adam—could have discovered how to help prepare people for the change."

"How so?" Adam asked. "What do you mean?" He'd noticed the change that'd come over Alexia and couldn't help but feel he was in the presence of something extraordinary.

"The prophecy of the Mayan calendar talks about the end of time approaching in just a few months; I believe…" Her mind grew quiet for a moment, as if it could go off and retrieve the knowledge it needed from somewhere else.

Adam watched her attentively. "What do you believe?"

Alexia smiled. And in that single smile, Adam saw the beauty and the light in her in all its radiant splendor. Her teeth were like priceless white pearls, her eyes two stars constantly twinkling.

"Adam, my father is a genius. I believe that the end of time is really the 'End of Time.' From passing from one dimension into another, we will see that the third dimension, the one we are living in, is the form of illusion, materiality, and the perception of everything in terms of eras, times, ages...If from the central sun at the center of the galaxy the ray of harmonizing light for our whole system and the people on Earth, if through this cosmic convergence or the portal of light evolution is generated, then we will perceive that time, such as it is, will cease to be a barrier for experiencing reality."

"What do you mean?"

"That we will come to understand that time doesn't exist! Can you even conceive of the consequences that would have?"

A slew of scenarios ran through Adam's mind. "There would be no more fear of death," he said.

"Exactly. Time does not exist. Everything would change."

"There would be no need for some future paradise; we would already be in communion with the Life Source."

Adam remembered that serious students of meditation who achieved spiritual enlightenment, like the Buddha, said that the state of *samadhi* or expansion of consciousness was a state in which there was no time, just the perception of eternity existing within the present moment. The Buddhist teaching had grounding in science, as researchers had learned that the human brain operated the smallest fraction of a second "behind" reality; it took the tiniest instant for the brain waves to transmit what was happening in the present to the consciousness. Adam remembered the words of his meditation teacher: *Enlightenment means grounding the brain in the eternal present and perceiving true reality, and it comes as a consequence of disciplined meditation practice.*

"We have to clearly understand exactly what it is we're trying to find here," Adam said, trying to get them back on track. "We still don't have a clear idea of what your father discovered, even after hours of looking."

Alexia's lively eyes darted all around the computer screen as she opened and closed files and documents. Adam stood behind her, resting his hands on the back of her chair, leaning forward to see what was on the screen.

Alexia read the titles of the computer files out loud: "Atlantis, prophecies, Mayans, Minoans, Map…"

She paused, looking at the screen more closely.

"Map?" she said, excited. She clicked on the file to open it.

"What is this?" she wondered aloud, uncertain.

"It's a bit strange, isn't it?" Adam said.

"It looks like a map with symbols."

"Zoom in on it."

"It looks as if it was scanned from the original," Alexia observed.

"It has a kind of gold color. Maybe it was etched onto gold or some kind of stone?"

Alexia shrugged.

"I'll make a copy. Make sure the printer is connected."

Alexia moved the mouse and clicked Print. A piece of paper slowly emerged from the printer.

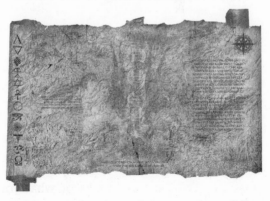

Adam picked up the piece of paper and carefully studied it.

"It has several esoteric symbols," he said.

"Do you know what they mean?"

He paused. He looked closely at the symbols; he knew what they were perfectly well: they were Egyptian, Hindu, Judaic, Greek...

"There's also a star of two triangles. It seems to mark a point in the sea."

Alexia's brow furrowed.

"This looks like a map of ancient Greece! If that's the case, then the star marks a point southwest of the island of Santorini and north of Crete," she said excitedly.

"That could be."

*A point in the Aegean Sea and ancient symbols.* Adam couldn't be sure of the significance.

# 16

The cardinal walked back into the room, ashen and pale. He could do nothing to slow his galloping heart rate.

Sopenski and Villamitre noticed the change in him immediately.

"Everything all right?" Sopenski asked.

Tous sighed heavily.

"There's a problem."

"What happened?" Sopenski's eyes opened wide in alarm.

"Something strange is happening with the sun," Tous replied, looking down at the floor.

"The sun?" Sopenski was confused. Things didn't just *happen* with the sun.

"Listen to me," the Magician said. Though he'd hung up with the Owl just two minutes before, he already had a plan. "I need you to stay here. I have to talk to the Organization."

Tous closed the distance between him and Aquiles in three long strides. "You win for now, Professor," he said, staring at him from just behind the spotlight. "Make no mistake, though—when I come back, you'll tell us everything you know."

He whispered something in Sopenski's ear and abruptly left the dungeon-like room.

The outside world, meanwhile, was in full alarm. Countries around the globe worked feverishly to evaluate and address the situation. The heat and the sun's vibration had set off solar storms. The storms weren't great in magnitude, but they were having an impact on information systems, causing some satellite communications to malfunction, leading to phone and Internet service outages.

"There is no reason to panic," authorities pleaded worldwide, "but we do need everyone to remain in their homes while we evaluate the situation." The United Nations called an emergency assembly meeting. Official representatives from every country were ready to take action.

In Athens, in the lobby of the Hotel Central, the Owl was pale, clutching an empty glass of gin and tonic and about to order another as he waited for Tous, his eyes glued to the television. Moments later the cardinal breezed through the hotel's doors and walked over to the Owl.

"I came as soon as I could," he said.

The Owl's eyes lit up with joy at seeing the cardinal. "What are we going to do?"

"Are you all right?" Tous asked, concerned, his voice betraying a measure of affection.

"Yes," the Owl replied, "just a little scared. What's the next step? What should we do? Has Vangelis said anything else?"

"We'll have to leave Professor Vangelis for later. My phone hasn't stopped ringing; the Vatican keeps calling. I have to return to Rome for an emergency meeting with the pope and some other members of the Secret Government's inner circle. We have to strategize."

"Do you have to go?" the Owl asked sadly.

"Yes, I'm afraid I have to be in Rome in less than three hours. Listen to me very carefully, though—I have a plan. I'll tell you just what we're going to do with that archeologist…"

# 17

Though their discovery of the map felt important, Alexia and Adam were frustrated they hadn't found more. Most importantly, they hadn't found Aquiles's emergency plan, the one he promised Alexia he'd leave in the event anything happened to him.

"It must not be here," Alexia said finally. "It must be in his official lab, in Santorini. I think we should search there, too. We've done all we can here."

Adam looked pensive.

"What is it?" Alexia asked.

"Your father's assistant. I just find it odd he wouldn't know anything at all. I think you should call him back before we go to Santorini."

"Call Eduard? Again?" Alexia looked skeptical. She'd never liked her father's assistant, but she knew Adam was right. "Hand me my bag. I'll call him on his cell phone."

She dialed and waited. "Hello, Eduard? It's Alexia. Are you okay?"

"Yes." The young man's voice on the other end of the line sounded surprised.

"Where are you?"

Eduard paused before answering. "In Athens. I got here a few hours ago."

"In Athens? What are you doing here?" Alexia didn't wait for him to answer. "Have you heard any news about my father?"

"No, nothing at all—it's as if the earth just opened up and swallowed him whole."

Alexia didn't find the comment the least bit amusing.

"We have to talk," Alexia said. "What did he tell you before he left Santorini? What had he discovered?"

Eduard was quiet. "Alexia, you know your father. I helped him, but he's intensely private about his work. He didn't tell me anything more than what, I would assume, he also told you."

Alexia took a moment to think. Then she said decisively, "Listen, I'm here in Athens with a friend of my father's, and we're going to Santorini. I want you to come with us."

"To Santorini?" Eduard was taken aback.

"Yes, to his lab. I'll call you back within half an hour."

Adam looked at her, admiring the strength and magnetic energy of her spirit. She possessed a fluid intelligence and confidence, traits she balanced with her sensitivity and sweetness.

"How are we going to get to Santorini?" Adam asked, snapping himself out of his reverie. "I can't imagine that flights are taking off under a red sun."

"Good point," Alexia said. She gathered up a few files, books, and the laptop, and put everything in her large leather bag. She grabbed Adam's warm hand and led him out the door. "Let's go to the port as fast as we can. A friend of my father's has a yacht there and can help us."

# 18

The red intensity of the sun diminished as the minutes passed, and experts predicted that by the end of the following day it would be completely back to its normal state. But many people didn't trust the news, reasoning that for every five forecasts meteorologists made, four were wrong. Nevertheless, airports had returned to their normal schedules.

Though weather experts felt calmer, Cardinal Tous did not. He felt full of a strange energy. With a mix of euphoria, fear, and survival instinct, his neurons worked full throttle during the flight to Italy. The cardinal's secretary was waiting for him at Rome's Fiumicino "Leonardo da Vinci" International Airport. His secretary carried a handsome black leather valise containing his official vestments, crucifix, the extremely valuable gold-and-diamond ring that he wore at all official church functions, and shoes just polished to a high luster. Tous went into the first-class lounge to change.

"What's the latest?" Tous asked when he emerged, feeling much more comfortable now that he was on home territory and wearing his official vestments.

His secretary explained they were waiting for two more cardinals, as well as other church officials and representatives. As soon as everyone arrived, a special assembly would convene.

"Very well," the cardinal said. "I need to pick up some things at my office. Please take me there right away."

They got into an official car, and the chauffeur drove them to the Vatican. Soon the sleek limousine was driving down the streets of the ancient city. The cardinal lowered his window slightly to let in a light breeze. As they stopped at a red light in front of a record store, the unmistakable melody of "Se Bastasse Una Canzone"—recorded by Luciano Pavarotti and Eros Ramazzotti—floated on the air. The cardinal felt a wave of emotion. He had a deep appreciation for classical opera and the arts of the Renaissance. More than anything else, they could provoke him to drop his rigid, carefully constructed armor.

St. Peter's Square was overflowing with the faithful, wearing sun hats and carrying parasols, stoically withstanding the heat, waiting for the supreme leader of their church to address them. They needed to reinforce their faith and push aside their fears.

Sitting comfortably on the car's black leather seat, the cardinal observed the mass of people from a distance. When the limousine slowly made its way down a street that ran parallel to the square, the cardinal had the disturbing thought that this would be one of the last times that such a crowd would ever gather there.

If that were the case, he would never get to realize his lifelong dream of being the pope.

## 19

Exercising her persuasion and charm, it had taken Alexia just under three minutes to persuade her father's friend to ferry her and Adam to the island of Santorini.

By yacht, the journey to Santorini would take only about an hour and ten minutes. It looked as if Poseidon had no plans at all to stir up the placid waters, and the sun was back to looking the way it usually did at that time of year, although the temperature was about fifteen degrees higher than normal—the thermometer registered 108 degrees Fahrenheit.

As Adam and Alexia completed the bureaucratic requirements for the trip, Eduard Cassas burst in. "The whole city's in a state of chaos!" he exclaimed. He wore large sunglasses, a short-sleeved blue T-shirt with an image of Bob Marley, and loose-fitting, khaki-colored pants. One could never guess what Eduard would show up wearing. Sometimes he wore comfortable, sporty clothes, like a casual schoolboy, and sometimes he played the part of a yuppie, looking more formal and serious, wearing a suit and tie. If he was going to be around younger people, he dressed more alternatively. Generally he dressed according to the company he kept, wanting to be accepted by whoever he was with at the time.

Eduard was exceptionally good looking. His celestial eyes glimmered like two coins over his strong aquiline nose. His chestnut hair, carefully cut, revealed a swath of gray hairs at his temples despite his young age, a typical mark of his Catalan genetics.

"It's lucky you managed to get here so fast," Alexia said as they went to find the ship's captain and finish the preparations.

The "little" yacht that Alexia had talked about was no less than thirty feet long, painted completely white, with a beautiful image of Zeus on its bow. The yacht's name was *Evlogia*, which meant "open mind."

"I'd like to introduce you to Eduard," Alexia said to Adam. "He's my father's assistant."

"I wish we could be meeting under better circumstances," Adam said as he shook his hand.

"Eduard has worked with my father for over a year."

As the men shook hands, Adam noticed that Eduard's grip was weak—he seemed very insecure.

"We should get out of the sun; it's not red anymore, but it's still extremely hot," Alexia said as she invited them aboard.

The landscape of the Athens coast had returned to normal, with turquoise waters and a clear blue sky. The red tinge that had seemed to color everything and had terrified everyone had disappeared. It was as if Apollo, the mythical Greek god of the sun, was no longer angry.

As they walked up the gangplank to the yacht, an unexpected wave caused Eduard to stumble, and he lost his grip on his cell phone, which fell into the water.

"Shit!"

Adam and Alexia turned to see the device disappear into the depths.

"You can buy another one in Santorini," Alexia said, trying to calm him.

"I hope I didn't lose all my contacts," he said, but had no inclination to dive into the water after the phone. Eduard had a powerful fear of the water. When he was eleven years old, some of his friends had tried to drown him at the beach in Spain. Ever since then, he had not wanted to set foot in the sea, or even in a swimming pool. And he was paralyzed by the fear of the mere possibility of falling into the water.

A few minutes after the yacht set sail, all three sat and drank sodas. The heat outside was stifling, but the cabin was more comfortable as the refreshing sea breeze came in.

Alexia sat down next to Eduard. "Tell me, when was the last time you saw him?"

He looked at her and sighed nervously. Whenever he found himself in a stressful situation, a nervous tic in his left eye surfaced, and it blinked uncontrollably like a flashing neon sign. Sometimes his nervous system betrayed him, and his left arm and leg collapsed, obstructing his circulation and causing him painful cramps.

"Before he left to meet you in Athens. After that I didn't hear from him at all." His voice sounded monotone and dry.

"And he didn't tell you anything at all about what he was working on?" Alexia pressed. "I find that hard to believe—you're his assistant!"

Eduard looked very pale. "I already told you, getting anything out of your father is like trying to get water from a stone." He avoided looking her in the eye. "He asked me to get things for him, but I wasn't directly involved in his research. I helped him with his scuba gear, made travel arrangements, arranged interviews, things like that, but he wouldn't even allow me to look in his files. He kept them in a locked cabinet."

"Scuba gear?" Alexia asked, losing patience. "That's all you did?"

Adam watched the young man carefully, observing how he reacted to the pressure. His nervous tic grew more pronounced. His masculine side manifested itself in the left side of his body, while his feminine side dominated the right side, where all of his nervous tension was directed.

"Well, that and some other things. I kept his calendar, got his lunch, returned phone calls for him…"

Alexia turned to look him in the eye. Her hardened expression was rather intimidating. "Tell me, who called him recently?"

Eduard swallowed hard.

"A British man called, a friend of your father's, and a few days ago I reserved a plane ticket for his flight from Santorini to Athens. He spent the past few days before he left alone in his lab. Then he got a package by certified mail. That's it."

"A package? What kind of package?" Alexia could hardly contain her rising irritation.

"A big box. It was from a lab, in…London, if I remember correctly. It was from a genetics lab, and the sender was somebody named Stefan Kruger. That's all I know."

Alexia knew Stefan—he was not only a geneticist, but also a historian and one of Aquiles's colleagues at the United Nations. "All right, Eduard," she said. "I can see you're tired. Get some rest in that cabin." She pointed to a lustrously polished wooden door toward the yacht's bow. "If you remember anything, anything at all, no matter how seemingly insignificant, please tell me."

Adam flashed her a questioning look. She shrugged.

"We'll be in the other cabin," Alexia said, about to open a smaller door. "We need to get some rest too, and clear our heads."

# 20

In Rome, the emergency meeting of the Secret Government was about to begin. Only a few cardinals were aware of it, and even fewer were permitted to attend. The pope himself was in attendance at this particular meeting in the ornate, handsomely appointed baroque salon, decorated with sculptures and paintings of incalculable historic and monetary value. Gathered in that room seated around an enormous table were about one hundred of the world's most influential and powerful from the spheres of politics, religion, finance, and high society.

Most of the members of the Secret Government were also members of the Freemasons, an organization that had begun their consolidation of power in the Middle Ages. Some even asserted that the Freemasons could trace their roots back to King Solomon. By the nineteenth century—especially in Boston and Philadelphia—they had shown themselves to be adept builders and had constructed some truly emblematic buildings. Many of the Freemasons' buildings displayed unusual architectural details and secret symbolism. The Freemasons brought significant influence to bear on the composition of the Constitution of the United States and even the dollar bill. The bill shows an image of George Washington—a famous master Freemason himself—but it also displays Masonic symbols.

The Secret Government was far more sinister than the Freemason Society. The former had been accused of artificially engineering diseases, of causing the hole in the ozone layer, of manipulating religious and ethnic struggles, and of starting wars. Their objective, always, was to reap dividends and consolidate their power. They sought nothing less than to control the planet. They protected their interests, always refining and expanding their intricate schematic to exert invisible, subliminal control over the masses.

Cardinal Tous sat just a few feet away from the pope. Stewart Washington, an American around seventy years old, was the leader of these high-level meetings of the Secret Government. Everyone called him the Brain. He was the first to speak.

Of slight stature, the Brain had a strong personality and an elegant, refined appearance. He looked like a modern-day Napoleon Bonaparte, especially within the grand setting of the Vatican. He wore an expertly tailored Armani suit, the expensive jacket draping his narrow shoulders. His crumpling, deeply lined face suggested a man who had been preoccupied for years, stuck in a permanent state of high tension and stress.

"Today is a very important day for the future of our organization," he formally began the proceedings. He arched a thick eyebrow over his glasses. "We must study very carefully the recent event that has affected the planet." He sounded extremely worried. The atmosphere in the room was charged with tension.

The representatives in the room had much more in common than not. The one thing distinguishing them was their manner of dress: some wore jackets and expensive ties, while others wore traditional religious garments. Although they sometimes differed on specific points of strategy, they all shared the same doctrine of power.

His Holiness the Pope, dressed entirely in white, looked expectant as he sat with his hands clasped just below his chest, where a large, ornate crucifix hung from a chain. He waited for the Brain to offer his solution to the problem. Although the pope occupied the most powerful position within the Vatican, his rank within the Secret Government was not comparably powerful. He would likely be listening today, not speaking.

As everyone present was well aware, the event that had shaken the world would have a huge impact on them. At the end of the day, they could not control the sun. Although they possessed technologies that could directly affect areas of the planet, they could do nothing to prevent solar storms.

Stewart Washington straightened his tie before continuing. His throat felt especially tight that day. He went on with his address. "Rumors are rapidly spreading through countries all around the world. People are talking about prophetic signs, the second coming of Christ, or the seventh Mayan prophecy. Some religious fanatics are sure it's a sign from the Bible—"

Too impatient to wait for his turn to speak, Cardinal Tous interrupted. "I beg your pardon, but I think that now is not the time to summarize all the rumors going around. Now is the time to act, and fast." His sonorous voice echoed off the vaulted ceiling. Everyone turned to look at him.

"That is the purpose of today's meeting, Cardinal." The Brain was always annoyed when anyone interrupted him, and few had the nerve to do it.

"We came here to discuss some rumors?" Tous asked, irritated.

The Brain gave him a withering look. "Among other things, Cardinal Tous. You have to read the latest reports and understand that our own team of scientists has studied the issue and agrees with recent reports issued by NASA and NOAA. They confirm that the sun has exhibited some highly unusual activity."

"And what of the prophecies—" Tous began, emboldened, leaning forward and striking his hands against the table.

Before the cardinal could interrupt him again, Washington cut him off, shaking his head. "We know we need to turn this to our advantage immediately. The masses are waking up, and we can't continue on the same track. The age of Adam's rib is over, Cardinal." These final words came out somewhat disjointedly, as if he was overwhelmed by the situation at hand. The power they were dealing with now was too much for him, or any of them.

"Everything that comes from the great beyond is our business," Tous replied, glancing around at His Holiness and the other representatives of the church. "I think our intelligence team can come up with a new plan."

The Brain waved his hand dismissively. "Yes, Cardinal, there are many plans. But this is somewhat, shall we say, different." The Brain stood up on his chair, as if to more forcefully underscore his words. "Our religious strength remains intact, but its power is waning. We need a renovation, or it may be too late. I'm not talking about changing the window dressing. We have a structural problem. As the leader, I need to look out for the organization's future."

Cardinal Tous seemed determined to interrupt again when the pope detained him with a slight gesture, as if he wanted to hear what the Brain was going to say next. Stepping down off the chair, the Brain took a sip of water. He was committed to winning majority support for the proposal he was about to present.

"All of our secret work," the Brain continued, "has been proceeding apace for many years. But now we cannot convince the people as easily as before. There are many independent researchers who don't accept our status quo. These are people who think for themselves, and every day we see more of them. Peoples' genetics are changing."

His words were like molten lava erupting from a volcano. He knew all too well that they could not keep on manufacturing more Iraqs, Pearl Harbors, 9/11s, witch hunts, Hiroshimas, or Nagasakis. Wars and persecutions had always been a lucrative business model for them, reinforcing their power base and the New World Order, but they were faced with something entirely new now.

The pope stood up. "I would like you to get right to the point," His Holiness said in a voice that seemed to emerge from a tomb. He did not want to waste any more time. The pope had his own reasons for worrying. He was all too aware that several texts of believers said that the sun's strange behavior signaled the end of the last pope's reign.

A murmur of approval ran through the cardinals present.

"Your Holiness," the Brain continued, "all I'm saying is that we cannot effectively use our usual tactics in the present set of circumstances. My job is to make accurate projections and devise adequate solutions."

Tous broke in again. "If the Mayan prophecies come to pass, and the secret texts of the Vatican and the Bible are right about there being a global change by the end of this year, then I have to—"

"Let me finish, Cardinal. What I'm trying to explain is that we can't keep bringing the people to their knees so often that they can no longer get up. Our organization, and our power, could be in real trouble. And know this: we cannot allow any individuals to communicate directly with whatever they think is up there." He raised his eyes toward the ceiling of the great room, ornately painted with religious imagery.

This last comment caused a stir around the room like a rushing brook. It wasn't like the Brain to speak so crudely, but there was no time for the usual decorum.

The pope abruptly cut in. "If the people are scared and confused, our job is to give them support. That is where our power lies." He said this as if it were a basic mantra that all of the popes had to memorize.

As a pragmatic politician, Stewart Washington had never been comfortable with the church's degree of influence on their decisions. "I don't disagree, Your Holiness."

Cardinal Tous was about to speak, but the pope silenced him with a gesture. "So what exactly do you propose?" asked the pope.

With a slight grimace, the Brain continued his discourse: "I believe now is the time to act, through a broader diffusion of information very closely controlled by us. We have progressed from a state of generalized fear to outright terror. And when this reaches a higher level still, of wild panic, we will seize the opportunity. Instead of causing fear, this time we need to calm it. The church should craft a message that will function as a panacea against fear, while our politicians and governments put protections in place. His Holiness should go out to address Saint Peter's Square. There are millions waiting."

Many members of the Secret Government murmured approvingly. Stewart Washington defended their interests tooth and nail. Stewart Washington felt in his bones that the time had come for them to change. They could not use fear as a currency anymore.

"And how do you suggest we make people believe we can protect them?" Tous asked tensely.

"The time has come to implant the microchip," Washington said. Stewart Washington was talking about the concept they'd been developing for years, of implanting a tiny chip under every person's skin like a human GPS. "We will tell people the chip will protect them from sun storms. Everyone will line up to get one."

## 21

Y ou're a bit fatalistic." Cardinal Tous's insubordina-
tion generated another round of murmurings.

"It's not fatalism, Cardinal. It's planning, execu-
tion, and results. We have to retool our organization for the
centuries to come. And with this current threat from nature,
with these astronomical movements…" he trailed off, peering
at the cardinal over his glasses, "we can't deny that people
might experience a great awakening."

"I have another plan," the cardinal announced.

"A plan?" Stewart Washington asked. "It would please
me and everyone else present to hear what your brilliant mind
has formulated to save us from disaster, Cardinal."

Tous stood and looked around the room. A hundred people attentively waited to hear what he had to say. Tous's plan
was to seize the archeologist's awesome discovery and use
it to increase not only the power of the Secret Government,
but his own power within it. Though he had no doubt he
would secure the object, the problem was that he didn't have
it yet. His challenge, therefore, was to sell the room on something he couldn't show them. "I'm about to obtain an object
of extreme importance," he remarked. "I practically have it
in my hands. It will arrive in very little time. It will change
everything."

Exasperated, the Brain drew in a long breath. "*That's* your great plan? My plan is concrete and tangible. You, Cardinal, aren't even talking openly about yours."

Tous opened his mouth to tell more about Aquiles Vangelis, but suddenly a deafening thunderclap tore through the room like an explosion, and all hundred faces of the Secret Government leaders took on the same expression of wild panic.

Milliseconds after the ear-splitting noise, the floor buckled beneath them. Some of the men fell down. Two columns at the far end of the room toppled over like sand castles at the beach. Chaos and confusion overtook the room. Everyone began screaming incoherently, some believing they were under attack.

The earth stopped moving after about thirty seconds. The pope, crouching under the table, was helped to his feet by two cardinals and asked, alarmed, "God in heaven! Is everyone all right?"

His suit covered with a layer of dust, Stewart Washington shot Cardinal Tous a challenging, triumphant look.

"I think that after this, my plan is the one we shall follow."

The rest of the attendees were in a daze. The room was a mass of confusion. Some men still sat on the floor, a few writhed in pain. They helped each other get up. Many coughed in the dusty air.

The Brain took control once more. In a loud voice, he announced, "Gentlemen, there is no time to lose. We must make a decision now and get to work."

## 22

**W**hile the yacht eased along over a calm sea at a speed of nine knots, inside the cabin Adam and Alexia sat in the middle of a bed that was covered with papers and books. Though Eduard hadn't shared much important information, both Adam and Alexia were intrigued by the package Aquiles had received from London.

"So what do you think it was all about?" Adam asked.

"I'm not sure. The last time he was in London, we met quickly for coffee, and he was excited about something—a discovery he'd just had confirmed through carbon-14 dating. He'd gone to see Stefan Kruger at his genetics lab."

Adam poured himself a glass of tonic water with lemon. "We need to get in touch with him. Quickly."

Alexia nodded. The topic of Stefan Kruger gave her an idea—clearly, whatever had happened in London was critical. She looked through Aquiles's laptop again. "Let me check on something," she said out loud, trying to focus her thoughts. Her mind took on a strange lucidity. Her eyes rapidly moved back and forth over the screen, quickly and methodically scanning through the files as she opened them.

"Look!" she said suddenly. "This file is called 'London Confirmation,' and there's a document titled 'Kruger.'"

They read through it together:

*-Words and frequencies can influence, program, and reprogram human DNA.*

*One can simply use words, affirmations, and mantras from human language to actually change DNA. As Siddhartha Gautama, the Buddha, said, "What you think, you become."*

*This represents a revolution that could change the world as we know it. For thousands of years, spiritual and esoteric masters have known that our bodies can be programmed through mantras or strong sounds, words, positive thinking, and above all through the states of consciousness achieved through deep meditation. Energy follows thought.*

*DNA activation has been scientifically demonstrated. Of course, not all people achieve the same degree of success changing their DNA. Individuals must work on their own spiritual development in order to establish conscious communication with their DNA.*

*Hyper-communication—which happens when DNA sends information to our consciousness—is most effective in states of deep relaxation and meditation. Stress, anxiety, and an overly active mind interfere with successful hyper-communication with the genes. In nature, various species have successfully practiced hyper-communication for millions of years, such as when some plants or animals intuit danger, fear, or an idea. It has been shown that the flow of life among all living things is organized according to a higher order, through synchronicity—the mislabeled "coincidences." Modern man understands only on a very subtle level. We know this overarching cosmic order as "intuition, a hunch, the sixth sense, or synchronicity."*

Adam stopped reading. He looked at Alexia curiously.

"What is it?" he asked.

"I feel strange."

"Strange? How, exactly?"

Alexia let out a long breath, closing her eyes, as if she were searching for something inside. Her expression was faintly joyous.

"I can't really describe it. It's like a really intense mental clarity."

Adam raised an eyebrow.

"And my chest is boiling," she added.

Adam gingerly placed his hands on the quartz necklace, which was hot to the touch.

"What's going on with that quartz?" he said. He stood up and began pacing around the cabin, his head down. "And what does it all have to do with changing DNA? Do you think your father found something that reprograms DNA?"

"I don't know," Alexia said. "Let's think for a moment more about Kruger. My father probably wanted Kruger to confirm his discovery, but Kruger's expertise is as a historian and a geneticist only."

Adam nodded slowly. "Go on."

Alexia looked into his eyes. "This all brings us back to you," she said, smiling.

"How so?"

"According to what we just read, DNA can be activated and reprogrammed with words, beliefs, fears, and mental power. Tell me, Adam, what's been the most effective negative programming that religions have used to block DNA and the way humans think and feel?"

"Sex, of course," Adam said. "Its repression and unnatural rules have caused problems, pathologies, and depravities for generations."

"Exactly! If my father found a way for people to set themselves free from all of these controlling mechanisms, they'd see who took their freedom from them in the first place. What if he found evidence that the church represses human sexuality as a means of control?"

"I don't know," Adam answered, uneasy. He walked over to the little porthole windows in the yacht's cabin. The horizon was blue. He could almost see the beautiful Santorini coast.

"I think I know why my father called you."

Adam gave her an expectant look. "Tell me."

"Think about it—what's the one thing that women and men have experienced throughout time, the thing that brings an entirely unique moment, bringing them outside of time, transporting them to a world where everything is unity, pleasure, and communion with life? Something that makes the duality of consciousness disappear, replaced with the sensation of being directly connected with the Life Force? Something that affects the glands, the skin, the psyche, even DNA…"

Adam Roussos finally understood why he was there. He had a key to hand over to his archeologist friend.

"Orgasm."

# 23

Even after the earthquake, Saint Peter's Square still overflowed with the faithful. The police issued an order to evacuate the square, but just a tiny fraction of people obeyed.

The atmosphere inside the Vatican was still very tense. Several members of the Secret Government, headed by Stewart Washington, had caught the first plane out they could. The leaders were now scattered around the globe.

In his private office, the pope had gathered members of his intelligence team and three cardinals, including Tous. Dim light from a few candles and two floor lamps gave the meeting a dramatic tone.

"His Holiness should go out to reassure the faithful in the plaza," advised Cardinal Primattesti, who, like Tous, fervently wished to one day occupy the pope's office himself.

"I think the present circumstances take priority." The pope was extremely worried.

"I don't understand, Your Holiness," Tous said, rubbing the knee he'd fallen on during the earthquake.

"My appearance could momentarily calm them and elevate their faith, but we have real problems." His voice sounded weak.

Everyone in the room froze at the sight of the lost expression of the man at the very top of the church's hierarchy. The pope turned to face the window that looked out over the plaza. Tous, Primattesti, and the other cardinals saw undisguised pain in the pope's expression.

Tous took control. "We shouldn't pay attention to books," he said, gesturing to the library adjacent to the pope's office. "It's entirely possible nothing will happen. We've heard about our ancestors' prophecies many times."

The pope and the other cardinals looked at him questioningly. "Cardinal Tous," the pope said calmly, "we must remember the words of Revelation 1:3." He turned to face the cardinals and recited, "Blessed is he who reads aloud the words of the prophecy, and blessed are those who hear, and who keep what is written therein; for the time is near."

Tous countered, "Your Holiness, those words were written more than—"

"Many years ago," Primattesti cut in, "and one day it will come to pass, do you not believe, Cardinal Tous?"

"Napoleon said it best," the pope broke in before Tous could answer. "History is the version of past events that people have decided to agree upon."

The cardinals gave the pope's comment a cool reception.

"What does that mean?" Primattesti asked.

The pope studied the cardinals with tired, compassionate eyes. He had access to and had read secret texts, reserved for the pope only, which the cardinals didn't even know existed.

"What do you think we should do?" Tous's body was taut with fury.

"I will go out so they can see me," the pope said, acquiescing. "The faithful will appreciate it."

"We have to be strong," Tous said.

The pope looked at him distantly. He knew the time had come to listen to the prophecies.

Everyone looked at the pope, expecting him to say more. His distant silence sent a shiver up the cardinals' spines.

"Should I announce your appearance on the balcony?" Tous asked, worried about what the pope might say to the throngs.

The pope nodded, looking slightly unsure.

"Your Holiness," Tous urged, "please, give them hope."

# 24

News stories circulated the globe at lightning speed. "Earthquake Hits Rome," "Cuba, Mexico, US, and Japan Rocked by Earthquakes," "The Earth Shakes," "Devastation in America," "7.1 Quake Rips Across Northern Hemisphere," "The Red Sun Made the Earth Move," "Earthquakes and Sun Storms Could Confirm Prophecies." The headlines frightened people as much as the events themselves.

Rattled believers waited for the pope's address, and as he went to greet them, Cardinal Tous retreated to his private office.

He took out his cell phone and dialed the Owl, but no one answered. Then he dialed the Vulture.

"It's me," the cardinal said hoarsely. "Listen, things are complicated here. Everyone's confused and panicking. How's the archeologist?"

"What's happened?" Shut in the windowless room, Viktor Sopenski had no idea about the earthquakes.

"There've been several earthquakes. People are terrified. What's happened with the archeologist? Has he confessed?" Without waiting for an answer, he continued, "I've tried to call the Owl, but there's no answer. Do you know what's going on with him? Is he there with you?"

"No," said Sopenski. "The Owl isn't here, and Vangelis is hard as a rock. We've tried everything, but he hasn't said another word. He only speaks in Greek, as if he's in some kind of trance. He's half-dead."

Tous was livid. "No! Don't kill him yet! Listen very carefully. We have to mobilize our contacts in England and find Vangelis's daughter. She lives in London. Go and get her," he said.

"Consider it done," Sopenski said obsequiously.

"She's the key. If we find her, he'll tell us everything."

# 25

In a well-appointed conference room of a luxury hotel, Stewart Washington met with the inner circle of the Secret Government, composed of twelve of its most powerful members. The air was thick with cigarette smoke and tension.

Patrick Jackson, a member who still had a head full of red hair despite his sixty years, spoke first. "Sir, I received a call from the leader of our armed forces. It's not good news."

"Yes, what is it?" Washington asked.

Jackson explained that he'd learned their nuclear weapons facilities were very vulnerable to the seismic activity affecting the globe. One more earthquake could set off a detonation.

Washington turned pale. "Have our satellites seen anything?"

"Four of our stations have detected sunspots and unusual solar activity," Jackson continued. "They've also picked up a strange point of light originating from a very distant point in our galaxy."

Washington was thoughtful. "A point of light?"

"According to NASA, it's spiral *formations* of light, several light years away from Earth."

"Gentlemen," Washington said tensely, "we need to activate the Secret Intelligence Plan. Events are transpiring just as the ancients predicted they would." He took several steps toward the center of the polished conference table. "We must alter the course of human evolution."

That utterance fell on the room like a finely honed guillotine's blade. Everyone looked intently at Washington again, waiting for him to continue.

"How?" one of the men asked.

"We have to activate the Secret Plan."

Those words caused every man around the table to break out in a cold sweat despite the heat in the room. Washington slowly turned to look around at the twelve men. His eyes were a television camera, filming their reaction. His voice sounded like a thunderclap.

"Gentlemen, you already know what we need to do next."

# 26

Santorini is a picturesque island southwest of Athens and north of Crete, surrounded by the crystalline waters of the Aegean Sea. Perhaps the most beautiful of Greece's islands, it is also the setting for most Greek myths.

The island is known for its volcano, although the volcano hasn't erupted for five thousand years. There is evidence that that last major event covered the sky in a giant cloud of gases and ash, traveling to Italy, Cyprus, Crete, and even as far as Israel and North Africa. That last eruption—the most powerful in history—formed a crater of fifty square miles at the island's center. The most popular of Santorini's myths holds that the volcanic eruption, accompanied by a devastating flood, buried Atlantis in the depths of the sea. Expert scientists predict that it will erupt again one day.

Adam Roussos was the first to disembark from the yacht. He held out his hand to Alexia, and Eduard led them both to the taxi stand. They grabbed a cab quickly and traveled a thousand feet from the port of Pireus up the narrow, winding road cut into the mountainside. Finally they turned onto the road that would take them to Oia, seven miles north of the island's capital.

When they reached the lab they went straight to Aquiles's office. The room had large windows, and its walls were painted white with a few blue accents.

"Where should we start?" Eduard asked, opening the refrigerator to get a cold drink. "I have to get my new cell phone."

Adam shot him a steely look. "First you need to help us here. I assume you know the combinations on the doors."

Alexia slowly turned around 360 degrees, carefully looking all around the room. "Open the combination on that door," she said, gesturing toward one on their right.

In a few seconds it swung open. They went inside and saw hundreds of papers, a night telescope, scuba diving equipment, maps, and strange drawings with notes written on them.

"Look at this, Adam," Alexia said excitedly, pointing to a file folder on the table. "It has the same drawings and symbols as the map we found in Athens."

Adam stood next to her to study the images.

"What do those signs mean?" Eduard asked.

"One's an Ouroboros, a serpent swallowing its own tail, symbolizing eternity," Adam said gravely, not taking his eyes off the symbols.

"There's the double helix, or DNA symbol, as well an ankh, the Egyptian cross representing eternity, and..."

He looked at Alexia before continuing.

"Go on."

"The ankh also has sexual connotations," he explained. "The masculine symbol of the pole in the lower portion represents the penis, and the open circle on the upper portion represents the vagina. The horizontal line bringing them together symbolizes the sexual act, or great union." Adam drew a picture so they could understand it more clearly.

Adam continued with his explanation. "In some religions, such as the Hindu faith, a point that looks like a seed symbolizes semen, or the seed of life. The Hindu symbol of the Om, the sound of Creation, is also a symbol for sexual union."

"And the superimposed triangles?" Alexia asked as the symbols came together in her mind.

A look of comprehension flashed across Adam's face.

"The Star of David. Aside from representing the union of the material with the spirit in Judaism, it also has a sexual connotation. The two triangles represent the union of the masculine triangle, pointing upward, with the feminine, pointing downward."

"Wouldn't my father have known the symbols' sexual meanings, though? He wouldn't have called you just for that."

Adam nodded. He'd been wondering the same thing.

"Let's compare this to our map." Alexia took the map out of her bag and studied it.

"Can I see it?" Eduard asked, and carefully examined the photocopy of the map and the symbols. "I don't get it. Does it necessarily mean anything at all?"

Adam looked him directly in the eye. "The mind learns through words, and the soul is moved by symbols." He turned his back, staring at the turquoise sea through the window. He was lost in thought, exhausted. "Excuse me for a moment," he finally said. "I need to think and recharge my batteries."

Adam took off his shoes and remembered how his yoga teacher always said the best posture for seeing everything clearly was the headstand, or *sirsasana*. In two quick movements he was balanced against the wall, standing on his head, his fingers laced behind his neck.

*What a time to be doing yoga*, Eduard thought.

Less than a minute later, Adam brought his feet down and stood up. His face was flushed from the flow of blood to his head.

"Eduard, give me the map," he said quietly. After a minute he said, "I think this map is upside down!"

Adam and Alexia both stared at it for another long minute, then said at the same time, "This isn't a map!"

"It's a picture of Adam and Eve!" They both got goose bumps.

Eduard approached to see it with his own eyes.

"There has to be something on this image," Alexia said, "something *you* have to solve, Adam, something my father didn't know. What do you *see* in this?"

"In some religions and Eastern spiritual practices," Adam explained, drawing on new energy, "the representation of Adam and Eve doesn't have the same connotations that the church assigns to it."

"Okay, then what does it mean? Tell us more."

"There's an Asian practice called Tantrism that gives a special meaning to these symbols. The Tantra is a science of sexuality, and it's over five thousand years old."

"So how would Tantrism interpret this?"

Adam ran a hand through his hair, remembering his studies. "The tree of good and evil, or the tree of knowledge, really isn't a tree. It represents the human spinal column, from the sacrum to the crown of the head, symbolizing the sacred in every human being. Points of energy called chakras are found all along the spinal column. These chakras are the motors of psycho-energy that activate the glands of the endocrine system. The spine is also where you find the serpent."

"What's important about the serpent, though?" Alexia asked.

"It represents sexual energy, the natural pulsation of life that is in everyone. They call it Kundalini."

"In the Bible, the serpent is a very negative image," Eduard remarked, happy to finally be contributing. "It represents the devil, tempting Eve, and all women."

"No, no, you're wrong," Adam said, looking up toward the ceiling, searching his memory. "'The serpent said unto the woman, ye shall not surely die: For God doth know that in the day ye eat thereof, then your eyes shall be opened, and ye shall be as gods, knowing good and evil.'"

"Where's that from?" Eduard asked, surprised.

"Genesis, chapter three," Adam said. "Aside from the serpent, the symbol of the apple, or the fruit, within Tantra represents the first chakra, a red circle of energy five centimeters in diameter. In the apple, or the sexual chakra, in the sacred zone, located here on Aquiles's drawing. It's said that this life energy in the form of a snake is located within the first chakra, and from there it ascends the spinal column to stimulate the six other chakras, eventually reaching the pineal gland, and the crown of the head."

"The coronation to the sublime," Alexia added.

"Exactly. In ancient times, coronation symbolized elevation to the highest levels."

"And within Tantra, does coronation mean something sexual? I don't understand," said Alexia.

"There are thousands of secret techniques to raise sexual energy up the vertebrae so individuals can reach their full potential and come into direct contact with the divine within themselves. They're based on transforming orgasmic energy into spiritual power."

"And that's how the ancients found spiritual elevation?" Alexia asked.

Adam nodded confidently.

"What about the half-moon and the dot or the seed?" Eduard asked.

"The half-moon represents the feminine principle, and the dot represents a drop of masculine semen. On this mystical path," Adam continued, "three things are important: the breath, control over the mind, and the retention of semen. In Tantra, it is believed that by retaining semen, that magnetic energy creates an electricity that travels throughout the nervous system, activating psycho-spiritual energy, the brain, and DNA."

"Semen is bad, though, right?" Eduard asked.

"Not at all, Eduard," Adam explained. "For Eastern civilizations, it's the primary material of life. It's sacred, and like blood, it shouldn't be wasted."

Adam paused a minute and studied Eduard's perplexed expression. "You know very well," Adam continued, "that after you ejaculate, you're left empty, tired, and sleepy. You fall from the 'paradise' that you inhabited just a moment before. But in these cultures, the elevation of the seminal material is literally the *seed* to create life within yourself. According to Eastern philosophies, the state of paradise is the expansion of consciousness to such a degree that you can feel the conscious connection with the Source of Life, the All. Various ancient cultures, such as the Atlanteans, Egyptians, Mayas, and Hindus, are believed to have practiced this kind of sexual alchemy. When Jesus tells Nicodemus that he had to be reborn in order to enter the kingdom of heaven, he's talking about an internal birth through the sexual alchemy practiced by the Tantrics. In Eastern traditions, it's called spiritual rebirth."

"I'm having a hard time believing this," Eduard said.

"You know," Adam said, "according to one theory, Jesus spent time in India as an adolescent studying these theories and putting them into practice."

"Are you saying that Jesus was sexually active?" Eduard challenged.

Adam threw even more fuel on the fire. "According to the theory, Jesus didn't just have sex, but through various initiation rites, some of which were sexual, he was transformed from the simple mortal man named Jesus into *Krestos*, which literally means 'anointed in fire' in ancient Greek. It's also said that Jesus was enlightened spiritually with Mary Magdalene. Remember that in ancient times, fire represented sexual energy."

"I just can't believe that Jesus might have had sex."

Adam shrugged. "Jesus himself said in Thomas 22, 'When you make the male and female into one, then you shall enter the Kingdom.'"

Eduard went pale.

Adam smiled slightly. "That's why the church condemned sex so harshly. It was dangerous because if people could become enlightened spiritually and find God within themselves through heightened, transformed, highly potent sexual energy, what use would they have for intermediaries? The whole world would be transforming sex into cosmic, liberating love!"

"What role did women have in this sexual rite?" Alexia asked, intrigued.

"The woman is the initiator, the power of life, the chalice from which power flows. The woman is the fountain, and she holds the counterpoint to masculine electricity inside of herself. That's where the electromagnetic current of sex comes from: the constant attraction, the joining of opposites. The woman is magnetic, and the man is electric."

"Okay, but what about the DNA symbol?" Eduard asked.

"I think I know." Alexia smiled, her eyes bright. "Your namesake, the supposed first man on Earth, is called 'Adan' in Spanish, right?"

"Yes."

She smiled mysteriously.

"Now, take the second 'a' out of your Spanish name."

Adam was shocked. "ADN! That's DNA in Spanish!"

Alexia nodded triumphantly, a smile lighting up her face.

"Now, let's call Kruger," Alexia said, rushing to find her phone.

# 27

Cardinal Tous had played a trump card with Viktor Sopenski. He'd promised him sixty thousand dollars if he could get his hands on Vangelis's daughter. The corrupt police officer didn't need to hear any more. "*No matter where you are, I'll find you...*" He was in full Vulture mode.

Sopenski didn't believe in any kind of prophecy. To him, the world simply kept on turning, and it would continue until he died as a very old man. Viktor Sopenski was not religious or spiritual. He was concerned mainly with imposing his own authority. And with money, of course. He amused himself thinking of all the ways he could spend his reward.

He impatiently waited at the airport gate. Having to travel to London made him angry. To distract himself he reviewed his plan. Once he arrived at the British capital, he'd go straight to Alexia's house. He'd break in when he knew she wouldn't be there and would quietly wait until, like a ravenous vulture, he could seize her.

He gulped down his coffee and anxiously paced through the Athens airport. Crowds passed through the wide hallways on their way to catch their flights, meet friends, or get in taxis. Just half an hour until boarding, he thought eagerly. He'd be in London in no time.

# 28

Eduard was deeply skeptical.

"Are you suggesting that the first Adam, or Adan, is nothing more than the symbolic abbreviation for DNA?" he asked, his mind spinning like the wheels on a bicycle.

"That could be," Adam said.

Alexia came back into the room with her BlackBerry. "Do you know where my father keeps his personal contacts?" she asked Eduard.

Eduard found Aquiles's rolodex and gave it to her. She dialed Stefan Kruger's number as the others waited in anticipation.

"Hello?"

"Dr. Kruger?"

"Yes, who is this?"

"I'm Alexia Vangelis, Aquiles's daughter. I hope you remember me. I met you a while ago at a conference my father organized in London."

"Alexia!" he said, happily. "How are you?"

"To be honest, not very well, Dr. Kruger. My father..." Alexia cleared her throat. "My father was with you two months ago in London; is that right?"

"Yes, exactly, we met here."

"I understand that he's made an extremely important discovery, although I'm not exactly sure what it is. But my father's...he's been kidnapped."

"What?" Kruger's tone sharpened. "Who did it?"

"I don't know—someone who really doesn't want my father's discovery to get out. Look, I need to talk to you. I imagine my father must have told you something about his discovery. Right now I'm looking through his lab, searching for anything that could help us, so I'd really appreciate anything you can tell me."

"We have to talk in person," he finally said after a long pause, not sounding entirely sure of himself. "It's too sensitive a topic to discuss over the phone."

"It's just that time is of the essence," Alexia said, exhausted and heartbroken. "I haven't heard anything at all from my father, and no one's asked for a ransom—nothing. I'm desperate."

"Trust me," the scientist said. "It would be best if you came here. We'll talk about it."

"Go to London?" Alexia was so tired her voice broke. "I just want to find my father." Her eyes filled with tears. She took a deep breath and resolved she'd do what she had to do. "Please give me your address. I'll get there as soon as I can."

# 29

When Stewart Washington gave the "go" order for the Secret Plan, his colleagues froze.

Finally Patrick Jackson spoke up. "We can't deliberately do that," he countered.

"So what do you want to do?" Washington said hoarsely.

"Let's try to come up with another strategy," Jackson suggested, looking around at the other men at the table. "I don't believe activating the Secret Plan would be the best course of action."

"If there's another solution, I'd greatly appreciate it if you would enlighten the rest of us," Washington said softly.

Jackson put the file folders he had in his hand down on the oval table and stood up. He felt inspired. "Let's see," he said, in a calm, firm voice. "I think we should design a protective layer to reinforce the ozone layer and block the cosmic energy from entering our atmosphere."

The other men looked at him, surprised.

"Are you talking about chemtrails? That we make the chemical flights more potent?"

Jackson knew he was opening a can of worms here. He drew in a deep breath before continuing. "What I mean is, if from the ionosphere our satellites and spacecraft could emit a strong vibrational field, supported by HAARP from the earth, then we could…"

"I think you're right," said Sergei Valisnov, a heavyset man with a thick Russian accent. "A vibrational protective field could be a good solution. It would form a kind of global shield around the whole planet, keeping the shower of photons out. It would never reach people's consciousness."

"Gentlemen, in my opinion, the most suitable option would be to set our Secret Plan into motion," the Brain said. "But I think we should also consider what the other members propose. Time is of the essence. We should bring it to a vote."

Just then Stewart's cell phone rang. He had given strict orders that he was to be disturbed only if it was a matter of life and death. He reluctantly answered. His personal assistant's voice sounded like the insistent buzzing of a bee.

"What happened? Didn't I tell you not to—"

His assistant cut him off.

The color of Stewart Washington's face changed dramatically, going from bright red to the blood-drained look of a cadaver. His body temperature experienced similarly dramatic changes; he felt hot and cold at the same time. His mouth was very dry.

"Are you sure?" he asked, then listened to the voice on the other end for a moment before hanging up.

"Gentlemen," he said, his voice breaking, "we have a bigger problem."

The Secret Government's inner circle maintained an uncomfortable silence.

"What's happened?" Jackson asked.

"My assistant has informed me that our center in Colorado has issued an urgent report, and that…they saw…"

The air was charged with tension.

"Just say it, please!"

Washington drew in a breath with some difficulty. "The scientists have said that Earth is threatened by a strange mass. They believe the point of light is actually a huge meteor and that it's headed directly for us."

# 30

The day had been one of the worst of Cardinal Raul Tous's entire life, and now he couldn't fall asleep. He was too anxious. More than anything, he was worried that his power was slipping away—his power in the church and his power in the Secret Government. He had to know what was going on with Viktor Sopenski in London and with the Owl in Greece. The cardinal felt trapped since he had orders to stay at the Vatican.

Tous just had to wait, the one thing he detested. He needed to have that powerful discovery in his own hands, and he needed it now. *They've searched the whole world over for centuries, and soon it will be mine,* he thought.

He paced back and forth like a tiger in a cage in his comfortable yet austere room. A crucifix hung over his large bed, and a Bible sat on the night table. He opened the Bible. He felt utterly powerless. The prophecies of some pre-Colombian Indians were not going to ruin all of his carefully laid plans! He had to find some error. A part of him felt that those prophecies were nothing more than myths, but another, very strong part felt a fear of the unknown.

He touched the gold ring on his right ring finger, as if it could somehow give him his strength back. *Think like the Magician. Find the solution to this problem! Why haven't I gotten word from the Vulture or the Owl? What is going on with that archeologist?* His insides began churning. *I'll call them again,* he thought as he went to the bathroom. *I have to act before it's too late.*

He started to feel desperation and took a sedative. The pills had a soothing effect on him. Now he needed strength, intelligence, and shrewd judgment. The voices in the his head were like a volcano erupting, a demon's restless clamor.

He closed his eyes, feeling the slight breeze coming in through the window. He needed to stop all mental activity for just a few minutes. At that instant, Raul Tous felt an overwhelming sense of loneliness. A dark abyss opened up inside of him.

He put on the heavy crucifix that hung over his solar plexus, although it hurt his neck more and more. He would get his hands on Vangelis's discovery. He knew he would. He had played his best card, and he was all in.

With that thought, he tried to fall asleep.

## 31

The next morning in Santorini, Adam Roussos woke up at six thirty. The first rays of sun peeked through the window. His back ached a bit from sleeping on an improvised bed on the hard floor. He took a shower and put on the same clothes he had worn the day before, as his bags were still at the Athens airport. As he got dressed, he saw that Alexia was beginning to stir. Eduard slept on a sofa next to her.

"Good morning," she said softly.

"Good morning," Adam answered, almost in a whisper. "I've been thinking. I'm going to go to London this morning. It's best if you and Eduard stay here to keep digging through your father's papers. There's a flight at nine forty-five, so I need to get going."

"I'll go with you," Alexia replied, still groggy, trying to sharpen her mind.

Adam shook his head. "It's better if I go. If Kruger knows something, I'll call you right away. You know your father's office better than I do. This way, we'll have two possibilities of discovering something instead of just one."

Alexia knew he was right, but she wasn't happy about being apart.

"Okay," she said, sitting up in her father's bed. She took a white shirt out of the closet and put it on.

She walked Adam to the door. "Listen, Adam," she said, and grabbed a piece of paper and a pencil. "Here's my address in London and my best friend's phone number. His name is Jacinto Urquijo. He works with me. He has the keys to my house. He said he'd stop by regularly to water the plants and feed my cat."

Adam took the piece of paper with her address and put it in his right pocket.

"If you need to spend another few days there, stay at my place. Jacinto can give you the keys."

Taking her hands in his, Adam aimed to be as soothing as possible. "Let's see what Kruger has to say," he said, "and then we'll decide."

"Adam...I..." Though they had talked little of their personal lives, Alexia felt a strong connection to Adam. "I want to thank you for everything you're doing, and please, be very careful." She gazed deeply into his eyes, and with a look, told him everything that she couldn't put into words.

"You too, Alexia. Be careful."

Adam wanted to pull her to him. She opened her arms first. They melted into a warm, intense embrace, as strong and connected as the roots of an elm with the earth.

"Ahhh!" Adam jumped as if he had just been shocked. "What's that?"

"My chest," she said, "it's the quartz crystal."

"Oh my God! What's going on with that thing? It's very hot. It felt like a release of energy."

She shrugged. "I don't know. Ever since all this started, it's been like that. Last night I even had some really strange dreams."

The two hugged goodbye once more. From across the room, Eduard watched them out of the corner of his eye.

# 32

In Athens, Aquiles awoke still tied up, exhausted and listless. The pain in his back was unbearable.

*I'll have to give him something to eat and drink. He can't die,* thought Claude Villamitre.

The Frenchman had slept fitfully on an old sofa. He was afraid the archeologist might somehow escape even though he was tightly bound and couldn't move. There was a great deal at stake, and Villamitre felt important. He was responsible for keeping their prisoner alive.

It had been hard to fit his gawky frame over the sofa. Wearing the same clothes he had been wearing for days, he went to the bathroom. As he came back in the room, he saw that the archeologist was faring very poorly.

"I'm going to let you have something to eat and drink, but I'm warning you: if you get out of line at all, I will shoot you," he said, pointing his gun at Aquiles.

Aquiles didn't say a word. He was too tired and dazed. Villamitre put a bottle of water and a glass on the table, with some bread, fruit, a can of tuna, some cheeses, and a few *spanakopitas* that had been in the room for two days already.

"You must forgive me, Professor. It's not the level of fine Greek dining you're surely accustomed to, but you should eat something," he said sarcastically.

Aquiles was still quiet, his head drooped down. The pain in his neck was excruciating.

"I'm going to untie one of your hands so that you can eat, but the other will still be tied to the chair. I repeat: one false move, and kaput." He traced a line across his own neck.

Villamitre loosened the ties around Aquiles's right arm, leaving the left one still restrained.

"Very well. Bon appétit," he said, gesturing toward the table.

Aquiles ate an apple, some grapes, and a banana and drank a full glass of water. After a few minutes, he spoke.

"Please, untie my other hand, too. I need to get my circulation going."

The Frenchman frowned. "*D'accord.*"

Aquiles stared straight ahead at the wall. Villamitre did not let him turn to see his punisher's face. Aquiles rested his bloodshot eyes since the bright light wasn't trained at him. The Frenchman sat on the sofa, looking at Aquiles's back.

Aquiles posed an unexpected question. "How much are they paying you?"

"That's none of your business."

"You're hypnotized."

"What's that?"

"I said, you're hypnotized." The archeologist's voice had regained some of its strength.

"What are you talking about?"

"You and your organization. You're just a slave of the machine."

"I'm just following orders," Villamitre said. "And they pay me very well to do it."

"You're motivated by money. You're living an illusion. You're completely replaceable," Aquiles said. "And you say you work because you want to make money? For what?"

"That's my business. Don't stick your nose where it doesn't belong."

Aquiles went on, undeterred. "You make money so you can spend it on cigarettes, whores, food...I could pay you twice what they're paying you."

Vangelis had hit the nail on the head. Villamitre was not a man of high-minded principles. Now he was really paying attention.

"I'm going to buy a house," Villamitre said, lighting up his first cigarette of the day.

"A house? How lovely!" Aquiles said sarcastically. "You'll own your own place that very soon will not be yours at all."

"What do you mean?"

"Very soon, the earth will once again belong to everyone."

"What are you talking about?"

"I'm just letting you know."

"Letting me know what?"

Wheezing, Aquiles struggled to breathe. He let out a dry cough. One of his lungs hurt tremendously. If he was going to die, he was going to say everything he wanted to.

"You're living in a trance. You work, probably at a job you don't like, eat, spend your money, dream of buying a house and meeting a partner who will make you happy. All of these things are an illusion. Have you never asked yourself why you are alive? What are you doing here? What is your mission? What is beyond the end of your own nose, out in the universe?"

"I see you want to talk philosophy," he replied, without much interest.

"With you?" Aquiles turned, although he could not see his face. "Philosophy is for intelligent people."

"Don't get smart, Professor."

The Frenchman hit Vangelis's back with a bat. "Now finish eating and face the wall, or I'll put the spotlight in your face."

Aquiles slowly sat up. His body was in more and more pain.

"You didn't answer me."

"What the hell do you want me to answer? Do you want to bribe me? Or lecture me?"

"How are you any different from the animals? They want to survive too, by eating, copulating, and having a place to sleep."

"Where are you going with this, Professor? How much money are you going to offer me? Will you save me from certain death?" Villamitre smiled tightly, then coughed.

"Your cigarettes will take care of your death."

"We're all going to die someday."

"Yes, you're right about that. But it's one thing to die when you've truly lived, and another for death to take you if you've been asleep. There's a huge difference between dying while you're doing what you came here to do, as opposed to wasting time planting your seeds over concrete."

"My seeds? What seeds?" Villamitre was irritated. He didn't understand what Aquiles was talking about.

"Your seeds, Frenchie, your dreams. I bet when you were young, the grown-ups asked you what you wanted to be when you grew up. Did you do it?"

Villamitre had not had a happy childhood. He'd always wanted to be a singer, like his idol, the French vocalist Charles Aznavour. But he hadn't thought about that in a long time.

"If you don't realize your childhood dreams, you'll never be free or happy. You'll live the life society programs you to live. You'll do what they say."

"Free!" Villamitre shouted angrily. "I am free!"

Enraged, he hit Aquiles again, harder and harder, over and over, until a trickle of blood ran down his back. Aquiles fell face down on the floor, motionless.

Silence.

Aquiles groaned, struggling to turn himself over on the floor, and after a few minutes, kept on talking.

"You are not free..." he rasped, passing a hand over his blood-covered face. "You escape from reality through television, drinking, and cigarettes."

"Go to hell, Professor! What do you care?"

"You're avoiding your personal destiny. You're a prisoner."

"You're making me angry! I already told you I'm free!"

"But you're wrong. People who are free go after their dreams."

"Destiny? Dreams? What are you talking about? I work like everybody else. I earn my money, then I do whatever I want."

"Money does not give you power."

"Oh, it doesn't? Then what does? Discovering some old statue? Digging in the dirt to see if I can find some lost treasure from an ancient civilization? What? Answer me, Professor!" Aquiles had successfully enraged Villamitre even more.

"Anger is a sign of fear. What gives you real power is knowing who you are and feeling that you have an immortal soul. You are not here right now because you are free. You follow orders. You are just a piston in a big machine, and if the piston breaks, it's replaced by another. You're expendable. And yet you have to answer to your bosses at an organization in which you don't even know the members."

On that point, Villamitre had to concede Aquiles was right. He had always received his payments from people he didn't know. "Then make me an offer. What do you think I should do?" he asked, skeptical.

"There's not much you can do. You're like a broken heart."

"A broken heart?"

"Yes, there's no cure for that," Aquiles said, suppressing a chuckle. He surprised himself, being able to joke at such a tense moment.

Overcome with fury, Villamitre attacked Aquiles, hitting him with all his might, in the back, the head, the legs…blood gushed from Aquiles's nose. A blow to the back of the neck knocked him unconscious.

Villamitre had a strange feeling that the message he'd just heard was dangerous. "Thanks for the advice, Professor," he said, looking down at Aquiles's crumpled, motionless body, "but I think it's time to tie you up and gag you again."

## 33

As Adam's London-bound plane took off from the Santorini airport, Sopenski was already in the British capital. Meanwhile, Eduard Cassas had purchased a new cell phone and dialed his first call. The brief seconds that it took for someone to answer seemed like years. The stress set off his nervous tic.

At the Vatican, the call was answered by Raul Tous.

"Hello," Eduard said, "it's me. Owl."

The cardinal's voice was strong and authoritative. "Where are you? I've been waiting to hear from you! Why didn't you call earlier?"

"I lost my phone and just got another one," Eduard said quickly. "But I have good news."

"Good news? Where are you?" The Magician felt a rush of adrenaline.

"I think I've accomplished what you wanted," Eduard said.

"Has Aquiles said anything?" Tous sounded impatient.

"I have something that will get him to. I'm in Santorini with Aquiles Vangelis's daughter."

The cardinal's eyes gleamed.

"What are you doing there?"

"She and a friend of hers brought me here. They were in Aquiles's laboratory looking for information about his discovery. He didn't tell her anything," Eduard said, barely opening his mouth. He had a strange way of talking, as if his jaw was wired shut. "Maybe there is such a thing as destiny, Raul," he said. Eduard was the only person who was allowed to call the cardinal by his first name.

"Don't leave her for a minute," Tous said. "Give it a few more hours to see if she finds anything. If not, we'll initiate the plan."

"Understood."

"Aquiles will talk!" the cardinal blurted out. He was ecstatic. Eduard's eyes lit up.

"Her friend went to see a geneticist in London. He's trying to find out if Aquiles left his discovery there."

"His name and address, quickly!"

Eduard gave him the information.

"I'll mobilize more people. Don't disappear again," Tous ordered. "Give me updates every hour." Tous felt as if he were back in the race.

Eduard rushed off to find Alexia.

# 34

Alexia was frustrated and tired. She'd looked over everything at least once and was going through it a second time when a date on her father's calendar caught her attention. The last entry he'd written, on the day before he was supposed to meet Adam, said, "dentist's appointment." He'd drawn a line through it and written "canceled." Below that, he'd written "45 Amalias Street." She decided to call Adam and tell him about it. After a few seconds, she was put through to his voice mail.

"Adam, I think I found another clue. The same day he was kidnapped, my father went, or was planning to go, to a place in Athens. I have the address. It was written on his calendar. I'm going back to find out what he was going to do there. Please call me as soon as you get this message."

# 35

Eduard quietly entered Aquiles's lab, trying not to make a sound. He looked through all the rooms, but no one was there. His nervous tic contorted his face. *You bitch! Where did you go?*

Her keys weren't there, but he did notice Aquiles's day planner open on the desk. It was open to the day he was kidnapped, and Eduard saw the notation with the address—the address where Vangelis was being held prisoner! Eduard had to catch up with Alexia. *She doesn't know what that address means...*

Among the papers, Eduard found a note:

*Eduard,*

*I have to go back to Athens right away. I found a clue about my father. Stay here in case we need anything.*

His face turned bright red, and he broke out in a cold sweat. As quickly as he could, he called the island's tourist information number to find out the ferry and flight schedules.

"Goddamn it!" he shouted as he listened to the recorded schedule. "There's a ferry in half an hour!"

If he lost her, Tous would be infuriated. Eduard took a pistol out from behind an armoire and rushed off as fast as he could, heading for the port.

hen Adam landed in London just after noon, he walked up to a news kiosk in the airport and looked over the headlines from the major newspapers.

"The Earth Collapses." "Baffling Chain of Earthquakes." "Summit Meeting at UN." "The British Government Calls for Calm Before the Olympic Games."

Shaking his head in disbelief, Adam left the airport, got in a taxi, and headed to the German scientist's institute. The streets of the English capital were choked with traffic, so the taxi driver was obliged to take a somewhat circuitous route.

"Please, I'm in a hurry."

The taxi driver wove around two cars next to them and skidded around a few corners until he found a less congested street that would take them to the city center. On the radio, the Bee Gees' mega-hit "Stayin' Alive" blasted through the speakers. Adam felt that he himself was "stayin' alive" in the middle of the chaos and confusion happening just then on the earth. Soon they were in the posh Belgravia neighborhood, with its luxurious homes and Victorian mansions.

A few minutes later the taxi came to a stop at a corner.

"You should get out here and walk down that street on the right. The place you're looking for is back there," the driver said, gesturing toward a dome-shaped building.

Adam did as directed. When he reached the building, he climbed a dozen white stairs and rang the bell to the right of the wooden door. It wasn't long before the door opened.

"Good afternoon." A young, attractive black woman greeted Adam. She was around thirty years old and athletic, and she had vivacious eyes and chestnut-colored hair that framed her face. She also had a nose piercing, which gave her a sensual look.

"I'm looking for Dr. Stefan Kruger."

"Your name?" the young woman asked in a classic British accent.

"I'm Adam Roussos. I have an appointment with him. We talked on the phone and—"

"Come in," a man's voice said from inside. He was over six feet tall, around fifty-five years old, and clean shaven. He had thick white hair and a solid, strong physique. "I'm Stefan Kruger," he said, firmly shaking Adam's hand.

Kruger smiled at the young woman.

"Thank you, Kate, I'll take it from here."

She walked away, her footsteps echoing down a long hallway.

"Come in, Mr. Roussos. Let's go to my office."

Pictures of children playing adorned the walls, along with photos of the solar system and DNA helices, and paintings of trees and landscapes. Everything seemed clean and well ordered. Adam followed Stefan to an office that smelled faintly of lavender.

"I was very worried after your call yesterday." Kruger opened a small refrigerator and took out two small bottles of juice.

"We all are," Adam said quickly. "Aquiles called Alexia and me to tell us he'd discovered something about the Atlanteans. We know it has something to do with sexuality...and we think it's also related to the Mayan prophecies. With the craziness with the sun, with the earthquakes, well, the timing of all of this is a little much to handle."

Kruger turned to face him. "It's okay. Just calm down." Kruger sounded like a father trying to soothe a child as he offered Adam a glass of juice. "Sit down, please. I see you're a little tense. Let's start at the beginning."

Adam told him about why he'd gone to Athens, the call he'd received from Aquiles in the middle of the night.

"What I'd like to know," Adam said gravely, "is what Aquiles told *you*, Dr. Kruger."

The geneticist raised an eyebrow. "Aquiles and I are colleagues, and we're friends. Our work has been very complementary, and—"

"Why did he come to see you? Did he tell you anything about his discovery? What does he know?"

Kruger paused, considering how to respond. "Mr. Roussos...may I call you Adam? I knew your father as well. I have his book. I have your book on sexuality, too."

"You knew my father?" Adam's heart leaped in his chest.

Kruger nodded. "We met several times. I was very sorry to hear of his death."

Adam's eyes gazed unseeing at a picture on the wall. For a few seconds he was struck by the always painful realization that his father was not around.

"So I suppose that I can trust you," Kruger said. "But why didn't Alexia come with you?"

"She stayed at her father's lab in Santorini to see if she could find anything useful there."

Kruger leaned forward in his chair. "Look, Adam. Aquiles came to see me with a very important discovery, but if it's applied in a negative sense, it could have very serious repercussions." Kruger stood and walked toward his bookshelves. "This is one of Aquiles's two discoveries. It's just a copy, of course. It's the less practical of the two things he found."

He held out a piece of paper. Adam took it with both hands. It was the drawing he'd already seen of Adam and Eve.

"We've already seen this. What does it mean?"

Kruger pressed his lips together tightly. "It's part of our origins."

"A part of our origins? As a human species? On a piece of paper?"

"It's not paper, Adam. It's the original tablet of orichalcum, the metal used by the ancient Atlanteans. According to carbon-14 tests, it's over twelve thousand years old. This is proof that they existed, and what's more—"

The phone on his desk rang. Kruger stopped in the middle of his explanation. "Yes?" There was silence as the voice on the other end spoke. "Very well, Kate." Kruger hung up the phone and looked at Adam. "That was the professor who let you in. In a minute you'll see the biggest part of Aquiles's discovery."

"What is that part?"

Dr. Kruger looked him directly in the eye. "First you have to analyze the first part. Look again at this drawing. Far from merely a piece of paper, it's an encrypted code of our original DNA. It tells us *where we came from*."

"I already know it's about DNA. But how does it explain where we came from?"

The geneticist smiled slightly. "We're at an extremely important turning point in history. Many people already know this, Adam. There are many spiritual groups working for evolution, and individuals who keep their genetics and their energy in harmony, in anticipation of the great moment." His gaze rested on a picture of the planets on the wall.

Adam looked at it too.

"They believe Earth will transition from the third to the fifth dimension."

"Do you believe that?" Adam asked.

Dr. Kruger sighed. "I know you've read your father's book. I know you've read the prophesies, but it doesn't seem as if you're paying much attention to them."

Adam frowned. Dr. Kruger was wrong—he'd read his father's book over a dozen times. Of course he was paying attention. "Look," he countered, "I'm doing everything I can to find Aquiles. I'm doing my best to understand what this is all about."

"I'll help you," Dr. Kruger said kindly. "Not to find Aquiles—I don't know where he is. But I'm sure of what he would say: 'Forget about me, Stefan, and go ahead with the plan.'"

"What plan?"

Kruger sat at his desk. "You see, Adam, there's another theory of life. Governments and traditional science feel creationism and evolution are the only possibilities, but that's not so. In reality, we came to exist because of an experiment."

"An experiment?"

"Yes. We're an experiment of more advanced beings. Millions of years ago, genetics masters came here to create the four different races of *Homo sapiens*.

"The ancient Atlanteans," he continued, "were an advanced civilization, coming after Lemuria, the first human civilization created by these beings of light from the center of the universe. The ancient Atlanteans answered to the Universal Consciousness, the Wellspring of Life. But humans don't call it that. We confused its essence by naming it God."

"So you're saying you believe in extraterrestrials," Adam said.

"Yes, Adam," Kruger said frankly. "There *is* life in other places. You can't think we are the center of the universe! Earth is an important place, full of valuable experiences, evolution, and learning, but it's just a minuscule entity among so many other galaxies, stars, and planets.

"After the cataclysms and floods that destroyed the Lemurians and later the Atlanteans over twelve thousand years ago, the survivors formed new cultures and went to Egypt, Greece, Stonehenge, and India," Dr. Kruger explained. "Others became the Mayans, who also wound up mysteriously disappearing, but before they did, they gave us their calendar, predicting the end of a cycle in our time, to take place this coming December 21."

"What's going to happen on December 21?"

"Earth will leave the third dimension and enter the fifth dimension."

"How?"

"The same way that a woman gives birth." Kruger smiled warmly. "It will be the birth of Earth. Twelve thousand years ago, when natural disasters destroyed Atlantis, Earth's magnetic poles were reversed. Now, all of these earthquakes lately are repositioning Earth's axis."

"Is that possible?"

"Yes, it is. Remember the Chilean earthquake in 2010? It was an 8.8, and it moved Earth's axis between seventeen and twenty-three degrees. It started even then. Earth is aligning itself with the new in order to evolve."

Adam was thoughtful. It was hard for him to believe that Kruger, a respected traditional scientist, was using words like "fifth dimension" and believed Earth was realigning. "Do you think what happened to Atlantis is going to happen again?"

"I believe Earth *will* raise its vibrational frequency to the fifth dimension," Kruger said. "Everyone who is prepared—by which I mean vibrating at that same frequency—will go on, but in a different way. We'll be on a more ethereal, less material plane."

"And what about the fourth dimension?"

"The fourth dimension is the world inhabited by the beings who have finished their experiences on Earth, whom we call 'dead,' although they're actually more alive than we are," he said.

"So if that's what the fourth dimension is, what's the fifth? What does it look like?"

"It's hard to explain. We'll use telepathy, communication through energy. It will mean the end of lies, the end of money, the extinction of lawyers, police, and the law as we know it. We will begin using clean energies—"

"But won't that lead to chaos?"

"Not at all," Kruger said. "When your consciousness expands and you understand that we are all one, the same

love, like spiritual energy, then you connect with everyone, and there's no need for control or laws. Consciousness
becomes the only authority over you, and it's what connects
you to everything."

"How do you know all of this?"

"Come on," Kruger said, leading Adam out of his office.
"I'll show you Aquiles's second discovery."

# 37

aptain Viktor Sopenski sat across the street from Alexia's house for over an hour. There wasn't much activity in Green Park, Alexia's upscale neighborhood—just a few passing cars and a couple of pedestrians. He wanted to make sure that if Alexia was home, she wouldn't run into him when she went to work. Sopenski didn't know her schedule. In fact, he didn't know much about her at all. Sopenski decided he'd casually ring the doorbell. If no one answered, he'd go in through the front door. If Alexia was in fact home, he'd point his gun at her, and she'd be his.

The captain's mind and heavy body were ready to spring into action. His heart pounded, and he could feel an adrenaline rush. He was excited but also slightly nervous this time. There was something different about this job: his target was a woman.

In his day-to-day life, his relationships with women were practically nonexistent. He'd only had a girlfriend twice, and since his last relationship had broken off, he slept with prostitutes, avoiding intimacy with anyone. Ever since he was a teenager, he'd had one weakness: beautiful women. In college, when he was about to lose his virginity to one of the prettiest girls in his class, his animal instincts got the better of him, and he finished before he'd started. He had the same problem several times until the pretty girl got tired of it and broke up with him.

His outward façade as a brutish, violent, crass man crumbled in the face of a beautiful woman. That was what worried him about Alexia. What if he couldn't control himself? What if she seduced him? He knew he was getting carried away in a web of fantasy. *Just breathe, Viktor, breathe.*

The sky was overcast, and a fine mist of summer rain began to fall. He crossed the sidewalk. A woman holding a little boy's hand passed in front of him. He waited until they rounded the corner before going up to Alexia's front door. He rang the doorbell. No answer.

*Once I'm inside*, he thought, *I should search the house carefully*. He'd examine Alexia's clothes, photos, and possessions. Maybe he'd find some unexpected information. Just thinking about it gave him an erection. He'd stay there until nightfall, when she'd come home.

He took an instrument out of his pocket to spring the lock. It gave easily. In less than fifteen seconds, the Vulture was inside Alexia's house.

He crept down the hallway and went into the bedroom. He donned surgical gloves and searched through all of Alexia Vangelis's drawers. He carefully leafed through books and folders for over an hour and went through her desk without noticeably disturbing anything. He couldn't find any obvious clues. He had to wait. He wanted to see her, to finally have her in front of him, face to face.

Sopenski found the perfume scent that permeated the house absolutely intoxicating. It made him daydream. He was no Don Juan and never had been, but he fantasized that he already had this woman. The mere sight of Alexia's underwear drawer had excited him. Little sets of lingerie that oozed sensuality. Delicate panties that invited him to dream about the soft-skinned body that would wear them. Her shoes lined up below the dresser. Just setting his eyes on a pair of high-heeled patent-leather shoes drove Sopenski mad with desire. Viktor Sopenski laid his sweaty frame over Alexia's crisp bed made up with white linens, clutching her panties in his hand. Without meaning to, he fell fast asleep. He didn't wake up until his phone rang.

It was the Magician, calling from Rome.

## 38

Adam followed Kruger down the long white hallway that separated his office from the rest of the building. An exquisite scent of violets and lavender filled the air. They turned down a hall to the left, and Adam noticed several closed office doors with nameplates: "Dr. Barry Cromptom," "Dr. Peter Ingals," "Dr. Kate Smith."

"Wait here," Kruger said, stopping in front of the door at the end of the hall. He punched in a numerical code as he pressed his right thumb to a security scanner. The door swung open.

They stepped through the secure door and headed down another hall that seemed to go on forever. They took a right turn and then a left. When they got to the next set of doors, Kruger picked up a white internal telephone installed on the wall.

"Kate, it's me. I'm here with Dr. Roussos."

"Come in," Adam heard the young woman say. The lock on the door clicked, and the door opened. Adam smiled at Kate as he went in.

"It's time for your lesson," Kate said cheerfully. She wore a light, very pleasant perfume. Adam noticed she had a smooth, soft complexion, a youthful glow. Ordinarily her beauty would have been distracting to Adam, but he was too preoccupied.

"A lesson? What do you mean?"

"You haven't told him anything, Dr. Kruger?" Kate asked.

Kruger turned to face Adam. "You're going to see the practical results of what our friend Aquiles discovered. His main discovery is not here. We have just a piece of it."

"I don't understand."

"First go look through that window," Kruger said, gesturing.

Adam stepped over to a large window that looked into an adjoining room. A few dozen children of all races played—some were writing, others were reading, some were sitting in groups of five or six on the floor, their eyes closed. Three adults wandered the room; Adam assumed they were their teachers or tutors.

"What is this? What are those children doing? What does it have to do with Aquiles's discovery?"

"It's like I told you," Kruger said, "these are the practical results of Aquiles's discovery."

"They're kids," Adam said. "This doesn't make any sense."

Kruger gestured toward a leather couch.

"Here, sit down. I'll tell you everything."

Adam sat down expectantly.

"Those are very special children with special abilities," Dr. Kruger explained. "They've developed a large portion of their brain capacity, and their genetic code is different. They have many capabilities that most ordinary people do not. Listen carefully—the original human DNA had twelve active strands, but they started to decay. Over the millennia we became what we are now: we have only two strands that are active. In spite of this, man progressed, of course. We've invented countless sophisticated technologies with just a fraction of our potential activated. Imagine how it would be if instead of only two strands..." Kruger gestured toward the children.

"The possibilities are limitless," Kruger continued. "And it all stems from Atlantis. Everyone in the world who has been interested in power knew that Atlantis existed, and what a grand civilization it had been. And what they were all looking for, well, it's exactly what Aquiles found."

## 39

Adam waited expectantly for more, his patience running out. "But, what is *it*? What did Aquiles find?"

"I'll show it to you," Dr. Kruger said. "Adam, it's incredibly exciting. We're on the verge of discovering the true origin of humanity."

"How can you possibly know that?"

Kruger smiled. "Two reasons: the children behind that glass told me, and Aquiles's discovery revealed it to me."

Adam felt a knot of anxiety in the pit of his stomach. He leaned forward. "How can you know through the children?"

Kruger gazed at him with compassion. "You'll understand all of this soon enough on your own. You need to let go of your tiny ant perspective and start to use your eagle eye, Adam."

"What do you mean?"

"Every person is a being with divine potential, a perfect representation of the totality, and within yourself, you will find all of the dimensions and cosmic energies. You just have to remember."

"Remember?"

Kruger nodded. "Remember and activate your DNA. You already have everything you need inside of you. These children," he gestured to the glass, "were born with superior genetic potential; this is a school for them. We stimulate their DNA, an effort Aquiles has helped us with."

"I find it hard to believe that those children told you what you're telling me."

Kruger nodded, smiling. "We've performed experiments on different children who didn't know each other, who never met, and they've all given us similar information, in their own words.

"Look at these panels," Kruger continued, going over to a small transparent panel hanging on the wall, backlit from behind. "These are the images of the children's brains. We grabbed images before and after scientific experiments with them."

Adam noticed some pronounced luminous circles within the brain scans.

"What are those?"

"Circles of light," Kruger said. "We've never seen anything like it. We believe it's the DNA activation. We think this activation is influenced by the new cosmic energy. This is the first sign of the hail of photons coming at us from the center of the galaxy."

Kate put a new set of transparencies on the screen.

"Kate and I have confirmed for ourselves the effects of Aquiles's discovery on our own brains. And as I said, we only have our hands on a small part of it. Imagine if all of humanity…" The geneticist paused to reflect. Then he added softly, "We are conscious beings in a state of constant evolution, Adam. Everything is unfolding exactly according to the Source of all Creation's intentions. Everything is progressing and evolving from one state to another, self-destructing, creating, and maintaining itself only to be destroyed and then grow anew, eternally seeking a higher degree of perfection.

"It's like a game, you see? Now, we are poised to leave this journey on Earth in the third dimension. What awaits us is a celebration. Still, many people fear the transition, and others try to prevent it in various ways. That's most likely why Aquiles was kidnapped."

Adam stood. He had an open mind, but this was a lot to take in. "Are you saying that those changes in DNA and in the brain are what's going to take us to another dimension?"

Kruger shook his head no. "I don't think it's going to happen for everyone. Only those who are vibrating in unison with the portal and with the energy of the Source, what the Mayans call the Central Sun, will evolve into the next dimension. It's not a question of chance, or goodwill, or performing charitable acts—rather, it's energy and consciousness. The change will happen for those who have reached an expanded state of consciousness and higher vibrational energy frequency. Those are the only ones who will be able to withstand the changes in their nervous systems, brains, and DNA."

"And what about the ones who can't cross through the energy portal?"

Kruger stepped closer to Adam and said almost in a whisper, "That's very hard to predict, but the cosmic energy itself will open up a path in the Great Spiral of Ascension. Those who don't perceive it will keep on living in another reality more closely attuned to their vibrational energy, brains, and DNA."

Adam took a step back. "In his book, my father suggests that the Mayans disappeared in this way, by entering a portal to another dimension. That's why they left their cities empty."

"Exactly." Kruger went over to the window in the wall to look in on the children.

"Doctor, I think I'm ready," Adam said. "Can I see Aquiles's discovery?"

Kruger turned and gave Kate a knowing look.

"Kate will show you the way."

## 40

Six more members had arrived at the meeting of the Secret Government's top inner circle. Stewart Washington was gazing out a window of the luxurious room, lost in thought, when Sergei Valisnov—also known as the Wizard—walked over to him.

"May I have a word?" he asked, standing to Washington's right.

The Brain nodded, though his face didn't change expression.

"Sir," he said, "I've received a report that you should be aware of."

The Brain's expression registered a subtle change. He turned to face the Wizard. He was exhausted and had a raging headache.

"Go on."

"My secretary called. At a CNN press conference, several former military leaders, air traffic controllers, and pilots made statements that seriously compromise us."

"What statements? What did they say?"

The Russian opened a black suitcase and took out a folder full of reports.

"Sir, they've revealed top-secret, confidential information of the US government. It's like the Disclosure Project all over again," he said, referring to the organization committed to outing what the government would rather keep under wraps—including extraterrestrial sightings. The Wizard Valisnov nodded. "It's even worse than what they put on WikiLeaks in 2010." Valisnov felt uncomfortable being so physically close to the Brain while he was in such an emotionally charged state, but he didn't have much choice. The minutes were ticking by, and they had to work fast to find a solution.

"There have been reports of sightings recently in Oregon, Texas, Colorado, New Mexico, Dallas, and other cities. Now in New York and other major cities around the world, groups are taking to the streets and demonstrating, claiming they've come into contact with intelligent extraterrestrials, and New Age groups are trying to get the word out to everyone." Valisnov's eyes burned brightly.

The Brain looked worried but said, "It won't be a problem. They're fringe groups with no credibility."

Valisnov paused to search through his papers. "We shouldn't underestimate them, sir. They've gotten very sophisticated. Their numbers are growing, and they're getting harder to sway. There's tremendous pressure building. There have also been sightings of a giant circle of spinning lights in the sky, over Area 51."

Area 51 was a top-secret military base built in 1955 that covered ten thousand square kilometers to the north of Las Vegas, Nevada. That territory, also known as the Box, was often the subject of various conspiracy theories, and it was said that, among other things, scientists inside Area 51 were secretly studying extraterrestrial technologies.

Washington's eyes bulged. "Over Area 51? This is extremely serious," Washington said, gravely concerned. He thought for a

moment. "Actually, this is a matter for the official US government and the CIA. What do they have to say about it? They
should be the ones to strike while the iron's hot."

"They're quickly assessing the situation to formulate a
response," Valisnov said confidently.

"Issue orders to the press and television networks that are
under our control to keep any news stories about this to an
absolute minimum. Don't let out any information."

"Already taken care of," the Russian said coolly. "The
media has been advised to censor all confidential information
on the prophecies and the UFO sightings."

"Very well," Washington sighed, his head throbbing.
"Find a new scapegoat that will buy us some time to find a
solution—a bombing or the death of a celebrity or something."

The Wizard Valisnov broke out in a cold sweat. If he was
going to make his proposal, now was the time. This was his
chance to move up within the organization.

"Sir, if you would permit me to explain something I have
in mind…I believe that if we put together all the pieces of
the global situation—the earthquakes, the solar events, the
hoopla over the Mayan prophecies, the meteor, and the dem-
onstrations—we can stack the deck in our favor."

The Brain was intrigued. He loosened his tie, receptive to
hearing the Russian's plan. As the other members took their
places around the polished oak table, placing their folders and
reports in front of them, Valisnov whispered in Stewart Washington's ear.

ate led Adam down a long hallway, through a conference room, then outside to a small yard beautifully landscaped with trees, plants, and flowers. They walked up to a circular, domed building. A circle of bright blue glass ran around the dome toward the top.

Kate opened the white door with a magnetic key. "Please leave your shoes and any metallic objects outside," she requested.

Adam complied. *What powerful energy this place has.*

Kate seemed to read his mind. "This place has a great deal of energy, Adam. Try to turn your mind off."

"What are we going to do?" he asked.

Kate looked at him with bright eyes. Her face glowed with a magnetic sensuality.

"You're going to see Aquiles's discovery. From what I understand, Aquiles expected a great deal from you, Adam." Adam noticed Kate's body again. It seemed to have been sculpted by an artist; her whole being emanated a palpable energy.

They went inside that mysterious cupola. In the center was a circle of quartz crystals about fifteen or twenty centimeters high, just under the circumference of blue glass on the roof.

"Quartz?" Adam asked.

"This is just a small part of Aquiles's discovery. This is where we performed the experiments with the children. Soon you'll feel it within your own body.

"First," Kate instructed, "close your eyes and take several deep breaths. As I mentioned before, it's very important to let your mind go blank, to be very still and quiet inside."

Adam Roussos was used to meditating, so he had no problem following her instructions. With a light smile, he indicated to Kate that he was ready. "Go into the quartz crystal circle," Kate directed confidently. "It would be best to enter the circle completely naked. I will, too. We'll go in together."

Kate seemed entirely natural and relaxed. She didn't seem to experience any shame or embarrassment because of their nudity. Adam, on the other hand, was a bit disconcerted by the situation.

"All right," Kate said firmly, "cross your legs in the lotus position, as if you were meditating, and keep your back straight. Close your eyes and breathe deeply. Hold your palms open, at the center of your chest, as if you were about to receive something."

Adam did as he was told. After a few minutes he was in an Alpha mental state, experiencing a feeling of profound clarity and focus in his mind's eye.

"You will receive Aquiles's discovery in your hands—a seed, which the ancient Atlanteans used to empower their DNA. After this experience, you will never be the same."

Those words sounded almost like a religious incantation. Adam remained calm and serene. After ten minutes of breathing in unison, facing each other to balance their feminine and masculine energies, Kate took a small object from a blue velvet pouch.

"Stay in a deeply relaxed state," she said, almost whispering. "Observe what is happening to you inside."

Adam felt a light weight in his hands, smooth to the touch and slightly cold. Kate had given him a small quartz crystal over twelve thousand years old. It was a small fragment from a much larger stone. Adam felt a subtle vibration, like a small electric charge, run up his spine and into his nervous system, making some muscles in his body and face involuntarily twitch. Gradually, he began to feel warmer and warmer. Then his energy levels increased, and he experienced the strange sensation of being able to see all of the cells within his body dancing, as if they were microscopic circles of light.

"Sit up straight," Kate said. "Keep focusing on what you are feeling."

The image of their nude bodies inside the crystal circle was beautiful, mystical. Adam felt the energy from the quartz rising up within him, and he felt Kate's feminine energy, warm and enveloping. He also felt a powerful connection to the quartz that Alexia wore around her neck.

*Is that why it's always so hot?* he wondered.

Kate took his hands, wrapping them and the small stone in hers. Adam felt a powerful heat and a charge as their hands met, and she leaned in close to whisper in his ear.

"Now your interior being and your DNA will start to change," she said, as if she were speaking to a child. "Prepare yourself for a journey inside."

She gently guided him to lie down on his back, and she placed the small quartz in the middle of his forehead.

He felt the stone with all of its power in his third eye, near his pineal and pituitary glands, and a flash of light, with all the symbols of the tablet that Aquiles had found, came to his mind. In that instant Adam Roussos, completely naked inside and out, began to experience a powerful feeling of *déjà vu*.

# 42

Alexia, onboard the ferry to Athens, was worried. It was almost noon, and she hadn't gotten any calls or messages from Adam at all. The ferry was packed with tourists, but she found a seat in a corner next to the window. She decided to surf the Internet on her BlackBerry.

The news headlines were grim. The newswire web pages reported serious damages caused by the earthquakes and the solar disturbances. More fallout was expected over the next few days. As a geologist, Alexia knew that when an earthquake struck in one place, within a certain time frame another disaster tended to strike some other point on the globe as a consequence. *Cause and effect*, she thought.

She saw photos from several places where earthquakes had wrought severe devastation—Taiwan, Japan, North and South Korea, and the Philippines. Buildings, bridges, and homes were destroyed. The images were dramatic. Alexia suddenly felt very alone.

She called Adam. She got his voice mail again.

Deep in her heart, Alexia thought the geological and astronomical events taking place had some hidden reason behind them. Maybe it was a divine reason.

Several rows behind Alexia, a man with dark glasses and a baseball cap was hunched down in his seat, quietly watching her.

It was Eduard.

## 43

dam's trance lasted a little over an hour. His mind opened up to an ancestral font of knowledge, as if he were reading a book or opening a file on a computer; he saw a parade of images flash through his mind, as if he were reading a comic book.

Several times, Adam's body arched and shook involuntarily; even though his eyes were closed, they moved quickly. The potency of the quartz over his hypophysis was even such that he had two erections without being aware of them.

After what seemed like an eternity, he slowly opened his eyes.

"How are you?" Kate said softly.

Adam just smiled, his eyes half-closed.

"It's been an incredible journey." His voice was very soft.

"What did you see? Can you tell me?"

Adam tried to describe it. "It was very intense," he began enthusiastically. "The first thing I saw was a light that erased all of my personal memories and made me feel as if I were floating…and I had the strangest sensation that a great void contained everything that existed."

Kate smiled sweetly.

"Then I saw how the planets in our solar system were connected by a kind of energy wave that binds the universe together, so there's no division. Earth looked far away and beautiful, a peaceful globe."

He furrowed his brow, struggling to put his experience into words.

"Then I had the strangest vision. In its earliest days, Earth was visited by beings who came from the stars, beings who emitted a very powerful light. They were very tall, with piercing eyes, more beautiful than humans. Those beings, who were connected to one another by the same light that unites the whole universe, conducted genetic experiments to create a brand-new race that went on to populate Earth.

"The same current of thought circulated among them; they all worked toward the same goal, a divine project: the creation of *Homo sapiens*. They were called Elohim, advanced beings from other corners of the cosmos, creators of humanity by order of the Life Source.

"Their first new creations were dark as ebony, then red, yellow, and white. The Elohim—beings of light, half feminine and half masculine—implanted the first organisms of their design within the uteruses of several female light beings and originated the *first* beings on the planet. They were little babies that the light beings protected for quite a while until they could look after themselves. They communicated telepathically.

"Then there was some kind of grand cosmic celebration," Adam explained. "Many beings of light came from all over the universe to see the new creation. They traveled in huge, round spaceships that flew through space at incredibly high speeds. It was a fantastic spectacle of lights and sensations. What I noticed most was how they all seemed to be made of light, with tremendously bright auras or something."

Kate arched an eyebrow.

"It seemed as if there were certain hierarchies among the light beings," Adam said, looking her in the eye.

"Hierarchies?"

Adam nodded. "Yes, some were teachers, others were scientists, and some were workers. I couldn't really tell them apart."

"Where did they come from?"

"From the stars," Adam said, sounding euphoric. "From the constellation of Sirius, from the Pleiades, and the stars known as the Three Kings, Orion."

Kate's expression was bright. "Go on."

Adam still sat with his legs crossed. Kate offered him a blanket so he wouldn't catch cold, but he didn't need it. He felt a strong heat inside.

"On Earth, animals lived together with a more rudimentary species of men, maybe the *Homo erectus* or the Neanderthals. They were very primitive and freely populated the planet."

"And the new babies?"

"They grew up. I saw how everything went by so quickly. The babies were children, then adolescents, then adults. But they had a conscious connection inside, they had a universal language, and they did not act like the *Homo erectus*. They were advanced, full of energy, power, and light. In what seemed to me like the time of a breath, the light beings who had created the first women and men left so that civilization could begin on its own."

Kate's eyes opened wide. "Lemuria."

Adam nodded his confirmation.

She said, "They were the first civilization, before the Atlanteans. Was that the end?"

"No. The light beings left the message that they would return every so often. They also left a special code so the people could maintain their cosmic consciousness and not lose their connection with the universe. They trusted that the seed of light that had been planted, the original DNA matrix, would prosper according to plan—which was to create a civilization guided by freedom of creation and unity."

"Go on."

"Those original archetypes of the first beings had powerful vibratory frequencies and the ability to communicate with one another through thought. They had a system of complex light codes inside of them, with twelve active strands of DNA."

"Dr. Kruger needs to hear this," Kate said enthusiastically. "None of us or the children have ever gone so far in our flights of consciousness."

Adam's gaze was fixed on the floor, his eyes unfocused, as he remembered his incredible experience. "The beings on Earth reproduced, increasing their numbers and creating the first advanced, intelligent civilization."

"How did they communicate?" she asked. "I know you said they communicated with one another through telepathy, but how did they communicate with their creators? The light beings from across the universe?"

"Through quartz crystals like this," Adam said, indicating the one in his hand, which had grown very hot. "Their cities lit up with huge crystals of over a meter high, as if they were streetlights. And people wore a crystal around their necks like a personal passport with their data."

Adam was struck by a realization. "The quartz crystal that Alexia has around her neck!"

"What is it?" Kate asked.

"I have to get in touch with Alexia. She must be worried."

"We will," Kate reassured him. "First, tell me more, while the experience is fresh in your mind."

Adam inhaled deeply, to oxygenate his brain.

"I sensed that Darwin's theory of evolution was correct only up until the beings of light arrived on Earth. But the missing piece of the puzzle, the first humans of four primary colors were created by extraterrestrials from space. They were all descendants of the first creations of the light beings. And I saw how civilizations advanced, reaching their zenith, and then were destroyed. I saw how a great city appeared and then disappeared. It may have been Atlantis—it seemed to all happen in an instant since there was no sense of time in my vision."

Kate could see him pulling back. "Why did we lose that conscious awareness? Could you see? Why did the ancient civilizations of Lemuria and Atlantis perish?"

"For the same reason it could happen to us." Those words spilled out of him from deep inside, unthinking, like a reflex.

"Why? You said those beings were practically ethereal, not material."

Adam took another deep breath. "After thousands and thousands of years, civilizations became corrupted, and they lost contact with their true origin. And just as I saw the extraterrestrial light beings who created the human race, I also saw how other, smaller extraterrestrials, gray in color, with dark intentions, started coming to Earth, disturbed by the new experiment. They began scheming to deprogram the DNA, neutralizing its original functionality, the light code; although the original light beings, who served the Source of Creation, would send solar messengers every so often to revive and guide the floundering civilizations."

Kate was deeply affected.

"Now, as the Mayans predicted, we've come to the end of a cosmic cycle so Earth can be reborn, and what's been obscured will rise to the surface. Secrets will come into the light. The year 2012 is our collective chance to reestablish contact with the Source of Creation!"

His face lit up as he said this. At the same time, a ray of sunlight beamed in through the top of the domed ceiling. The light projected a beautiful image of a nude man and woman onto the wall.

"The sun," Adam murmured.

"The sun?"

Adam felt entirely transformed by his contact with the Atlantean quartz. "Yes. The sun has been more active than usual, which means it's already receiving energy from the galaxy's Source of Creation. The transmission will be completed on December 21, when a wave of energy will activate all of the helices of people's DNA. The sun has always been on our side! It's alive! It's the representation of the divine in our planetary system!"

Kate was impressed by how much Adam had learned in his trance. "We've all done the experiment with the quartz crystal," she said, "but no one's gotten this amount of information."

Adam shrugged his shoulders. "I don't know," he said. "Maybe I went into different files, like going into a different folder in a computer."

"Tell me more about the sun," Kate said. "What makes you think it's on our side?"

"Because it's destroying their control systems!"

"*Whose* control systems? What do you mean?"

"Different governments have put control systems in the ozone layer, to keep us from contact with the light beings," he explained. "The sun isn't destroying the ozone layer; instead, it's clearing a path."

Adam stood up to get dressed.

"I think I understand what's going to happen now with the planet," he exclaimed. "The Mayans were connected with the light beings, and they knew what was going to happen on December 21."

Kate was visibly disconcerted. "What do you think is going to happen?" she asked. She stood and began dressing.

"The earth will raise its frequency. A great many people will remember our origin. The original genetic program will be reactivated, empowering our DNA. It will be a great evolution for all of the races and beings who are in harmony with the new vibrational frequency. It will be the end of alienation, unconsciousness, and fear!"

Adam was suddenly struck by a revelation. "Kate, if I got all of this information from one tiny little fragment of quartz," he pondered this, a smile playing on his lips, "which comes from a much bigger quartz, over a meter high...think of what the mother quartz Aquiles found could do! Now I understand what he wanted to do! He was going to prepare the people's consciousness at the Olympic Games with that quartz, to cause a chain reaction!" It seemed as if his heart would leap from his chest. "The collective reaction would be explosive!"

He started for the door.

"Hurry, Kate. Let's talk to Dr. Kruger and Alexia. We have to find the mother quartz!"

Just as he spoke those words, he saw the silhouette of a fat man with a gun in his hand and several police officers trying to force open a door of the main building.

aul Tous took a walk to clear his mind. He slowly headed toward the Vatican's Signature Room to look at the works of art, thinking he might find some inspiration there.

Now that he'd initiated the hunt, he had to wait. Alexia would soon be in Eduard's hands, and Sopenski was after Adam Roussos and Dr. Kruger at the genetics lab. He'd called Sopenski when Eduard had informed him of Alexia's whereabouts. Tous let Sopenski know he'd be supported by an elite group of officers from Scotland Yard.

When he stepped into the grand room, he came face to face with Raphael's *The School of Athens*, a fresco depicting Plato at the center, holding a book in his hand, surrounded by many other Greek wise men. Tous squinted to get a sharper view. He could hardly believe his eyes when he recognized the book. The *Timaeus*! It was the very book in which Plato described the continent of Atlantis in great detail.

Tous's heart began to pound furiously. His emotional response wasn't exactly from a deep devotion to art, but was a product of sheer nervousness. He felt as if Plato were looking at him in triumph, saying, "The truth will come to light, no matter what you do."

The fresco that Raphael painted in the year 1512 portrayed Plato with Leonardo da Vinci's face, pointing up at the sky, while beside him Aristotle pointed down to the ground, holding his book *Ethics*. Both Greeks were surrounded by other famed philosophers such as Diogenes, Pythagoras, and Plotinus.

Tous left the room in quick strides. The cardinal frantically headed to his office, like a frightened animal fleeing from hunters in hot pursuit. When he finally got there, his assistant knocked on his door.

"Come in," Tous said, waving him in without raising his gaze from the papers in front of him.

His assistant set down a folder containing four or five sheets of paper.

"Thank you," Tous said curtly, then gave his assistant instructions that he was not to be disturbed since he needed some time alone to think. He picked up the folder and read the pages. The color in his face drained until it was ghostly white. The report revealed nothing but bad news, but the worst was the headline: "Six Consecutive Earthquakes Strike the Earth."

A shiver ran up his spine. The cardinal had a chilling premonition. A verse from the Bible, Revelation chapter 10, verses 6 and 7, ran through his mind:

*There should be no more delay, but in the days of the trumpet call to be sounded by the seventh angel, the mystery of God, as he announced to the servants his prophets, should be fulfilled.*

"There have already been six earthquakes!" he cried. It had to be a sign. His face became a mask of pure horror. His back spasmed as he buckled under a powerful wave of nausea. He rushed to the bathroom as quickly as he could. He vomited violently, his blood pressure dropped precipitously, and he collapsed like a rag doll onto the floor. As he fell, his head struck the porcelain sink, and he lost consciousness.

# 45

Sergei Valisnov's plan struck Stewart Washington like a refreshing breath of air in the midst of the stifling tension. Valisnov had proposed positioning a cadre of floating nuclear bombs in space to destroy the meteor and then contaminate Earth's energy. Of course, it would be a top-secret operation, as always. They would allow the official government to put their best face on it, presenting it as the latest American superpower feat. They would be the great "saviors," rescuing Earth from a threat, becoming the leader of the world, and making people think that everything that came from space was harmful.

People would now see the stars as a threat more than a symbol of hope. They would inject a new, powerful dose of nihilism and materialism into modern life, devoid of all spiritual seeking.

"I like it," Washington said, with the suggestion of a smile on his lips.

Just then Patrick Jackson walked up to them, looking terrified.

"Sir," he said, his face ashen, "please forgive the interruption. The other members are waiting…there's something important I think you need to know."

Washington and Valisnov turned to face him.

"Go ahead."

"We just received another report. All around the globe, groups are announcing the end of the world, and some others are claiming they've had contact with extraterrestrial space-ships." His eyes opened wide in fright. "It's chaos and jubila-tion mixed together."

"Did our media outlets minimize the significance in their stories?"

Jackson nodded. "Yes sir, but there are still some other outlets that—"

"And what about the order I gave to censor those kinds of news stories?"

"The information getting out to the public is going through independent channels. We've tried, but they won't cooperate. And," Jackson added, "there are new sunspots… and the aurora borealis is exhibiting bizarre patterns, not only at the pole, but in several cities, at night now."

The three men looked at each other tensely. Washington was motionless. Although he was deeply disturbed, he seemed imperturbable.

"It's time to set the new plan in motion, before everything slips through our fingers," he said firmly.

His steely gaze was as cold as ice. All eyes in the room were on him.

"Proceed with what we've discussed," the Brain finally said to Valisnov in a sure tone. "We are going to remove from our path everything that flies over the face of the earth."

# 46

Drenched with sweat, an impatient Viktor Sopenski was trying to force open the door that stood between him and Adam and Kate. He'd received orders from Cardinal Tous to capture Adam Roussos and Dr. Kruger. Though he and his hired guns from Scotland Yard had arrested several scientists and were interrogating them about the children, Dr. Kruger had gotten away.

Kate looked frightened and stunned but quickly pulled herself together. "Hurry, Adam! We have to get out of here through the back way!"

Kate grabbed Adam by the hand and pulled him away. Running down a long hallway at the other end of the cupola, they opened a door, dashed down a flight of stairs, and ran down a short hall. Then Kate extracted a set of keys from behind a picture hanging on the wall.

Adam turned to look behind them. The police had managed to break down the glass door. There was a loud noise. They were getting close.

"Hurry, Kate! They're inside!"

Kate deftly opened the two locks on the heavy door. As it swung open, a gust of fresh air hit them. The door led to the street. They looked all around but saw only a few people on the sidewalks, who paid them no attention. A small park lay amid the handsome Victorian buildings.

"This way!" Kate shouted, pulling Adam by the arm and running to the end of the block. "My car's on that corner!"

Viktor Sopenski and the other police officers were only a few hundred feet away, as they'd just gotten outside.

"There they are!" Sopenski yelled when he saw Kate and Adam running toward the corner. "You two, go after them, and you go bring the cars around!" he ordered.

Adam and Kate reached her car, but she realized she didn't have her keys. Beads of cold sweat ran down her back.

Adam turned to see a white Volkswagen pulling around the corner at low speed. He frantically waved his hands. The woman driving stopped the car.

"Please, get out!" he ordered. "It's an emergency!"

The woman hesitated for a second but then did as she was asked. Adam got in the driver's seat. He wasn't used to having the steering wheel on the right side. Kate got in as the car began to move. The driver's side door was still open. As the car accelerated, the door hit a parked car and fell off its hinges.

"The door came off!"

The owner of the Volkswagen watched helplessly as her car door landed heavily on the pavement just a few feet from her.

"That wasn't very nice," Kate said.

"The ends justify the means. She'll find out that she's helping to accomplish something much more important."

Adam hit the gas and drove down a street parallel to where the police were.

Meanwhile, Sopenski was about to fire his gun at the fleeing car when another officer from Scotland Yard stopped him from behind.

"This isn't New York!" the British inspector said. "You can't just go shooting at people willy-nilly in the street."

Sopenski gave him a contemptuous look. Just then, two police cars screeched to a halt in front of them.

Viktor Sopenski and the inspector jumped in, and both cars turned on their sirens and sped off after Adam and Kate.

aul Tous's assistant had managed to drag his boss's heavy frame to the office sofa. Almost twenty minutes had passed since Tous had passed out in the bathroom.

"Are you all right, Your Excellency?"

Tous stared up at him blankly, his eyes wide.

"What? What happened?"

"You fainted."

The cardinal struggled to remember. He brought his hands to his temples. His head was throbbing. He'd given himself a good whack on the sink.

"I'll bring you some ice."

His assistant was frightened but acted calmly and efficiently. Tous was quiet. His assistant returned with a few ice cubes wrapped in a handkerchief, which he placed on Tous's forehead.

"Better?"

Tous nodded slowly.

"Now I remember," he said softly. "I fell down in the bathroom."

"Something you ate must have made you sick, Your Excellency."

Then Tous remembered why he had thrown up his breakfast.

*The six earthquakes. The prophecies. One more earthquake and it will be fulfilled!*

He began to think clearly again.

"These last few days have been very difficult," his assistant said. "You should get some rest."

"I'm feeling better, thank you. I'll stay here on the sofa. But please leave me; I need to get my thoughts in order."

"But Your Excellency—"

"Thank you," he repeated sharply, "now please leave me alone."

"I'll be here if you need me," the assistant said, then closed the ornately carved wooden door behind him.

Tous drew in a deep breath. He wanted to get moving and find out what was going on with his plan. He picked up his cell phone. He had a voice mail from the Owl. It must've come in while he was still unconscious.

"Call me as soon as you get this," the Owl said urgently. "I'm about to get off the ferry in Athens with Aquiles's daughter. She's going to where we're holding her father, but she doesn't know he's there. I'm going to surprise her, and then we'll have what we want. When we get to Athens, I'll call again. I hope you're happy. I'll…always be at your side."

# 48

Adam careened down the streets of London. He'd put some distance between them and the police cars, but he was worried.

"Now we're suspects!" he said as Kate turned to look for the police cars.

"You can slow down now; I think we've lost them."

Adam looked in the rearview mirror.

"But they'll have alerted other patrol cars. We have to be careful. Tell me what just happened!"

"I don't know," Kate replied. "They don't have the right to enter the institute like that. Let's go to Green Park. Turn right here."

As he made the turn, Kate's phone rang. She pulled it from her bag.

"Dr. Kruger!" she exclaimed. "What's going on?"

"I don't know, Kate. They just broke in and took all the doctors and children. I assume they're going to interrogate them. I was able to hide, and then I left through the back door of my private office."

"How can they treat us like this? Who are they? What should we do now?"

"Do you have the quartz?" Kruger asked.

"Yes. Just the small fragment from the original, nothing more."

"Fine. I'll tell you what we're going to do. Listen carefully…"

## 49

Alexia, exhausted and frantic, walked down the ferry's gangplank and stepped onto solid ground at the Athens port. She scanned the street for a taxi.

"Alexia!" Eduard yelled from a few feet behind her.

She turned and studied him coldly.

"Eduard, what are you doing here?"

"I saw your note. I didn't want to leave you alone."

"But I told you to stay in Santorini."

"Yes, but I think I'll be more useful to you here. There's nothing in the laboratory."

"It doesn't matter now anyway," Alexia sighed, resigned. "I haven't gotten any calls from Adam, and he's not answering his phone. And based on the articles I've been reading for the past hour, now it looks as if the world is falling apart." Alexia couldn't recall a time when she'd felt more defeated, and Eduard's presence irritated her to no end. She hailed a taxi.

"Get in," she said, although she wasn't entirely sure she wanted to go anywhere with Eduard.

The Owl went around the other side of the taxi and got in.

"To Plaka, please," Alexia directed the driver. "We're in a hurry!"

"I have something important to tell you, Alexia. Listen," Eduard said, clearing his throat. "I talked to a friend of mine in Athens, and he said..." His voice deepened, and his nervous tic grew even more noticeable. "He thinks he saw your father near the city center."

Alexia turned to look him in the eye. "What? Someone saw my father? Who? Where?"

"He said it was near downtown Athens, in Sintagma Plaza."

Alexia's eyes lit up. Her heart started to pound.

"What else? What else did he say?"

"Well, he said he seemed disoriented."

"Disoriented? But who told you that?"

"I already said, just a friend of mine from Athens," Eduard said.

Alexia's mind worked quickly, constructing several hypotheses about why her father would be downtown. Had he been drugged? Had he managed to escape his captors? Had he hit his head and lost his memory?

"I think it would be best if we went to see my friend."

Alexia was quiet, thinking. She felt a gnawing hole in her heart and an overwhelming, piercing desire to find her father. She began to slowly nod her assent, as if trying to convince herself that it was the correct course of action. Her gaze rested on a photo of Aquiles on her BlackBerry. Her intuition won out.

"First let's go to the address I found."

# 50

dam was still deep in reflection when his cell phone rang.

"Alexia!" he exclaimed happily.

"Where have you been?" she asked, calling from the taxi.

"I've been meeting with Kruger and another researcher at the institute. So much has happened. I'll tell you all about it. Where are you?"

"In Athens. I found an address in my father's datebook I'm going to check out."

"Are you alone? That's dangerous, Alexia. The police were after us. Be extremely careful."

"Listen. Get in touch with my friend Jacinto Urquijo and tell him to take you to my apartment. I remembered there's a flash drive there that could have some computer files my father sent me a while ago."

"A flash drive? What made you think of that now?"

"I've gone through everything else!" Alexia said, exasperated. "I don't know, maybe none of it will be useful, but we can't leave anything to chance. Maybe it has some important documents, or addresses, I don't know…something. It's in a blue box in the armoire in my bedroom."

"I'll find it, Alexia. Then I'll head back to Athens and meet up with you. Let me talk to Dr. Kruger about a plan, and I'll let you know. Be very careful."

"Write down the directions to where I'm going—"

Just then, Eduard grabbed the phone out of Alexia's hands and ended the call.

"What are you doing?" Alexia was stunned.

"The game's over, bitch!" Eduard yelled as he pulled a gun from his jacket.

dam stared down at his BlackBerry screen, puzzled. *Her battery must have run out. Or maybe she wanted to text me the address.*

"What did she say?"

"She's going to an address in Athens she found written in Aquiles's date book."

"I hope she finds something," said Dr. Kruger. "We should hurry up and get out of here. The police could be here any second."

"Why run away, Doctor? There's nothing illegal going on at your institute."

"Because they want the quartz!"

"Before we go, we should get organized," Adam said. "We have to think."

"What do you think we should do now?" Kate asked.

"Two things," Adam said forcefully. "First, we need to find Aquiles or some trace of where he could be. And second…"

Kruger seemed to read his mind. "Talk to the media!"

"Exactly," Adam said. "We have to let people know about this, to start a chain reaction so people will get ready." His face was as firmly set as a statue of Apollo. Then he remembered Alexia's request to get her flash drive. "I just had a thought.

We pass information from one USB port to another, from one disk to another, from a computer to a memory chip. What if we could pass the information in one quartz to another?"

Dr. Kruger and Kate's eyes blazed with excitement.

"If that could be done…" Kruger marveled. "If we could program any quartz, even just from the small fragment of the Atlantean quartz that we have…"

Adam finished, "We could give thousands and thousands of charged, preprogrammed quartzes out to people!"

"Would that trigger a collective revolution of energy?" Kate wondered.

"Precisely, although first we'd have to do some tests," Kruger added, his face flush from emotion and excitement. "It'd be a chain reaction. Perhaps we *can* get people to understand what's going to happen on December 21."

Adam nodded happily.

"Kate," Kruger said, "let's work on how we can transfer this information. I'd like you to be in charge of testing it. If it works, call all the quartz mines in the world and buy all the quartzes that you can that are five, seven, or nine centimeters long."

Adam imagined the thousands—perhaps millions—of quartzes they could program. Suddenly, something clicked. "Now I know why the quartz Alexia wears around her neck is so hot," he said. "It's being activated."

## 52

Eduard began to sweat inside the taxi.

"What are you doing, you idiot? I was talking to Adam," Alexia said angrily, watching Eduard point his gun at her.

"From now on you're going to do exactly as I say."

The terrified taxi driver saw what was going on through the rearview mirror. A huge crowd had gathered in the heart of downtown Athens, in what looked like a massive demonstration.

"This street has been blocked off," the driver said, thinking he'd be much better off just letting them get out. He didn't want any trouble.

"You'll do as I say, too!" the Owl snapped, still training his gun on Alexia.

"But what do you want?" Alexia asked, stunned and confused.

"Right now I want you to shut up. Let's go—drive!" he ordered the taxi driver.

"But there's no way to get through this street."

"Then turn down that one," Eduard said, pointing to a deserted side street. They were only two blocks from the house where Aquiles was being held.

The driver turned down the side street as he was told, avoiding the demonstration. They went about 150 feet before Eduard ordered him to stop.

"You'll have to forgive me, I don't have any money to pay for the ride," he said sarcastically. "Hurry up, get out of the car!" he barked at Alexia.

She followed his order, opening the door and planting one foot on the pavement.

Eduard quickly climbed out on the other side.

In a quick movement, Alexia threw herself back inside the taxi and the driver hit the gas, with the doors still open, leaving the Spaniard outside.

The Owl didn't hesitate. He raised his gun and aimed directly at the driver. One sure shot made the taxi crash into a lamppost. The noise from the impact made a dog up the street howl in terror. The Owl sprinted the distance to the car. He saw Alexia in a daze in the back seat, watching a stream of blood trickling from the driver's head. Eduard grabbed Alexia by the hand and roughly pulled her from the car. The dress she had on tore up to her hip.

"Come on, you stupid bitch! Walk!"

She stumbled along beside him while he put the gun back in his right inside jacket pocket.

"If you get smart again, I will shoot you in the head."

Alexia had hit her forehead when the taxi crashed. She was dizzy and could barely stay on her feet. The Owl dragged her along, and soon they were out of sight of the taxi. Luckily for Eduard, no one had witnessed the scene. They turned a corner. They were only a few hundred feet away from the house where Aquiles was guarded by the Frenchman.

"After everything that's happened, you should be happy now. You're going to see your father."

# 53

Back in Dr. Kruger's house, Kate heard a strange sound. She looked out the window onto the street and saw a black car and three patrol cars.

"The police!" she exclaimed.

Adam and Kate looked at each other in a panic. Kruger sprang into action.

"This way!" he said, heading for the kitchen in the back of the house. There was a dark wooden door that let out on a small alleyway with some trash cans. Kruger quickly opened the door, and they ran outside. "They'll be in any second. It's best if we split up. You both have your cell phones?"

They quickly nodded.

"You both know what you have to do," Kruger said solemnly. "Be careful."

They went out the back of the alleyway and quickly walked off in different directions. At Kruger's front steps, Viktor Sopenski and the English police broke down the door.

# 54

They'd agreed that Kate and Dr. Kruger would work on testing and programming the small quartz crystals they planned to distribute during the Olympics. Kate would contact the media while Adam would go back to Greece to continue the search for Aquiles and the mother quartz from Atlantis.

After fleeing the police, Adam had jumped in a taxi and quickly left the neighborhood. He called Jacinto Urquijo, as Alexia had asked, to get the keys to her apartment. They planned to meet at the well-known Westfield shopping center in downtown London.

As the taxi approached Big Ben, the famous clock tower of Westminster palace read seven o'clock in the evening. The car drove down the street alongside, near the seat of the British parliament.

Gazing at the palace, Adam reflected on the events of the past several days. Ever since he'd left New York, he'd become entangled in an escalating spiral of unpredictable events and prophecies, riddles, hypotheses, premonitions, and metaphysical experiences. Accustomed to his very organized, albeit busy routine, he felt as if his life had been turned upside down. And now everything was speeding up.

He needed time to process everything. Ever since Aquiles's phone call, he'd been running nonstop from one place to another, devising theories, interpreting symbols, and testing his powers of comprehension to their limits.

A flurry of images danced in his mind: the earthquakes, the bizarre solar activity, the mystical use of sex, the orichalcum tablet, the quartz infused with Atlantean wisdom...

He tried to figure out how all the pieces fit together.

On top of everything, he was now a fugitive without ever having committed a crime. He didn't like being persecuted. He lowered the taxi window to get some fresh air. He asked the driver to turn up the radio and listened to news about the countries hardest hit by the earthquakes. The planet's situation was very delicate. Meteorologists continued to observe solar storms, and who knew what was next?

London had been untouched by the devastation, so the Olympics were still scheduled as planned. When the taxi stopped at a red light, Adam saw groups of demonstrators carrying signs with antigovernment slogans, and many more announcing the end of the world. The city seemed like a human cocktail of color, confusion, and surrealism.

Adam tried to take his mind off the news for a minute. He closed his eyes. He thought of something Kate had said to him after his experience with the quartz.

"I don't know if it's because of this moment," she'd said, "but I have to confess I feel very connected to you."

Adam wasn't thinking about love or sex, although he couldn't deny that a sexual experience with a woman like Kate would definitely be memorable. Or maybe something more; he didn't know. He felt a very strong desire to see Alexia again. He decided to push thoughts of both women out of his mind.

The taxi pulled up to the shopping center. Adam took out his cell phone and called Alexia's friend again.

## 55

Jacinto Urquijo waited at the entrance to a Dolce & Gabbana boutique. He was holding a large shopping bag with "D&G" emblazoned across it. He was short and slight, but with his stylish way of dressing, he never went unnoticed. He wore fashionable gray pants, a white shirt, and large black sunglasses. His hair was cut short and had been styled with gel to point straight up. He wore a ring on each finger and always had a smile on his face. He'd been born in Puerto Rico but had lived in London for many years now.

"Hello!" he called out brightly, waving as he made his way through the crowd of shoppers. "Here I am!"

Adam introduced himself as soon as Jacinto was in the taxi. "Were you waiting a long time?"

"No, I got here early. I wanted to go shopping. I got tired of working, and all the chaos." Jacinto gestured with his hands as he talked.

"You work with Alexia, right?"

"Yes," he said enthusiastically. "I'm a geologist too. I adore Alexia, I truly adore her. She's divine…a goddess."

"I feel the same way," Adam said. "She's an amazing woman."

Jacinto gave the driver the address, and they were on their way.

"Look, Jacinto, Alexia and I have a big problem. It's very complicated. Her father's disappeared."

"I know. She called me from Santorini and told me you'd come by to pick up her keys and some files or something. This is crazy! I'll help you any way I can." He paused before going on. "I already told Alexia about this, so I'm going to tell you, too..." His voice faltered, and his expression grew serious.

"What is it?"

"You see, Adam, we've gotten several e-mails at the geological institute with aerial photos of strange geometric symbols, agro glyphs—crop circles."

"Go on," Adam said. Crop circles were strange, sophisticated patterns in the fields, anywhere between sixty-five and five hundred feet long.

"Are they recent?"

"Yes," he confirmed, his eyes wide. "They're not just in England. They've shown up in fields around the whole world. It's the big news story today. It's all over the Internet and TV."

"What do the symbols show?"

"It's bizarre."

Jacinto took a folder out of his bag and showed him a picture. Adam's heart leaped. An electrical current seemed to pass over his entire body.

The taxi driver looked at them curiously through the rear-view mirror.

"What are these symbols? What do they mean?" Jacinto wasn't sure why, but the hairs on the back of his neck stood on end.

Adam didn't take his eyes off the photo in his hands. "Jacinto, these are the same symbols Alexia's father found on a tablet more than twelve thousand years old!"

"Seriously?"

Adam nodded.

"Let me see it again. What do they mean?" Jacinto took the papers and photographs back.

"Those are the alpha and omega, and there are several symbols for Elohim, the sacred sexual union of the feminine and masculine."

"Amazing!"

"Even if they never find out who or what made these crop circles, I haven't the slightest doubt that those symbols are the work of advanced, enlightened beings. Tell me, where have they been sighted?"

"Everywhere," Jacinto replied. "From Argentina to Canada, in China, Malaysia, Greece, in Australia..."

"Unbelievable," Adam said. He was about to say more but cut himself off, not wanting the taxi driver to hear more. He brought his index finger to his lips, making a shushing gesture. They were quiet for the rest of the drive.

The taxi driver took a right turn and sped down the street at top speed, then crossed over two blocks, avoiding the main avenues. After five more blocks, Jacinto gestured to the driver to stop.

"We'll walk down the block," Jacinto said. "Alexia's house is the white one down there."

# 56

I'm nervous," Jacinto said as they walked toward Alexia's house. "I don't understand what's going on."

Adam tried to fill Jacinto in as best he could, but it was a lot for anyone to take in. As Adam spoke, Jacinto was quiet and looked thoughtful and slightly afraid.

Just outside of Alexia's house, Jacinto's cell phone rang. He took it out of his pocket and looked at the screen. Adam looked on, hoping the caller was Alexia. He was anxious to tell her that the quartz on her necklace could be a fragment from the Atlantis quartz. He wanted to explain how she could access its information.

"It's not Alexia," Jacinto said, looking down. "It's a friend. You go on in, and I'll be right there." He handed Adam the house keys.

Adam unlocked the front door and stepped inside the tastefully decorated entryway. A carefully tended box of flowers filled the window. He closed the front door behind him and smelled the slightest hint of Alexia's perfume in the air. Everything looked like her—minimalist and warm. She'd made the best use of the space, which was thoughtfully furnished. He took a few steps down the spacious hallway.

Alexia had said he'd find the flash drive in her bedroom. He headed toward the spiral staircase at the end of the hall, which was painted a very light shade of lavender. He climbed the stairs imagining Alexia there, living alone, self-sufficient, filling up every corner of the house with the vibrant energy of her luminous spirit.

As he reached the top of the stairs, he saw a half-open door to the bathroom and glimpsed the toilet with the seat up.

*How strange,* he thought, *Alexia wouldn't have left the seat up.* He assumed that Jacinto must have used the bathroom a few days before, when he came by to water the plants. Then he walked into the bedroom. On the wall were a few framed paintings of sunsets in Santorini. He noticed right away that the bed wasn't made. It was a detail that stood out immediately in the otherwise neat and well-ordered environment.

He opened one of the lower drawers of the armoire. Underneath some folded towels, he saw a small blue box. He opened it. He found the flash drive inside. Just as he was about to turn to leave the house, he felt the touch of a cold metal barrel of a pistol on the back of his neck.

Behind him, Viktor Sopenski firmly gripped the weapon.

# 57

Sergei Valisnov sat on Stewart Washington's right at the summit meeting in Washington, DC. The meeting was top secret, as its attendees didn't want to attract attention from the independent media. The Brain inwardly fretted—he knew that some members of the Secret Government and the official administration might veto the plan to detonate nuclear bombs. He had to make his case, forcing them to see it was their only option. They needed to not only destroy the meteor heading straight for Earth, but also to quell the fervent hope spreading around the world about the winter solstice.

Top leaders of several countries joined representatives from the Vatican, the highest-ranking members of the Secret Government, and a few other individuals responsible for controlling the world media and the pharmaceutical industry.

"We must make some decisions," the Brain said forcefully. "As you are already aware, we need to urgently focus our attention on several fronts."

An air of uncertainty hung over the room, and the faces around the table all wore extremely serious expressions. Stewart Washington continued, "On the one hand, we have the imminent arrival of the meteor that our scientists at NORAD and the NASA observatories have recently detected, which will surely strike Earth if we don't do something to stop it.

The problem is compounded by the addition of our second main concern: the rumor about the solstice—the stories about the Mayan prophesies."

Several of the attendees were visibly discomfited by this.

"It's not hard to understand why these rumors have gained so much power. Just consider the events of the past few days: the changes in solar activity, the earthquakes. People are afraid and confused."

Washington paused and looked around the table before continuing.

"If the people find out about the approaching meteor, they will go into a state of severe psychological crisis. They will turn en masse to the Mayan prophesies for meaning."

Washington locked eyes with an emissary from the Vatican, who gazed back with an uncertain, doubtful expression. The Brain had ensured Cardinal Tous did not attend the meeting, ordering him to stay in Rome. He wanted to avoid arguments. But even so, the tension in the air grew with each word Washington spoke.

"We also have the sightings to deal with," said the Brain, referring to reports that intergalactic spaceships had been sighted around the world. Though he didn't say so, there were also financial ramifications to all the recent crises—billions of dollars and euros were lost as the financial system grew shaky.

"What do you propose?" asked the president of the United States.

"Our proposal may sound rather drastic at first, but I believe over the long run, it will be an investment that will ultimately grant us total world dominance. It is the only way to impose our long-awaited New World Order in the near term. The fears of most of the 6.3 billion people on Earth will be

replaced by the security we'll offer them. After our intervention...pardon me," he corrected himself, "after *your* intervention as official standing governments, it will be clear that you
are their saviors from the Apocalypse."

"What *is* the plan, then?" the United States secretary of
defense asked.

Washington cleared his throat. "The plan we have
designed," he said, looking at Valisnov, "is to detonate several
nuclear bombs, activating the shield we've already installed in
space. We will take care of the meteorite and the extraterrestrial spacecraft at the same time."

A murmur ran around the room like a babbling brook. A
spokesperson from the Vatican quickly spoke up. "I'm afraid
His Holiness will not support this plan when he finds out
about it."

Washington shot him a look as burning as a laser beam.
"His Holiness will simply have to understand the gravity of
the situation we're facing. The church has always shown itself
to be firm when it comes to protecting the word of the Bible
at all costs, imposing by force 'what was in the past,' but it's
demonstrated a clear reluctance to talk about 'what will be
in the future,' and our future depends on the outcome of this
meeting today."

"You think you are so powerful that you can change the
Word of God?" the papal representative retorted smugly.

"Now is not the time for a religious debate," cut in the
Wizard.

All eyes turned to him.

"I would like to explain to you the seriousness of the situation in technical terms," he said loudly, opening up a folder
on the table in front of him.

Washington nodded his assent, gesturing for him to continue.

"This next threat of impact will not be an object of little significance," Valisnov continued, his eyes blazing. "It's not just another meteorite. What is approaching Earth now was not detected in advance by telescopes or satellites, and yet it's going to reach us in a matter of four or five months." He wore an expression of an ancient gladiator poised for combat. "In fact, the latest studies suggest it's not necessarily a meteor at all."

The room hummed with low whispers.

"Then what is it?" the secretary of defense asked impatiently.

"We aren't sure. The latest reports from our scientists say the unidentified object could be some type of comet. It's aflame, and if it makes contact with Earth's atmosphere, it would produce giant, fiery rocks that would rain down on the planet, destroying it."

A heavy silence enveloped the room.

"Imagine for a moment that if there is a collision," continued the Wizard, "this fiery material would be all that was left on Earth, and none of us, quite literally, would ever see our bodies again on this planet."

"But nuclear weapons can't be the only option," said the secretary of defense. "Is there a plan B?"

"I'm afraid there is no other option. This is our ace in the hole," Valisnov said firmly.

# 58

Viktor Sopenski was tense. He was irritated that he'd had to go through such an ordeal just to capture Adam.

"One false move and your brains will be splattered on the wall."

Adam stood motionless, doing as he was told. Sopenski snorted like an enraged buffalo.

"Put your hands on your head! Don't move!" Sopenski screamed angrily.

Adam slowly raised his hands and laced his fingers behind his head.

"What did you just take out of that box?" Sopenski asked. "Give it to me!"

Adam's mind raced as he tried to think of some way out of the situation.

"It's…"

"A flash drive? What's on it?"

"I don't know."

"Give it to me! We'll know soon enough," Sopenski said. He went over to a laptop on Alexia's desk, still pointing the gun at Adam.

"I can help you," Adam said, trying to gain the upper hand. "I can give you more money than they're paying you."

Sopenski kicked him in the kidneys. Even though Adam was a strong man, he let out a loud groan.

"You're going to tell me what's on this flash drive. Turn on the computer! One false move and I'll shoot."

Just then a sound from the stairway distracted Sopenski. The bulky police officer hid behind the door, still training his gun at Adam's head. The feminine, languorous frame of a cat stepped through the door, with a regal, majestic gait, as if she were Cleopatra herself at the height of her reign in Egypt. The creature was looking for her owner. She meowed, as if posing a question.

"Get out of here, goddamn cat!"

Sopenski threw a small decorative pillow from the bed at the animal. She ran out of the room and raced down the stairs.

Holding the gun out in front of him, Sopenski roughly gestured for Adam to move to his right. Sopenski had his back to the door.

"My patience is running out," he barked furiously, practically foaming at the mouth. "Let's see what's on this, and then we'll get out of here."

Adam sat down at the desk and opened the laptop.

"You need a password. I don't know what it is."

Sopenski's eyes seemed to bulge out of his skull. "Password?" The policeman clenched his jaw helplessly. He thought for a moment. "Get the password now!"

Adam hesitated for a second. Just as he was about to take his BlackBerry out of his pocket, Viktor Sopenski's oversized frame collapsed in a heap on the floor. A swift blow to the head from a porcelain vase had rendered him unconscious.

"When I gave this vase to Alexia, I had no idea it would end up knocking this thief in the head." Jacinto's voice was music to Adam's ears.

Adam turned, relieved. "He's not a thief exactly," Adam said, pulling himself together. "Quick, let's find something to tie him up with."

## 59

You say there's no plan B?" the secretary of defense repeated.

"And we need to act fast," Valisnov added, "since very soon the asteroid will be visible to independent astronomers all over the world."

"What should we say to the press, though? We can't exactly justify sending nuclear warheads into space," said the secretary.

"They report our version of events, as always," soothed the Brain. "This operation will grant the official US government and other allied nations absolute power. They will be the definitive leaders and the 'heroes' of the world if everything goes according to plan."

The secretary of defense countered, "This isn't about heroism. It's about preventing disaster. When the first amateur astronomer talks to the press about his discovery, the whole world will dissolve into chaos. We have to make the announcement ourselves first."

Valisnov took a deep breath. "We believe that the outbreak of global panic will give us the opportunity to finally implant personal microchips. People will do it voluntarily and willingly—they'll think it will protect them."

"I think we've heard more than enough to let us agree to launch a defense," said the Brain, taking back control of the meeting. "I propose we bring it to a vote."

Several of the men around the table nodded in agreement. The president of the United States did not say anything, thinking it over.

"Those who support sending nuclear warheads into space cast your vote," the Brain instructed.

Over the next few, quiet minutes, the members of the Secret Government and the heads of state in attendance cast their votes on pieces of paper. In less than ten minutes, the results were in.

"Gentlemen," the Brain intoned, as he coolly looked around the table, "the ballots show that of seventy people present, forty-nine are in favor of launching nuclear missiles into space."

Stewart Washington's heart pounded as he made the momentous announcement; he could feel the blood pulsing through his veins.

"We don't have much time," he said triumphantly. "We only have a few months. We must set our plan into motion now."

The countdown began. There was no going back.

## 60

dam knelt in front of Sopenski, whose hands were tied behind his back. He reached into the man's inside jacket pocket and found his wallet with personal identification.

"It seems his name is Viktor Sopenski. He has some ID from the United States," Adam told Jacinto.

"What's he doing here?"

"Soon he'll tell us for himself what he's doing here," Adam said, "but first we have to wait for him to come to."

"He'd better hurry up." The small-statured geologist went to the bathroom and came back with a bowl of cold water.

He turned abruptly and threw the water in the policeman's face, as if he were spitting on him. Sopenski began to move. He opened his eyes and blinked.

"Who are you and what the hell are you doing here?" Jacinto demanded.

"Wait, give him a chance to come to his senses; you gave him quite a knock on the head."

"What should I have done? He was pointing a gun at you!"

"Okay, good point. I'm just saying we have to give him a minute to fully regain consciousness."

Sopenski's glazed eyes looked as if they had been staring at a bicycle's spinning wheel for the past couple of hours.

"What the hell," the police officer muttered when he realized he was tied up.

"What are you doing here?" Jacinto asked again.

"I'm not telling you anything."

"Well you're going to have to." Jacinto went to grab him by the hair, but Adam stopped him.

"Whoa, hang on," he said, taking Jacinto by the shoulders and guiding him to sit on Alexia's bed. "Let me question him.

"Mr. Sopenski," Adam said calmly. "You entered a private home without permission, and in this country, that's against the law."

Sopenski looked contemptuously at Adam. Who was he to talk about what was legal?

"We'll call the police! The Brits will make him talk," Jacinto said.

Adam shook his head and paused thoughtfully. "This is all very confusing, Mr. Sopenski. You'll have to tell us what you were doing in this house and whom you work for."

Just then, Viktor Sopenski's phone buzzed from inside his jacket pocket.

"I think you just got a text message," Adam said, reaching into the jacket to examine the phone. "If you don't mind, I'll read it myself."

Sopenski struggled, flailing his torpid body about to somehow keep Adam from seeing the phone, but he only managed to cause himself more pain. He was like a furious bull, foaming at the mouth, full of rage.

"Cut it out, pig!" Jacinto shouted.

Adam took the phone and read the message, first to himself, and then aloud.

*Return to Athens immediately. The Owl has her. He's taking her to where the archeologist is. Hurry.*

The number that sent the message appeared as "the Magician."

"Now you're really in trouble," Adam said soberly, his expression stern. "Call Alexia, quick," he told Jacinto.

"She's not answering," Jacinto said as he waited for her to pick up, a pained expression on his face.

Adam frowned. Alexia was in very serious danger.

"Who is the Owl? And the Magician?" he asked Sopenski, who looked nauseated.

The police officer was tight-lipped.

"We have to move fast," Adam told Jacinto. "Listen carefully." Adam placed a hand on each shoulder and looked him straight in the eye. "Jacinto, listen very carefully, here's what we're going to do: You're going to call the police and tell them what happened. I'm going to Athens right away to find Alexia." Adam had some misgivings about calling the police, considering they'd chased him without cause. But he wasn't sure whom else to call for help, and he did fundamentally believe that the police were on the side of good—the earlier scenario must have been brought on by a misunderstanding.

"But how are you going to find her?" Jacinto asked.

"I'll bring his phone," Adam said, glancing at Sopenski. "I don't know, I'll send a text asking for the address for the meeting. I'll think of something on the way."

"But what should I do with this pig?"

"Just tell the police what happened. I'll call Kruger and explain on the way. We can't waste any more time."

Jacinto nodded as he shot Sopenski a hateful look.

"I'm counting on you, Jacinto. Think of Alexia. Call the police right away. I'm on my way to Athens right now."

Less than a minute later, Adam had gone down the stairs and was outside, closing the front door behind him.

## 61

Adam stepped into the street and hailed a taxi. He asked the driver to take him to the closest airport, London City Airport, which was only six miles away.

He lowered the window, and as the fresh breeze hit his face, he felt renewed energy. As they drove through the city, a spectacularly chaotic scene unfolded before them. Near London Bridge, throngs of people of all ages protested, carrying posters and signs. They chanted and shouted, and several protesters threw rocks at the riot police who were trying to calm things down.

"What's going on?" Adam asked the driver.

"Haven't you heard?"

"No, I guess not."

The driver gave Adam a worried look through the rearview mirror.

"They want to cancel the Olympics."

"Why?"

"Mostly because of all the damage from the earthquakes. Many countries were affected. The governments of the hardest-hit countries sent petitions to the Olympics organizers about how it's not the right time for the games since so many people died or lost their homes. It's really bad."

Adam felt his heart race. If they canceled the Olympic games, then they wouldn't be able to spread the message of the prophecies through the quartzes. And the outlook world-wide was bleaker than it seemed. The atmosphere hummed with tension, chaos, confusion, and a strange combination of energies. He sighed heavily. He was tired. Overwhelmed. He felt as if a giant snowball was rolling out of control over the planet. Was there some kind of order behind it all that he just couldn't see?

"The whole world is blowing up; it's a real drama," the driver said.

Adam knew that the worldwide outburst wasn't because people were upset that the Olympics, the biggest global event, might be canceled. They were upset because of what was going on deep within the earth and out in the galaxy.

He pulled out his cell phone and called Kruger.

"Doctor?"

"Yes, Adam, I was just about to call you." His slightly accented German voice sounded energized.

"Something very serious has happened."

"What is it?" Kruger's tone was more subdued.

"We had a run-in with a strange man at Alexia's house. He pointed a gun at me. Luckily, Jacinto took him by surprise, and we tied him up. Jacinto's waiting for the police to get there."

"But what was the man doing there?"

"I think he was looking for information. He got a text message while we were there, and I read it. I still have his phone."

"So what did the message say?"

"That they have Alexia in Athens."

"Oh my God! What's going on? Who's behind all of this?"

"I don't know. Right now I'm on my way to the airport to fly back to Athens. I'm going to somehow use his phone to find out where they're taking her."

"Adam, it's dangerous…"

"You don't have to remind me, believe me. What's going on with the quartzes?"

"We're starting to run some tests. I think it will work—we've already been able to pass information from the small quartz crystal to other ones."

Adam smiled brightly. "Really? That's great news! How did you do it?"

"The quartz crystals can be programmed through respiration and mental intention," said Kruger.

"Respiration?"

"Exactly. Respiration and intention. I have lined up the Atlantis quartz in sequence with other quartz crystals. Kate and I went to the home of two special children who weren't at the institute. They used their third eye and their pineal glands, just as you did in your experience with the quartz. What we do using technology, like sending e-mails, they do using thought and respiration."

"That's truly amazing."

"Adam," Kruger said, his voice becoming grave, "you're in danger. Be very careful."

"Let's call each other as soon as we have any news."

## 62

Eduard dragged Alexia toward the house. It was getting dark, and a light breeze began to blow. They were in for a very long night. The Spaniard took out his phone and called Villamitre.

"Is everything okay? Open up. I'm outside with the daughter."

Villamitre greeted this news without much enthusiasm. He'd been stuck inside for days, guarding Aquiles. The door opened halfway. The Frenchman looked shocked by the sight of them. Eduard touched a finger to his lips, telling him to not make a sound.

The doorway was dark with shadows. Eduard roughly gestured to Alexia to walk down the three steps and go inside. He glanced all around the street. The night was on his side; no one saw them enter the house. Villamitre led the way into the other room, turning toward the exhausted archeologist sitting tied to the chair, barely conscious.

"You have a visitor," he said ironically.

Villamitre bared his yellow teeth in a smile, making him appear even uglier.

"Cheer up, Professor Vangelis. Your daughter came to see you in person. I think it's time you got ready to talk—if you don't want to watch her die right in front of your eyes."

# 63

Alexia saw a figure in the shadows. The fetid room reeked of sweat. Neither Aquiles or Villamitre had bathed in days.

"Don't move!" the Owl barked. "You can't see him yet. You, what are you waiting for? Tie her up! Hurry! And have her sit on this chair," he ordered Villamitre.

The Frenchman did as he was told. Eduard stepped toward the other room and quickly called the Magician in Rome.

The voice of Cardinal Tous came through the phone loud and clear. "Where are you?" he asked. The cardinal had recovered from his fainting spell but was still on edge.

"I'm here with Alexia in the house in Athens; he's about to see her."

"It's now or never. Turn on the computer and call me on Skype. I want to see everything. You know what you have to do…"

"I'll call you in a minute." Eduard had been expecting a bit more appreciation from Tous. "Are you happy?" he couldn't help but ask.

"Yes…of course. You are a treasure."

Eduard liked hearing those words. And it was true—he'd been the one to capture Alexia, and he'd been the one who'd fooled the famous archeologist for so long. He was the one giving the Magician what he wanted. He set the computer up so the cardinal could watch it all. He knew that *now* was his moment, and he wanted to enjoy it as much as possible. He'd been waiting for a chance like this for a very, very long time.

He didn't care at all about betraying Aquiles. Eduard didn't have any pangs of regret, even though the archeologist had taught him many things. He wasn't going to let any sentimental obstacle keep him from getting what he wanted so badly.

# 64

The Secret Government's preparations were carried out to the letter. Stewart Washington, Sergei Valis-nov, and the United States secretary of defense had jointly designated the team responsible for the all-important operation. All of the tasks were carried out with the precision of a Swiss watch: the team in charge of launching the bombs into space carefully prepared the missiles and detonations, and everyone worked in tandem, those directing the press campaigns as well as the official government leaders. They'd named their endeavor "Operation M," for missile, meteorite, and the Mayans.

Through the media, they would announce that the meteorite was going to pass very close to Earth. The widespread panic and alarm among the world population would benefit them when they swooped in to save the day. They would inform people that thanks to sophisticated technologies already in place, such as a nuclear laser, and the influence that HAARP could exert on the ionosphere, everything was under control. They would be the providers of peace and calm and would be considered the "saviors" of humanity.

Stewart Washington sat in his private office, meeting with a half-dozen high-level members who specialized in intelligence. A range of issues was on the agenda, including the possible cancelation of the Olympic Games.

"It is not in our interests to have the games canceled," Washington said. "It would be better to keep the people entertained and distracted as we carry out our operation." *Bread and circus*, he thought to himself.

"We will convince the Olympic Committee," the redheaded Patrick Jackson stated.

"When will the missiles be sent into space?" the Brain asked, looking exhausted as he quickly swallowed two aspirin.

Valisnov, who was now the Brain's right-hand man after devising Operation M, rushed to answer. "According to the latest updates, sir, the first missiles will be launched exactly ten days from now. Four intercontinental missiles will be prepared, especially designed for striking such a large object."

A look of wonder passed over the Brain's face. Operation M was the most important mission of his life.

# 65

L et me go!" Alexia screamed at Eduard as he tied her hands behind her.

"You're not in any position to give orders or ask for anything, bitch. Walk!"

Eduard pointed his pistol to indicate where she should go. Alexia did as she was told. She could make out the shadow of a man tied up toward the end of the room. Her heart beat wildly. It couldn't be. It was too much for her exhausted mind to process.

"Papa?" she murmured uncertainly.

Eduard smirked sarcastically. "How touching!"

Villamitre led her to the other side of the room. Alexia could see Aquiles's poor condition, bloody and battered, with a broken, weary expression. His back was covered in blood. His eyes were half shut and glazed.

"Papa!" she yelled, frustrated that she couldn't throw her arms around him. "You're alive!"

The archeologist seemed as if he couldn't believe his ears. He struggled to open his eyes wider and focus them.

"Alexia…" he rasped weakly, "is that you? They found you?"

Aquiles's eyes were very bloodshot.

"You idiot!" Eduard shouted at Villamitre. "This guy is half dead! You should have taken better care of him!"

Villamitre felt humiliated. Eduard had never talked to him like that. And besides, he'd followed Captain Sopenski's direct orders. *Who does this Spaniard think he is, talking to a Frenchman like this?* Villamitre looked disgusted. He'd been stuck in that airless, smelly room, day and night, guarding the archeologist. He hadn't seen the sun for several days. He was sick of it.

"I did the best I could," he stammered. "You could have come yourself!"

"Father, oh my God!"

Aquiles nodded his head slightly. He was so tired. His arms were lacerated and bruised from the tight ropes cutting off his circulation.

"Papa, I love you…" Alexia had tears in her eyes.

Eduard relished being in control of the situation, although deep in his heart he felt a pang of jealousy. He'd never experienced such an obvious show of affection with his own parents.

"All right. Now that we've had this emotional reunion," he said sarcastically, "I'll tell you what we're going to do."

Alexia suddenly raised her head like an angry lioness.

"What do you want? Have you lost your mind? Traitor! You're the one who kidnapped my father! Goddamn worthless troll! You're nothing but a conceited bastard who thinks he's better than he is!"

She was furious, her eyes blazing.

"That's of no concern to you. What you do need to be concerned about is that your father gather his strength because he's going to have to tell us where his big discovery is, once and for all."

"Or what?" Alexia challenged defiantly.

"Or we'll let him watch my colleague here do what he wishes with you, and then…bang!" He pretended to shoot her with his gun.

"Son of a bitch!"

Eduard couldn't suppress a giggle. He wished Cardinal Tous were there to see him act with such ruthless determination.

"I always told my father I didn't like you, that you couldn't be trusted. Don't you see how hurt he is?"

Alexia felt utterly powerless. Eduard stepped close to the archeologist, who struggled to look up. The Owl looked at him contemptuously.

"Oh, brave Professor Vangelis. Surprised?"

The strong scent of patchouli from the cologne that Eduard always wore penetrated his nostrils. The archeologist crinkled his nose, trying to inhale deeply.

"I knew I remembered that cologne from somewhere," Aquiles murmured.

"And what are you going to do about it, Professor?" Eduard sneered. "Go out and buy me a bottle? This is no time to be discussing cologne. Hey, you!" he barked at Villamitre. "Get him some water to drink and some fruit, quick! You'll need your strength, Professor. You're going to have to start talking if you don't want to see your daughter die." Eduard pointed his pistol at Alexia's head.

Aquiles was in no position to negotiate. His most precious treasure was at stake.

"Don't tell them anything!" Alexia said vehemently.

"Shut up!" Eduard was infuriated. He could not tolerate being challenged. His inflated ego had taken him over, like a dangerous virus of the psyche. "I'm in charge now! You'll do what I say!" he screamed at the top of his lungs. His nervous tic pulsated rhythmically on his face like the second hand on a watch.

"Alexia, I have to save your life," Aquiles said, resigned.

"Papa, they're not going to let us out of here anyway!"

"I told you to shut up!" Eduard said, apoplectic. "He's the one who has to do the talking!"

Unnerved, he went over to the computer and opened Skype. Seconds later, the Magician watched the scene unfold through the camera.

## 66

Villamitre set down a plate of dried fruit, a dish of fresh fruit, and a bottle of water on the table next to Aquiles.

*Now the boss is watching everything,* he thought.

The room simmered with heat, sweat, tension, and nerves. But even though Aquiles was at a distinct disadvantage, the archeologist seemed to be the calmest one of all. He was resigned. He knew there wasn't much time left, and escaping would be extremely difficult. Even though it wasn't likely, he still held onto the hope that they would let his daughter go if he talked.

"Well, Professor? My patience is running out."

Aquiles turned and gave his daughter a look filled with compassion.

A pained expression on her face, she shook her head slowly, silently pleading with him not to say anything.

"Okay," Aquiles said after drinking two glasses of water in quick succession. "If you want to know about my discovery...I'll tell you all about it."

Eduard's eyes shined malevolently. He made sure the Magician was watching.

"Turn on the digital recorder too!" he ordered Villamitre.

Aquiles took a deep breath.

"I'll talk, but first untie us."

Eduard and Villamitre exchanged a look. After a few seconds, Eduard nodded.

"But I'm only going to untie your arms," Villamitre said.

He went over and untied them.

"Professor?" Eduard said dryly, still training his gun on Alexia.

Aquiles talked directly to Alexia, as if he didn't care whether anyone else was listening.

"I've been searching for Atlantis my whole life," he said softly. "I've always believed that a highly evolved civilization existed before the great flood and the cataclysms that shook the earth. I studied the references in Plato's writings and dedicated my life's work to researching Atlantis. I thought my work in this life, my destiny, was to find the remains of Atlantis and tell the whole world about it, finally drowning out the skeptics."

"We already know all that, Professor. Don't get off course here. What did you discover?"

Aquiles felt reenergized, although he still had some difficulty breathing, and he still ached all over.

"Go on!" Eduard ordered.

"The ancient Atlanteans were highly evolved. They had advanced technologies and paranormal powers. They understood their place in the universe and had direct contact with the Source of Creation. They knew that not only Earth, but the entire universe has no borders and belongs to no one. No one is the owner of anything; everything is a divine gift. Everything is one in the cosmos, even if the human mind cannot comprehend this."

Villamitre listened distractedly. Alexia was very moved to see the intense effort her father made to speak.

"The Atlanteans could travel by astral projection; they could leave their bodies and make contact with other dimensions; they could stimulate their energy and expand their consciousness. The full potential of their DNA was activated."

"Move along, Professor," Eduard prodded, growing increasingly impatient.

"Very gradually, they came to see their civilization as better than the others, and they became...shall we say, more rigid and less spiritual, and a problem emerged."

"What problem?" Eduard asked.

Aquiles raised his tired eyes to look directly at the young Spaniard before answering.

"The ego."

"Talk about what you discovered! We don't need a lecture on ancient history or metaphysics!"

"If I don't explain this first, you will not understand the significance of my discovery at all. Do you want me to give you my discovery without the instruction manual?"

Eduard stamped his foot like an angry bull before going out into the ring. He checked to make sure the recorder was on and that the cardinal could see everything; he was terrified that the Internet connection could be lost.

"Go on."

Aquiles turned to gaze at Alexia, who smiled at him warmly.

"The ego germinated in them like an invisible virus and started to overrun an entire civilization, just like an army of rats or termites devours everything in its path. Little by little, egotism…" he looked pointedly at Eduard, "took control and ruined their world, and their powers began to wane. People began to identify more with their egos than their eternal consciousness, and that led to a fall."

"What fall?" Eduard asked.

"We've all heard of the original Fall from Grace. The loss of paradise."

"I don't get it."

The Magician listened intently in front of his laptop.

"The legendary Fall from Grace in the Bible refers to the loss of cosmic consciousness. When the ego comes into play and takes over the reins of a person's destiny, the consciousness becomes unconscious, or asleep. When people started to live according to external belief systems, they lost awareness of direct experience and evolution by experience. They moved away from the present, the gift of the moment, the eternal now. It is not the same to believe that water exists as to know it does by drinking it."

"And…?"

"Along with the ego, fear began to grow in human beings. And they went from being human-divine with an awareness of unity to gradually becoming frightened, and ended up as…" he gave Eduard a disdainful look, "something with no scruples, competitive and vain."

"Don't get smart, Professor. Just tell us what the hell you discovered. About Atlantis?"

Aquiles Vangelis cleared his throat.

"I found something that proves that it existed. Something that could return men and women to the state of paradise that was lost."

That was exactly what Cardinal Tous wanted to hear.

"A new birth. A new cycle. The Mayans foretold that on December 21 of this year, people who were energetically and spiritually prepared would begin a new cycle filled with light."

Eduard raised an eyebrow.

"In what way? How?"

Aquiles paused.

"For a long time they called it…enlightenment."

Alexia realized that her father was stalling and was not going to tell them what they wanted to hear.

"And what exactly are you trying to say with this cute little story, Professor?"

"Well, I discovered that Atlantis existed."

"How? Where?" Eduard was irritated. He didn't think Cardinal Tous was particularly interested in discovering the whereabouts of Atlantis, but something more practical, some instrument of power.

Aquiles continued, "Enlightenment or reconnection with the Source of Original Consciousness is a transforming process…" Aquiles paused, his back screaming in pain, and asked if he could drink a little more water.

Villamitre roughly pushed the bottle of water toward him.

"When consciousness is fully enlightened, human DNA functions at its maximum potential, with twelve helices and sixty-four codons. We know that cells have light," he said to Alexia. "And that initially, the human body was created with a type of cell capable of absorbing and consuming ninety percent of the light and the cosmic forces. But the cells began to deteriorate until they were only operating at ten percent of their original capacity. In antiquity, they understood that we recharged ourselves energetically and spiritually through the sun. What I've discovered will serve to fill everyone with light once again, from the physical cells to the consciousness."

Aquiles's information clearly posed a real threat to the church. Eduard could see why the cardinal was so interested in knowing about a possible mass awakening of consciousness—they'd need to stop it.

"Talk!" Eduard yelled, very aware that Tous was watching.

"That's what I'm doing…"

"Then what, Professor? Hurry up, talk or I'm going to shoot your daughter!"

Aquiles grimaced in pain. He stretched his neck.

"What do you have to do to program DNA?"

"It's easier than you would think. Humans have been trained to go through life with their minds focused on the past or the future, and in that way they lose the present. The present, as the very word implies, is the *gift*, the illumination of the eternal now, the essence of ultimate reality, the origin of life. The mystics have many names for it."

"And how would that change people's lives?" Eduard asked.

Aquiles smiled. "You can't imagine the consequences this would have. It would be a quantum leap…"

The archeologist feigned a cough; he did not want to go any further into that subject.

Alexia smiled. She was so proud of her father.

"Go on," the Owl ordered, extremely unsettled.

"Thanks to what I have discovered, I also found out that we are all connected by a Unity Consciousness Grid."

"Grid of consciousness? What's that?"

Aquiles sighed. He made an effort to keep on talking in spite of the blazing pain in his back.

"Most people are completely unaware of this, although the most powerful governments in the world know about it. I suspect that whomever you two work for are aware of it. They know there are electromagnetic fields laid out in a geometric pattern surrounding and containing Earth, like a warrior's shield. There are millions of them, and from space they look like bright lights enveloping the globe, like the planet's 'coat.' Some governments have set out to destroy this coat. But each person also has this energy field, the aura, which is simply a combination of electricity and magnetism."

"What are you doing?" Eduard yelled. "Giving us a lecture on electricity? Do you think we're that stupid? What did you discover?"

Aquiles kept going, to get him to stop yelling.

"We humans also have three electromagnetic grids connected to consciousness. The first grid was connected long ago by wise, ancient, indigenous peoples, the survivors of Atlantis.

"The second grid was designed geometrically in triangular patterns—that's why the Egyptians built the first pyramids of Giza. They were meant to be a laboratory for those who wanted to regain their lost consciousness of unity and reestablish their powers.

"The third is the Unity Consciousness Grid; it is literally based on a geometric form known as the dodecahedron pentagon. This is the Web of Consciousness that is growing stronger and which will act as the collective consciousness. People who are prepared will become re-enlightened in the extraordinary planetary alignment...this coming December 21."

"But what do those grids have to do with your discovery? You haven't told us anything!" Eduard was losing control.

"It has everything to do with it, Eduard. You just don't understand it." Aquiles tried to break it down into its smallest components.

"I want to know! Talk!"

"In order to understand how these grids function, first you have to understand something very important," Aquiles said firmly. "Without the Unity Consciousness Grid, there would be no way for consciousness to evolve. The leaders in control know this, and that's why they are trying to change it by any means they can."

Aquiles took a deep breath. He continued, looking at his daughter, who was listening carefully to every word, drawing her own conclusions.

"You're delirious," Eduard said.

"You're wrong. You can prove scientifically that what I've said is true. The United States discovered the second grid, and Russia discovered the Unity Consciousness Grid."

Alexia listened intently.

"The Unity Consciousness Grid has been weakened *ex professo* by the governments in order to weaken humanity. They want consciousness to keep on shrinking."

Eduard grimaced. His nervous tic began pulsing again.

"Go on!"

"I've told you enough. Now let my daughter go."

Eduard shook his head no.

"Keep on talking, Professor, and I'll let her go later."

"Don't say anything else, Papa. They're not going to let either one of us go anyway!"

Eduard shot her a look. "Don't force me to gag you or shoot you. Keep your stupid mouth shut."

Aquiles grimaced. The throbbing pain in his wrists tormented him.

"The Unity Consciousness Grid discovered by the Russians has three important energy components. One is masculine, in Egypt; one is neutral, in Tibet; and the one that will awaken next, the feminine, is in Mexico."

"How is it going to 'awaken,' exactly?"

Aquiles gazed at his daughter. "The feminine energy will reach its full potential all over the planet at the next equinox. Many things are going to change."

"What's going to change?" Eduard asked, on edge. He was anxious to get this over with, to liquidate them.

"Feminine energy is the energy of the goddess."

"The goddess? What goddess?" asked the Spaniard.

"The Life Source," Aquiles explained, smiling.

Eduard was quiet.

"The patriarch seized power, leaving his mark on everything: reason and logic, violence and war, philosophy and politics, competitiveness and ambition. Only the Minoans conserved their matriarchy and the cult of the goddess, up until 4,500 years ago in Crete and Santorini."

Eduard was perplexed. Alexia nodded knowingly.

"In ancient cultures, life was steered by wise women. The matriarchy was guided by the vibrations of intuition, free love, telepathy, divine magic, and artistic sensibilities. But this has been slipping away, partly because the wise women were burned at the stake. Soon this vibration will be reactivated when the photon energy of the cosmos fully activates our DNA."

Through the computer screen, Tous watched as attentively as a cougar closing in on his prey.

"There's something very important," Aquiles added.
"This feminine power will be activated only if there are two
or more people receiving it."

"Just say it clearly," Eduard said, irritated.

"Newton's law of motion says, 'For every action there is
an equal and opposite reaction.' The mutual forces of action
and reaction between two bodies are equal, opposite, and col-
linear."

Villamitre scratched his head.

"The existence of only one force is impossible. There
must always be, as in effect there are, a pair of equal, opposite forces, since electricity is a phenomenon of repulsion and
attraction, the interplay of oppositely charged electrons and
protons."

"You're making my head spin! I want to know everything
you discovered, and I want to know it *right now!*" Eduard got
right in Aquiles's face and fixed him with a hateful stare. He felt
powerless. He had expected something clearer, more concise.

"I'll try and make it easier for you, Eduard. Feminine
electricity joins with masculine magnetism. That is light. Just
like the electrical outlets in a house."

"What the hell does electricity and magnetism, the Unity
of Consciousness Grid, Atlantis, and some goddess waking
up have to do with anything?" Eduard shouted, not understanding the theory at all.

Cardinal Tous understood it very well.

Aquiles stifled a laugh and then coughed.

"It's something very natural that everybody does, even
though they might not understand what it's for. The church

has condemned the union of electricity and magnetism for many hundreds of years. They just know it by another name."

"And what is that name?"

Aquiles paused, as if what he was about to say was sacred.

"Sex."

ex?" Eduard asked. "What does sex have to do with all of this?"

"Sex is an energetic-mystical medium to produce Unity Consciousness and regenerate light in the cells and the psyche. In this way, the DNA's full potential is activated. But sex is usually practiced in an animalistic way, to satisfy base instincts and pressures rather than as a spiritual bond and mechanism for cellular reprogramming."

Alexia started to understand why her father had asked Adam to come. Just thinking about him, she felt a swell of emotion. She was sexually attracted to Adam—her pull to him felt magnetic.

Eduard's patience was tested to its limits. He took a deep breath. "What do the Atlanteans have to do with sex, electro-magnetism, and enlightenment?"

"The Atlanteans practiced sex in a sacred, scientific way. Their sexual encounters were long, and through them they entered a state of ecstasy and communion with the original Unity. They worshipped the power of the goddess, cosmic and sexual energy. They awakened more powers through the inner light they generated with alchemic sex." He stopped suddenly. Aquiles looked at the quartz crystal necklace he'd given his daughter. "And through the sexual energy they generated, and using the power of their thoughts, they programmed quartz crystals."

"Quartz crystals? Oh, please! Where are you going with this? I have no more patience for you, Professor. You've always been a storyteller."

"Silence!" Cardinal Tous ordered through the computer screen. "Let him talk!"

That's what the Magician was after. Alexia and her father turned toward the computer.

"Oh! I see we have company," Aquiles said upon hearing his voice. "Only a cockroach like you could be behind all of this."

Tous said coolly, "An attitude is not in your best interest now, Professor Vangelis."

Eduard wanted to remain in charge. "Pure conjecture!" he exclaimed.

"You're wrong, Eduard. It's science, and there is proof."

"What proof?"

Aquiles turned to look at his daughter, choosing his words carefully before proceeding, his eyes welling with emotion:

"I have found a quartz programmed by the Atlanteans, a quartz that is over twelve thousand years old."

There was silence. Tous swallowed hard. *He has it,* he thought.

"A quartz?" Eduard asked, unsure.

Aquiles nodded. "A quartz that could help reprogram DNA, and above all, prepare people to receive the new cosmic energy."

"That's enough, Papa! Don't tell them any more!" Alexia's earlier guess was wrong; her father was holding nothing back.

Villamitre did not have the head for pondering these ridiculous theories. He saw Aquiles as a loony old man. But Eduard felt a glimmer of doubt arise in him. What if Aquiles was right? The Secret Government and the church would be in trouble. They'd lose power and control and would disappear forever.

Cardinal Tous wanted proof.

"Give me the quartz," Tous said, "and we will let your daughter go."

He knew that for centuries many people had tirelessly searched for that stone. Men had killed for it, and theories of its whereabouts abounded.

"It's hidden."

Eduard's eyes opened wide and round, showing why he'd earned the nickname the Owl.

"Don't tell them, Papa!"

Eduard slapped her hard across the face. Alexia tumbled to the floor, injuring her arm and her back. The Owl was quaking with rage. He was sweating heavily, his breathing jagged.

"So, a stone with special powers," Eduard said mockingly, his voice a menacing whine. "What goddamn rock are you talking about, Professor?"

Aquiles looked at Alexia. His eyes filled with tears, he loved her so much. He could not let them hurt his daughter.

"You and everyone else on the planet have heard it mentioned at least once at some point." The archeologist paused. "Usually it's known as the Philosopher's Stone."

# 68

Eduard was flabbergasted by Aquiles's revelation. He'd heard of the Philosopher's Stone, of course, but he thought it had something to do with alchemy and could change lead into gold.

"Professor," he said, incredulous, "you're telling me the stone you found from the Atlanteans is the Philosopher's Stone? I'm not buying it."

"Let him talk, you idiot!" Cardinal Tous yelled, really angry now. "And don't interrupt him again! Speak, Professor!"

It was the first time Tous had spoken to Eduard like that, and he felt just as he had when his father had yelled at him. He didn't like it one bit.

Aquiles continued in the same tone as before. "It doesn't matter whether you believe me or not. I'm not trying to convince anyone. All I'm trying to explain is that through the Philosopher's Stone, the Atlanteans could find what is commonly known as 'the elixir of life,' or simply, sexual energy used in an alchemic way. The Atlanteans were masters of the use of energy. Not only could they create gold, their very bodies were filled with the highest vibrational and energy frequencies. That is what produced a whole era of 'spiritual gold.'"

"Go on," Tous ordered.

Aquiles looked at Alexia, still sprawled on the floor.

"The Philosopher's Stone that I found can transform human DNA so that through..." Aquiles had a sudden fit of coughing.

"So that what? Talk!" Eduard picked up a glass on the only table in the room and hurled it through the air. It just missed Aquiles's head and smashed against the wall behind him, sending shards of glass everywhere. Aquiles fixed him with a defiant, angry glare.

"You imbecile!" Tous growled. "Let him talk!"

"I will not tell you how it's used!" Aquiles shouted. "And I'm not telling you where it is!"

Eduard strode over to Alexia and kicked her hard in the stomach. She howled in pain. Villamitre grabbed hold of Eduard's slender arm and pulled him away.

"No matter what I tell you, what good will it do?" Aquiles asked.

"Don't test our patience!" Tous commanded through the computer screen, nervous and impotent, back in Rome. "You have my word we will set you free. Tell me where it is and exactly how you use it, and I will let your daughter go. And you, Eduard, do not dare interrupt again."

"You already know what it's used for. You've just chosen to ignore it," Aquiles said. "The brilliant splendor that the Philosopher's Stone activates can result in the golden aura that highly evolved people radiate; in the East with the Buddhas and gurus, and in the West the auras of Jesus, the saints, and the enlightened mystics. That light is, simply, DNA that has been one hundred percent activated."

Eduard swallowed hard. Now he understood the urgency behind the cardinal's quest.

"I don't have to tell you, Cardinal, that the aura around the head symbolizes direct, conscious contact with the Wellspring of Life, the Universal Consciousness, the Source. It is a crown. If people could obtain it on their own, your institution would lose its reason for being."

Eduard was quiet. He remembered on the yacht to Santorini, Adam had said that sexual energy could rise to the head and that "coronation" was produced through a ritual of sexual alchemy. That unnerved him even more.

Aquiles paused. He was only interested in making sure his daughter understood *all* of the teachings around his discovery in their entirety. Alexia was astonished to see her father's aura, the energy field full of vibrant greens and purples all around him, radiating from him. After so many days in darkness, the archeologist was clearly inspired. It was the first time she had ever seen a human aura.

"What was first known as *lapis exilis*, which derived from *lapis ex caelis* and in Latin meant 'stone from heaven,' became, through its wise use, the *lapis philosophorum*, the stone from which sacred knowledge comes, to spiritually enlighten human beings," Professor Vangelis added. "This knowledge is *inside* of the Philosopher's Stone I have. The church has been searching all over the globe for it for centuries, isn't that so, Cardinal?"

"The church knows about this?" Eduard asked.

"Of course. The church has always had the very best 'detectives' on the case looking for it," Aquiles said ironically.

Eduard checked every minute to make sure the computer was still on and the connection with Tous had not been lost.

Aquiles shifted his weight in his seat, trying to somehow get comfortable or at least ease the pain.

"Where do you have the stone?" the cardinal asked pointedly.

"Why do you want it? So you can keep your beloved institution alive?" Aquiles asked, goading him.

"It's time for you to tell me where it is," Eduard said. "Choose. Sacrifice your discovery, or your daught—"

Mid-sentence, he stopped. The table had moved. Villamitre looked suddenly terrified. The overhead lamp hanging from the ceiling swung back and forth like a pendulum. The earth manifested its power once again. First, there was a relatively minor tremor, strong enough to knock some glasses and folders off of the table. The computer fell off the table too—Cardinal Tous disappeared as the screen smashed against the floor. Then there was a stronger tremor, followed by a devastating quake. The light from the only bulb in the room went out. The floor moved, and shattered glass tinkled. With an unearthly, deafening roar of a thousand lions, the earth thundered. A deep, powerful, awesome sound.

Aquiles fell on his side, hitting the floor hard on his shoulder. Villamitre's slight frame was thrown violently against a wall. Eduard fell on his face.

The room's inhabitants were overcome by blind panic as the earth unleashed its seventh quake in just three days.

Several more even stronger jolts struck, irregular and sharp. One of the old columns supporting the building collapsed, and a large piece struck Villamitre in the temple, killing him instantly.

Eduard, overcome with panic, his nose gushing blood, dropped his gun when he fell. He tried to search around the darkened room for it, but he was knocked down again by a violent tremor, dislocating his shoulder and fracturing several ribs. The roof of the old house that had sheltered several generations of Greek families came crashing down, leaving a large hole overhead.

Aquiles saw an opening in the debris. For the first time in days, he caught a glimpse of sunlight. It was just for an instant—he breathed in a cloud of dust from the falling building and was struck by an uncontrollable fit of coughing. Everything went dark.

"Papa?" Alexia called from somewhere in the darkness. "Where are you?"

Silence.

Another tremor struck with terrifying power. Several bricks fell on Eduard's still-intact shoulder, and a slab of concrete knocked him unconscious.

Aquiles was still breathing, but he was hurt and dazed.

"Papa! Where are you?" Alexia called again.

She heard a noise—a cough—coming from several feet away. Alexia freed her hands and clawed her way through the debris. Through a pile of fallen bricks, she could just make out the silhouette of her father lying on his side, the chair stuck to his body, his legs still tied.

She scraped her knees against the floor as she struggled to make a path through the debris. She inched along as best she could, barefoot, one arm so injured it was useless. She crawled over the mound of collapsed bricks between them, and using every bit of strength she had, reached her father's side.

Aquiles was battered and bleeding. Alexia's dress was in tatters, and dust swirled in the air like a lethal gas.

"Papa," she said softly, not knowing if her father would be able to, "we have to get out of here."

# 69

The news was everywhere. The violent earthquake in Greece had been the strongest of the seven in recent days, measuring 8.1 on the Richter scale. Chaos reigned in the wake of the worldwide disasters. Hundreds of thousands of people lost their homes. There was still not an accurate count of how many had died.

The seismic movements, like an alligator thrashing its tail, had also unleashed powerful tsunamis, demolishing buildings on the coastline. Activity had been registered in several volcanoes as they acted like chimneys, relieving some of the pressure building up deep within the earth. To make matters worse, hurricanes struck many cities, wreaking havoc over the ruins caused by the earthquakes and tsunamis. It was as if the planet wanted to cleanse itself. This intensive cleansing was coming at a very high price.

Devout Christians were convinced the Apocalypse had arrived. The Red Cross and other humanitarian agencies and NGOs around the globe worked tirelessly to provide support, organizing relief efforts in the disaster zones.

One BBC commentator, whose career as a reporter spanned over thirty years, lost all sense of professionalism and wept uncontrollably in front of the cameras as he watched the horrific images being broadcast on the program. He could not complete his report and had to be replaced.

All over the planet, the earthquakes were the main story. The television networks tried to enlist expert geologists to offer explanations in every possible language. It was a world-wide tragedy.

Despite his long, prestigious career in the sciences, Dr. Stefan Kruger had a very hard time getting some air time on the BBC. At first, the producers at the network thought he was just another crazy person. But finally through a friend with contacts, he managed to land an on-air interview for himself, Kate, and four of the children working on the project, so they could send a very different message out into the world.

The news broadcast's theme music lasted less than fifteen seconds. Then the anchorwoman began introducing the scientists and the children.

"We are here with Dr. Stefan Kruger, a geneticist and director of the Genetics Institute of London. We also have with us the geneticist Dr. Kate Smith, and these four children." She read their names from a piece of paper: "Amalia, Miguel, Pedro, and Gertrude."

The children giggled. Kruger had an eager, enthusiastic expression.

"All right then," their interviewer sighed, "what do you have to tell us, Dr. Kruger?"

"You see," he began, "we are here to tell you about a very important discovery while also providing a bit of understanding about what is happening on the planet."

Skeptical, the interviewer arched an eyebrow. "You believe, Doctor, that the people can truly *understand* the chain of disasters?" She pronounced the word "understand" as if she were speaking to a very small child.

"They will have to," Kruger said pointedly. "For a very long time, humanity has been asleep, programmed, on automatic pilot. It is time to wake up. Now—"

His interviewer interrupted. "Wake up?" She was tired and irritated after having interviewed a dozen people with very different theories; her mind was too exhausted to hear another one.

Kruger smiled, ignoring her negative attitude.

"I mean we need to wake up to what's happening to us. Everything has a cause. These reactions of the earth are the result of a purification, a purge, a kind of preparation for the energy that—"

The reporter interrupted again, her irritation rising. "A purification?"

Kruger's own patience was waning. "If you would let me continue, I can explain," he said with a sober expression, piercing the reporter with his gaze. She crossed her arms and sighed.

"Go ahead," she said unenthusiastically. "Surprise me."

Kruger knew he didn't have much time.

"We believe the earthquakes are the planet's way of preparing to receive an energy—an energy that will cause many things to happen. I don't mean material, physical changes, but..." he looked at the children, "changes in consciousness and changes at a fundamental, genetic level, altering and activating the DNA of people who have prepared themselves for the shift."

The reporter smiled cynically. "Pardon me, Doctor," she began, "but are you trying to tell us that the earthquakes are actually good? That they're a means of preparing us to elevate our consciousness?"

Kate jumped in to answer. "The argument that Dr. Kruger is trying to summarize," she said calmly, "is based on ancient knowledge of pre-Colombian America, specifically the wisdom of the Mayans, when people understood that Earth is itself a living being; they listened to its heartbeat and studied its cosmic cycles."

"Excuse me, but you two talk more like astronauts than geneticists, Dr. Smith."

Kate shook her head. "The key point here is about human evolution. Our DNA. But Earth is the planet we live on, and the galaxy we are in, among thousands and thousands of other galaxies, is *sharing* the universe. We must not limit our vision. We are geneticists," she affirmed, "but as scientists, we are also trying to understand in a holistic way how other energies and events can alter our DNA."

Kate's soothing voice and warm sensuality seemed to have a calming effect on the interviewer.

"And what do you think we should do?"

"Prepare ourselves to receive the energy that will activate all twelve strands of our DNA."

The journalist thought about all the pain people were experiencing and imagined that they wouldn't have much energy to devote to such preparation, but she kept her thoughts to herself. Kate had won her over.

"Correct me if I'm wrong, Doctor. As I understand it, we only use two strands, right?"

Kate and Kruger both nodded.

"Exactly," Kate said. "If modern men and women activated all twelve strands, human life as we know it would experience a quantum leap forward. We're not the only ones working on this. Scientists all over the world have been researching this subject for years, but they haven't always been taken seriously.

"These children who are here with us today," Kate continued, "have three active strands. They can read minds and perceive things through their heightened powers of intuition. They can read an entire book simply by placing their hands over the cover—"

"Let's go back to what you said before," said the interviewer. "What did you mean by a quantum leap?"

"What I mean is that we're about to experience dramatic changes in vibration and light in our solar system. As a human race, we will evolve this coming December 21—"

The interviewer abruptly cut her off. "Thank you so much for being here and sharing your views with us."

She'd seen the show's producers urgently gesturing to her from behind the cameras that they were out of time. They had to go to a commercial break and end the show.

"I'm sorry," their interviewer said, "we ran out of time."

Away from the microphones, Kate whispered to Kruger. "That was really rude. They didn't even let the children say anything, and we didn't get to mention the quartz crystals."

"I know," Kruger replied, "but I think in spite of that, people who were watching and paying attention, who are awake and ready for the change, will understand the message."

But even Kruger couldn't guess the extent of the brief interview's impact. In less than half an hour, Kruger's institute would be overrun by a crowd of fully awake, conscious people, waiting for Kruger and Kate to return.

# 70

Adam Roussos's flight to Athens was delayed from landing for half an hour. The Olympic Airways pilot had to go into a holding pattern since the control tower had instructed him that he could not land the plane until the tremors had subsided. In order not to alarm the passengers, the flight crew didn't tell them about the earthquakes.

Adam was nervous. He was very anxious to land and start looking for Alexia. He turned to his meditation and deep breathing practice again.

The minutes felt like centuries. As soon as he stepped off the plane, he turned on his BlackBerry. He called Alexia. He needed to hear her voice.

Silence.

No one answered. Not even the voice mail message.

He heard shouting and a lot of commotion. He went over to one of the airport televisions with a crowd of people gathered around it and saw reports of the earthquake. Now he was even more worried than before.

*What am I going to do?* he thought. *Where should I go to try to find her? Did she make it through the earthquake? Did she manage to find Aquiles?*

His mind raced. He paused for a moment to find his center. He let himself tune in to an inner voice to guide him.

Between his intuition and common sense, he supposed that if Alexia was okay, she'd go to her father's house. But he also thought about the message on Viktor Sopenski's phone, which he still had with him, saying that Alexia was being kidnapped.

*I could send a message to make them tell me the address.* But instead he felt pulled to Aquiles's house.

It took him over half an hour to find a taxi to share since the throngs of people passing through the airport had completely overwhelmed the local transportation services.

The driver gave them the latest news. The earthquake had caused serious damage all over Athens and had even affected the city of Kalamata, to the west of the capital.

Adam rolled down the window. He needed air. The oppressive summer heat clung to him like flypaper.

The driver had to go down narrow side streets. Some main avenues had collapsed in places, and traffic police worked to close them off around the gaping holes in the pavement. Live electrical cables danced and sparked on the ground. Piles of wreckage from collapsed buildings lay everywhere, while some intact buildings looked as if they could give way at any moment.

When Adam stepped out of the taxi in Aquiles's neighborhood, he could sense the suffering in the air. Teams of medics loaded the wounded and the dead onto stretchers. The landscape was bleak.

*Alexia! Please, God, give me a sign!*

Determined, he started walking directly to Aquiles's house. On the way, he helped some children pass over a big hole in the ground, assisted a woman who had fallen into a ditch, and consoled another who was sobbing hysterically.

His heart was overwhelmed. He felt as if that earthquake had touched the deepest parts of Gaia, the Earth Goddess.

He was thirsty and sweating profusely. Though he'd rolled up the sleeves of his white shirt, he was hot, and the shirt clung to his chest and back. He felt he was using up his very last reserves of strength. He'd been going nonstop, his days filled with anxiety, wonder, and confusion.

The first words Aquiles had spoken on the phone echoed in his mind. *"Adam, please, I need you here in Greece!"* But even now, he still didn't entirely understand what he was doing there. *The designs of destiny are strange,* he thought. *I just want to find Alexia and get out of here.*

He was overcome by a feeling of pure love as he felt a passionate desire to be by Alexia's side. And he realized that he wanted to be with her for a long time, maybe even for the rest of his life. He could see himself living with the beautiful geologist, working together, loving each other, and raising children. For a fleeting instant, he had a waking dream, his mind evoking a tantalizing vision of beauty and togetherness.

It took him over an hour to get to Aquiles's house, an hour spent dodging people running around frantically, stumbling over piles of rubble and even dead bodies, trying not to touch any live electrical wires. He wasn't sure if what he saw when he turned the final corner was actually real or not.

He looked down the street and made out the heavyset form of Aquiles, dragging a leg behind him, his head covered in dust and filth, bleeding and struggling to move, leaning on his daughter's shoulder.

Adam felt as if his heart would explode. The synchronicity of the universe was manifesting itself right before his eyes.

# 71

I n Rome, news of Greece's deadly earthquake hit Cardinal Tous like a slap in the face. Tous tried to call the Owl, but with no success. So he busied himself talking with several highly influential people, gathering the latest reports and strategizing about the most effective ways to deal with the global crisis.

The pope had once again stood on the balcony of the Vatican to address the crowd gathered in St. Peter's Square, delivering a message of calm and faith that was broadcast on all the major television networks around the world. His Holiness had a very tough job before him, trying to quell the people's rising panic in the face of one disaster after another. And as if that weren't enough, an amateur Australian astronomer had reported to the independent press that a large meteorite could be headed straight for Earth.

Conflicting rumors swirled around the globe. Most of the Christian population believed that the earthquakes and sun storms were clear signs of the Apocalypse, while the most devout members of other religions, mainly overcome with fear, fervently prayed to their god, not sure what to do. In the poorest countries afflicted by earthquakes, looting and robberies were widespread. People took whatever they could, while others simply cried inconsolably after losing their homes and loved ones. The panorama around the globe was positively Dante-esque. The landscape seemed straight out of the brilliant surrealist painter Salvador Dalí's wildest imagination.

"All lines are busy," a recorded voice informed Tous in a monotone each of the eleven times he tried to call the Owl. *I just hope he's alive,* he thought, breathing heavily. He felt angry and powerless, like a mighty lion in a cage. He hated waiting; his anxiety overpowered his intelligence. But he didn't have a choice.

In Athens, amid the ruins, Eduard Cassas managed to drag his mangled body with a dislocated shoulder and a broken leg toward the only way out. He progressed a few feet. The pain was excruciating, and blood oozed from a head wound. Everything was gloomy shadows. A single ray of light peeked through a gap in the roof that had collapsed, and he could make out a tree over it. Eduard could see the lifeless body of Claude Villamitre lying a few feet away, completely crushed by a block of concrete. He looked all around but didn't see Alexia or Aquiles anywhere. Even stronger than the physical pain, he felt an inner emotional pain because he'd failed in his mission. The digital recorder had been smashed by a door that had come off its hinges. He had no confession, no prisoners, nothing. He felt like a total failure.

Though he still had his phone in his pocket, he didn't feel like finding out if it still worked and calling Tous. He was ashamed by his failure, destroyed.

His expression was akin to an ancient warrior's after a particularly bloody battle. Bringing his right hand down to feel his broken leg, he passed out from the shock and pain.

lexia! Aquiles!" Adam yelled loudly as he ran toward them. He felt a surge of adrenaline course through his body.

He looked at Alexia, exhausted from trying to support her father. Adam quickly stepped between them, supporting one of them with each arm. Alexia hugged him tightly. Her mascara had run down her face, giving her a ghostly look.

"You're alive! You're alive! I'm so happy!" Adam exclaimed, his face lighting up in a broad smile.

Aquiles, totally exhausted, could only nod slightly in response. Alexia smiled weakly.

"We have to go to the hospital."

"No," Aquiles managed to say.

"What do you mean 'no'? You're both hurt," Adam said.

"We're exhausted, but we're not hurt."

"But look at yourself, Aquiles!" Adam said. "Your back is covered in blood."

"My back can take it," said Aquiles, who had always been proud of his strength and stamina. "I just want to go to my bed and rest. We really have to talk."

Alexia looked at Adam. *He's stubborn,* she thought but said nothing aloud.

The three turned down a side street and headed toward Aquiles's house, stepping around spilled trash bags, cars crashed into each other, and fallen trees across the sidewalk. Aquiles hoped that somehow his house had escaped all the damage.

"We're almost there," Adam huffed, his heart pounding, breathing heavily. He was straining with all his might to keep them both on their feet.

Once they were in front of his house, Aquiles saw that the earthquake had knocked the front door off, and part of the wall was damaged.

"Well, we won't need a key to get in," he joked.

"Papa!" Alexia reproached, although she was happy to see her father was able to crack jokes.

Once inside, Adam helped Aquiles take off his tattered shirt, cleaned his wounds the best he could, and laid him down on his bed. Alexia sat down on the sofa, exhausted.

"I can't believe I found you!" Adam was still so happy, stunned by his good luck. "Are you sure you don't want to go to the hospital? You might have broken a rib or some other serious injury."

Alexia shook her head no and took a sip from a bottle of mineral water. Adam placed a damp cloth on Aquiles's forehead. The older man's eyes were already half-closed.

"Get some rest," Adam said, gazing at Alexia tenderly. "We'll talk in the morning. We need to gather our strength. I'll look after your father."

Alexia looked at him, her eyes glistening from emotion. "I'm so happy to see you," she said, drawing him into her arms.

"Me too," Adam whispered in her ear. "Alexia, I want you to know how important you are to me."

They stayed wrapped in each other's arms for a long time, each feeling the heat and energy from the other. Their souls were united in that embrace. It was a healing balm amid all the chaos. And there, only there, with Adam's arms around her, could Alexia finally relax.

Adam woke up with a start. He'd fallen asleep on the sofa. His back ached, but his energy had returned. He was alive, and Aquiles and Alexia were too. That was reason enough to celebrate and face the new day. He got up and made some coffee. Alexia woke up a little while later.

"Would you like some coffee?"

"Yes, please," she replied.

"Your father's still asleep."

"That's what you think," Aquiles said from his bed. "I've been awake for an hour, lying here, thinking."

Alexia and Adam exchanged a look. Aquiles was as indestructible as titanium.

"Tell me, what happened?" Adam asked as he served Alexia coffee.

Alexia had to make a real effort to remember it clearly, as if the story had begun centuries ago.

"Eduard betrayed us," she said. "He was part of the plot to kidnap my father."

Adam nodded. In a way, he wasn't surprised at all to hear this news. "Traitor," he muttered.

"Yes," Alexia said. "I told you I never liked that guy."

"Listen, don't be alarmed, but your friend Jacinto and I came across a creepy guy snooping around in your house. He pointed a gun at me, and he tried to get me to tell him where you were, but Jacinto saved me. He hit him in the head from behind and knocked him out. Now the guy's in police custody in London. Hopefully he'll confess who he's working for."

Alexia was obviously disturbed by this. Adam gently took her hand. "I found out you'd been kidnapped when I read a text message on the guy's phone," Adam explained. "So what happened with Eduard? Where is he? Did he survive the earthquake?"

"We don't know," Alexia answered, and took a sip of coffee. "It was a miracle that we managed to get out of there. It was so horrible!"

"We have to come up with a plan right away," Aquiles said.

"First you have to rest and recuperate from all your injuries," Alexia said.

"There will be plenty of time for that. First we need to talk." He turned to Adam. "You were in London? Did you see Kruger?"

"Yes. He's done something really amazing. He was able to pass the information from a small quartz fragment that you'd given him on to thousands of other quartz crystals. He wants to distribute them to the people."

"That's perfect!" Aquiles said.

"Is it true," Alexia began, "that the Atlantis quartz you found, that you told Eduard and me all about, is the Philosopher's Stone?"

Aquiles nodded. "You have a fragment of it around your neck."

A shiver ran through Alexia as she brought her hands to her chest to touch it.

Aquiles looked at Adam. "Once you open up the 'archives' inside the quartz, the information gets downloaded directly into your mind. Whoever opens it will understand the actual origin of the first man—his creation at the hands of evolved extraterrestrial beings from another dimension." Aquiles chose his next words carefully. "The ideological structures of religion will be devoid of all meaning; they will eventually become nothing more than forgotten fables."

As he spoke, Aquiles got up from his bed and took a picture off the wall to reveal a secret shelf where he kept his safe. He dialed the combination and opened it, then took out a slim package wrapped in blue velvet. It contained a sheet of shiny metal, around the dimensions of a standard piece of letter-size paper. It was the Atlantean tablet, over twelve thousand years old, made from the rare metal known as orichalcum.

"It's beautiful!" Alexia exclaimed.

Aquiles nodded, placing it in his daughter's hands.

Alexia and Adam couldn't take their eyes off of the tablet. In spite of its age, the metal was in perfect condition. They were both filled with wonder.

"Papa, don't you think people will be skeptical about all of this?"

"No," Aquiles said vehemently, "not if they come into contact with the quartz. This isn't something you believe. You *know* it firsthand, by direct experience! How can you deny what you're experiencing? The stone transmits knowledge as if it were a computer. It sends it directly into the person's mind."

Adam nodded.

"If Dr. Kruger has been able to transmit the information from the quartz into others, and if he's planning on handing out a small quartz to each and every person, then they could program brand-new quartzes, and it will be like a chain reaction," Adam said, excited.

"That would be glorious," Aquiles agreed.

Alexia looked unsure. "I don't want to be negative, but I don't think it's possible. You would need 6.5 billion quartzes if you wanted to hand one out to every single person on Earth. And a little piece of quartz wouldn't have the same effect as the mother quartz you have, right Papa?"

"Just one little piece of it contains all of the knowledge," he said simply.

"That reminds me," Adam said. "I have a few questions for you. First, where is the Philosopher's Stone? Where did you find it?"

Aquiles smiled slightly. He put a hand on Adam's shoulder.

"I'll tell you where I found it and where it is now. But just a moment." Aquiles paused. "Everything is happening exactly as it's supposed to. Don't you remember the teachings from your father's book?"

"My father taught so many things. What do you mean specifically?"

"Your father said that nature was guided by a sacred triangle of life, encompassing everything from climate changes to human relationships."

"Creation, conservation, and destruction." Adam recited the concept in his father's book.

"Precisely," Aquiles said with a smile. "Everything created is conserved until it is useful, and then it must be destroyed in order to create something new and more evolved. It's as it is with buildings—old buildings must be torn down to make room for newer, taller ones. I think it's also what will happen with human evolution."

"Papa, how will you publicize your discoveries? Everyone's so absorbed by the disasters."

Adam nodded his agreement. There were so many stories in the news just then, it seemed impossible to break through.

"Just a minute, relax." Aquiles said. "Before we can plan anything, you need to know a few more very important things."

"Tell us, Papa," Alexia said, anxious.

Aquiles looked her in the eye. "We believe the practical use of the Philosopher's Stone would be to prepare the human race's DNA to receive the new cosmic energy, right?"

Alexia and Adam nodded.

"Here's the most important part of all," Aquiles continued. "I didn't tell Eduard about this. You've heard about Rupert Sheldrake's work, haven't you?"

"Well, I know a little bit about it," Adam answered, rubbing his chin. "I know he's popular in England, less so in the United States. Why? What does he have to do with this?"

Alexia furrowed her brow. "Who's Sheldrake?"

"He's a British biochemist who popularized the theory of morphic fields. I spent some time with him years ago. He works on the most hidden aspects of the mind. He believes that all humans and even all species have a seventh sense. A dormant sense."

"What do you mean, exactly?" asked Alexia. "And how does Sheldrake's theory relate to the Atlantis quartz?"

Adam was fascinated. He felt he could intuit where Aquiles was going. "Go on, please. I'm all ears."

"Rupert Sheldrake said there's an invisible mental network. If an individual of a certain species—for example, an animal—learns a new ability, it will be easier for all the other members of that species to learn it. That ability, no matter what it may be, resonates in each one of them no matter how far apart they are physically. And the more individual members of the species learn it, the easier it gets for the remaining members of the species.

"Sheldrake's theory partly grew out of the hundred monkey theory, which resulted from observing a large number of primates on a Japanese island. Japanese scientists gave the monkeys sweet potatoes to eat, setting them down on the beach, which of course had sand. Normally the monkeys would just eat them covered in sand. Then one morning, a female discovered that she could wash the sweet potatoes and eat them without a layer of sand stuck to them. The rest of the monkeys began to imitate her, eating the sweet potatoes after they had washed them."

"So? What's so special about that?" Alexia asked.

"The Japanese scientists observed that if ninety-nine monkeys out of a hundred had learned the new technique, once the one hundredth monkey learned it, other monkeys scattered around the island learned it, too. It didn't matter how far away they were. Even in other countries, different types of monkeys learned to wash the sweet potatoes."

"A genetic chain reaction!" Alexia said, wide-eyed.

"Specifically," Aquiles added, "Sheldrake's theory posits that once approximately seventeen percent of a species learns something new, a critical mass is reached, and the species as a whole develops and integrates this new skill instantly, through a holistic genetic relationship. The collective mind acts as a pathway for directly passing information, a conduit from the subconscious into the DNA. It's like an electric web encompassing the entire species."

They were all quiet for a moment, ruminating over the scientific theory.

"Could it be that..." Adam paused, collecting his thoughts. "If this theory is applied to the collective use of the Philosopher's Stone of Atlantis, reprogramming the DNA of the human species—"

"It would happen all over the world!" Alexia exclaimed.

"A collective spiritual enlightenment!" Aquiles affirmed, smiling broadly.

# 73

"Correct me if I'm wrong," Alexia said, "but if Sheldrake's theory is applied to collectively activate the DNA of the human race, then it could also be used in a negative sense, to disempower it, right?"

"That's exactly what Adam's father thought," Aquiles replied. "We have been collectively programmed to lose the little power we have."

"By whom?"

"You already know…" Aquiles said, and trailed off.

"Let's focus on what we're going to do from now on," Alexia said, trying to be proactive. She didn't want to think about Eduard, and whom he really worked for.

"Yes," Aquiles said. "We have a real problem. Those who don't have their vital systems in harmony and are not vibrating at the same frequency as the new cosmic energy will not pass through the vibrational gateway."

"What do you think will happen to those who aren't on the same frequency?" Alexia asked.

"I'm afraid they won't be able to withstand a mental and energy impact of such an awesome magnitude. They'll either die or go insane, I don't know. That's why it's so important to get the quartz crystals distributed and put people in contact with the Philosopher's Stone: so their consciousness can awaken immediately."

"Forgive me for being the one who has to inject reason and logic into the discussion," Alexia said, aware that those two attributes had always been exclusively, and often erroneously, ascribed to male philosophers, "but our first order of business should be getting out of here."

"Perhaps this is also part of the change," Aquiles reflected. "Men will become more intuitive and sensitive, and women will become more practical and logical."

"I don't know, Papa," she said, "but we have to find out what's going on in the world. And we need to leave here. We don't know what else the Secret Government knows about us."

"We'll go," Aquiles promised. "There's just one more thing—it's important and will help us get organized."

Alexia knew that when her father felt inspired, time did not exist.

"Go ahead," she said. "What is it?"

"Sheldrake also talked about the theory of formative causation, which held that all things were organized following a common pattern. Atoms do not have to be created by an external agent, but are formed by themselves. A molecule and a crystal are not constructed by humans piece by piece—they crystallize spontaneously."

"Where are you going with this, Papa?"

"We have to see how we can apply his theories to individuals and synchronize the quartzes with the energy of unity. It will be a kind of mental colony, organizing the mind to receive the energy that will allow us to pass from one dimension to another."

Adam stood and took a step toward Aquiles. "Aquiles, the only way to activate the quartz in a collective mind would be through group meditation."

Suddenly, the sound of Adam's cell phone pulled them back to the harsh reality of the physical world. Adam's face drained of color as he listened to Dr. Kruger on the other end of the line. After a few seconds, Adam replied, "Are you sure, Doctor?"

Aquiles and Alexia exchanged a look.

Adam hung up.

"What did he say?" Alexia asked anxiously.

"I didn't even get the chance to tell him that I had found you," Adam said to Aquiles, dejected. "I don't think everything's going to go according to your plan, Aquiles. Now we have to deal with a problem that falls completely outside of any theory."

"What problem?" they both asked at once.

"There's a new story in the news, and it's not good."

"Another earthquake?" Alexia asked, a knot forming in the pit of her stomach.

Adam shook his head.

"I'm afraid it's even worse." His expression hardened. "Astronomers have discovered a gigantic meteorite headed straight for Earth."

## 74

**W**e don't have much time," Aquiles said, surprisingly calmly. "Remember the old proverb: From the darkest storm clouds falls the clearest rain."

"We're in no mood for proverbs, Papa."

"I have the Philosopher's Stone—it's our greatest hope."

"The Atlanteans perished," she reminded him. "The stone didn't save them then."

"Don't be so negative, Alexia. At times like this, we need to put our wisdom into practice."

"Your father's right," Adam said, and stepped behind her to gently wrap his arms around her.

They were quiet for a moment.

"My father's book," Adam began softly, "talked about the sacred Mayan text *Chilam Balam*. It said, 'In the thirteen *Ahau* at the end of the last *katun*, the *itza* will be overrun and Tanka will roil, there will be a time when they are plunged into darkness, and then they will come bringing the sign of the future men of the sun; the land will awaken in the north and the west, and the *itza* will awaken.'"

Alexia was very solemn, her head bowed, as if she weren't listening.

"I think the Mayans knew what would happen," Adam said. "They predicted everything exactly. And the Atlanteans knew that they originally came from the constellations of Orion and Sirius.

"Where is the mother quartz?" Adam asked Aquiles, suddenly changing his approach.

Aquiles sighed deeply. "I had it sent to Mexico, to the geological nexus of feminine energy. I was planning on presenting it to the United Nations, along with the Atlantean tablet, with all the requisite scientific confirmation. Right now, a shaman I have known for quite a while is working with it, along with a group of his people."

"In Mexico?" Adam reiterated, surprised by this new development.

Aquiles nodded. "In Chichen Itza. It's not only the safest place, it's also the most important location on the planet in terms of energy."

"What? You let the mother quartz get away? Why would you do that?" Alexia asked anxiously.

"It had to be done," Aquiles said. "Adam, to help her understand, can you please explain what you said about the *Ahau* and *itza*."

"It talks about the thirteen *Ahau*, which is what the Mayans called the sun, and the time it takes the sun to pass through all twelve constellations—'the end of the last *katun*,' a period of about twenty years, from 1992 until 2012. The Mayans called that period of twenty years *the time of no time*."

"Go on," Aquiles prodded.

"The *itza* will be overrun, they said..."Adam paused to think. "*Itza* means 'mouth of water.'"

"The tsunamis," Aquiles said.

"And Tanka will roil," Adam went on, "meaning the earth. Then it basically says there will be a period of darkness, and then they will come bringing the sign of the future men of the sun; the land will awaken in the north and the west, the *itza* will awaken."

Adam felt a rush of adrenaline.

"The *itza* will awaken…Chichen Itza!" Aquiles said.

Adam nodded.

"So what should we do now?" Alexia asked.

"We'll go to London," said Aquiles with renewed energy, "to the Olympics. We'll tell the world about the discovery and how to use the quartzes. And then we'll go to Mexico. We'll reunite with the Philosopher's Stone."

# 75

J ust a few blocks away, the specter of Eduard Cassas, bloody and weak, shuffled along, having somehow emerged from the collapsed house. He took a few wobbly steps before collapsing onto the sidewalk, blood trickling from an open wound. He was barefoot, and his clothes were tattered rags. He looked like a ghoulish street urchin.

Two medics from the Red Cross saw him fall and ran over to him. One of them put his hand on Eduard's jugular.

"His pulse is very weak," he told his partner. "He's lost a great deal of blood." The other medic went back to their ambulance and quickly set up a stretcher.

Once the Red Cross workers had loaded Eduard into the ambulance, they drove off as fast as they could with the siren wailing.

The seventh earthquake to strike had already claimed nine hundred victims in Athens alone.

Back in Rome, Cardinal Tous was sick with worry. He'd tried to call Eduard eighteen times just in the last half hour. He was anxious and overcome with an empty, painful loneliness. Not only was Eduard his right-hand man, but he was also his lover, his confidante, his foundation of support. In solitary silence, Tous suddenly realized everything Eduard meant to him. Just then, the Magician felt a deep, gnawing pain in the center of his chest. For the first time, a real guilt, a tremendous psychological weight, fell on him like a bomb over his heart.

With this dark shadow over his soul, he determined to play his last card to seize the Philosopher's Stone. Later that night, he made two phone calls: He issued the order to search for Eduard over every square inch of Athens, and he ordered the release of Viktor Sopenski, who was in British police custody.

The Vulture would strike, and this time he would not fail.

# 76

Dr. Stefan Kruger's voice resonated like a clap of thunder at the press conference broadcast by the BBC. His goal was to help people understand how the quartzes worked, to allow them to achieve a state of receptivity. Already, over five hundred people had received their personal, preprogrammed quartz crystal. Dr. Kruger spoke without any notes, looking directly into the television camera. His speech was inspiring and convincing:

"In this current worldwide climate of confusion, chaos, and uncertainty, we've begun distributing quartzes with properties highly beneficial to the nervous system, and especially to human DNA. Through our Institute of Genetic Studies, we will give everyone who wants one a quartz with the ability to enact positive changes on individual genetics.

"Reality as we know it is going to change. A great quantum leap is about to take place all around the globe. We must prepare ourselves. The worst mistake you can make at this time is to be afraid. Fear weakens us. We must open our minds to a different future."

Kruger was hopeful. He, Kate, and many others had already felt the quartz crystals' beneficial effects. They experienced an inner clarity and a broader, more heightened sense of perception than usual. The television studio was completely silent, charged with a magnetic aura.

*He's a messiah,* some thought.

*Just another charlatan exploiting the situation to make some easy money,* others thought.

Kruger continued with his speech, explaining everything he could about DNA, the quartz, vibrational programming, and the importance of being prepared.

"This is not a game. It is a matter of life and death, a matter of transformation. The time has come to leave behind false beliefs and base fears. The time has come to forget our differences and human limitations. It is time to accept our divine nature.

"It is a wonderful opportunity, and I hope you can understand the magnitude of this moment."

The throng of reporters crowded inside the television studio began shouting out questions all at once:

"What happens if someone doesn't accept the quartz?"

"What are you getting out of this, Doctor?"

"Is this the sign of the Apocalypse?"

"What should be done about the meteor that they say is going to strike Earth?"

"Whom do you work for?"

"How exactly will the quartz affect us? What will we feel?"

"Does this have to do with the end of the world prophecies?"

"If there's another earthquake, I'm going to shove that quartz straight up me arse!" an obviously drunk English reporter called out.

The room erupted in shouting and chaos. Though many people understood the message, most of the population was in the grip of a paralyzing panic.

The British reporters were like a pack of ravenous bloodhounds. The tension began to subside when Kate started handing out the quartz crystals.

After a few minutes, the hostile vibrations changed. A palpable wave of calm swept the room. Just a couple of people who'd received quartz crystals left them on their seats, shouting, "It's a fraud!" But no one else said anything. Those who now held the quartz crystals in their hands began to feel the effect.

Kruger and Kate had managed to arrange an interview with one of the few reporters who'd volunteered to take a quartz home with him earlier and experiment with it. The geneticists knew they had to take advantage of that interview.

The reporter asked many of the same questions the others did, questions about what was happening with the planet, and how it was possible to change DNA. Dr. Kruger and Kate patiently explained everything, and the reporter gave them ample time to do so. Finally the reporter said, "But, Doctor, the world is in a state of chaos right now. Can you actually see a silver lining in all of this?"

"We think the most intense aspect is still to come. This is just the beginning," Kruger explained. "The dimensional transformation will not happen all at once. First we will experience expanded levels of consciousness that have been developing for many years, and on December 21 the portal to the new dimensions will open up completely."

The interview was over. Kruger and Kate were satisfied. In less than an hour, a line had formed outside the BBC studios of people wanting to get their own quartz crystals, stretching around the block.

Now the second part of the work they had planned was coming to fruition.

## 77

## LONDON, JULY 27, 2012
## OPENING DAY OF THE OLYMPIC GAMES

In spite of the latest news about the meteor, Aquiles, Alexia, and Adam were full of enthusiasm. They were getting ready to go to the opening ceremony of the Olympic Games, their faith in the Philosopher's Stone unshakeable.

A massive crowd had gathered in the Olympic stadium to watch the great spectacle. Aquiles was very excited. After a great deal of effort, he'd been granted official approval to address the crowd, although his time slot had been shortened because of scheduling constraints. The Olympic Committee wanted people to feel optimistic and hopeful, even in the face of such somber events and news stories. Aquiles knew that the mass of energy that would accumulate among the tens of thousands of spectators would help to fully activate the quartz crystals.

A group of over two hundred, including Kruger's staff and some volunteers, would coordinate the distribution of the quartz crystals among the opening ceremony's audience.

"Let's hurry," Aquiles said to his daughter as she got ready in the bathroom. "I'll go down and get the car ready. Now don't dawdle."

"I'll take care of it," Adam said with a complicit wink.

Aquiles went out of Alexia's house to the street to start the car. Even though it was a rainy day, the sidewalk was filled with people. Police patrol cars drove by frequently, as the Olympics organizers had received a bomb threat. The threat had turned out to be baseless, but the level of police paranoia had increased.

"I'm almost ready—I just have to put on my earrings," Alexia called from the bathroom.

Adam gazed at her through the open door. She was radiantly beautiful. He felt a rush of desire for her. Outside, Aquiles dug into his pockets, searching for the car keys. London seemed more bustling than ever, and people drove more chaotically than usual, causing traffic snarls. Aquiles didn't want to be late.

*Come on, let's go,* he thought impatiently.

A black car pulled up just behind him. Aquiles found the keys and was about to unlock the door. Just then a man got out of the black car and quickly walked up behind him. Aquiles didn't see the man, but he felt something cold on the back of his neck. The muzzle of Viktor Sopenski's .38 revolver pulled Aquiles back into a nightmare he did not want to relive. In a fraction of a second, Aquiles lamented, again, not having taken the necessary precautions.

"It's all or nothing, Professor. Where is the stone? Tell me, or I'll blow your brains out."

A lump rose in Aquiles's throat. The giddy enthusiasm he'd felt just a moment earlier turned to a dark feeling of powerlessness. He didn't turn around. A rush of adrenaline clouded his judgment. He thought if he could hit the Vulture, he could knock him down. He flung his arm backward as fast as he could, but Sopenski arched back, dodging the blow. Seeing that the archeologist was not going to cooperate, he put his finger on the trigger, ready to fire.

"Son of a bitch!" Aquiles seethed.

"It's all or nothing, Professor Vangelis," the Vulture goaded.

"I'd rather take my secret to the grave than give it to you."

"You always have to play the hero, don't you, Professor?"

Aquiles watched as the obese policeman pulled the trigger. The bullet took a hundredth of a second to enter his chest. The archeologist's body crumpled to the ground. The Vulture looked him right in the eye just before he took off running down the street. At that instant, Adam opened the front door, horrified by what he saw. His heart pounded as he ran to Aquiles.

"Stop that man!" he yelled as loud as he could.

A police patrol car at the end of the street blocked Sopenski's path as he ran as fast as he could, holding his gun, a wild look on his face.

"Stop! Drop your weapon!" a police officer shouted.

He stopped. He was sweating and breathing hard as the rain picked up. Sopenski couldn't think straight; he was in a daze after impulsively killing Aquiles. He knew he wouldn't get the reward money or the Philosopher's Stone or any recognition. There was no way out. He was not going to prison for murder. He decided to go for it. He trusted the speed of his weapon. He suddenly raised his gun and fired. The police officer did the same.

Alexia came running when she heard the commotion in the street. She saw Adam bent over her father, who was lying on the ground. It was a scene out of her worst nightmare. All of her childhood rushed before her eyes: her father hugging her, making her laugh, teaching her about archeology, nurturing in her a love of the earth and the gods...

"NOOO! Papa!"

Adam tried to keep him conscious.

Aquiles's gaze rested on his daughter.

She couldn't cry.

Aquiles swallowed and slowly shook his head.

The look that passed between them said it all. Aquiles was saying goodbye. His dream evaporated. But he felt at peace, knowing that he'd done all that he could to help humanity.

"Papa! You must hold on! Please!"

Aquiles gestured for Adam to move closer. Adam turned his head so his ear was close to Aquiles's lips.

Aquiles murmured something, and then breathed his last breath.

Down the street, Viktor Sopenski had been shot by the policeman's bullet. Death would reunite the archeologist and the Vulture once again, as if their destiny was to continue their struggle in another life.

# 78

In Washington, the Brain and the entire Secret Government investigation team were extremely bothered by the widespread use of the quartz crystals. Although the Brain's primary concern was the meteorite's status and the progress of the missiles, he ordered the media outlets under the Secret Government's control to cease all coverage of Dr. Kruger and his collaborators.

In Rome, Tous heard of Aquiles's and Sopenski's deaths. It seemed as if the world was falling apart. He looked as if he'd aged ten years overnight. He was ready to disobey the order not to leave the Vatican. His normally insatiable appetite for power had suddenly vanished. His natural instincts were contained, like a wild beast in a cage. His anger gave way to a feeling of defeat, and indignation. Aquiles had never given up his secret. A whirlwind of emotions swirled in him. The cardinal realized that he might lose the battle. His powers of reason indicated this was the case even though he was the Magician. A magician always needs new tricks, but he couldn't see any at hand that might help. Something inside of him gave up, and he lay down on the couch in his office, succumbing to defeat. With Sopenski dead, and no news of Eduard, his grand scheme had suddenly vanished into thin air.

## 79

# CHICHEN ITZA, MEXICO, DECEMBER 15, 2012

**L**ocated in the Mayan Riviera, Chichen Itza was a popular destination for tourists and spiritual seekers. Lush with tropical vegetation, the small enclave in the jungle was surrounded by hundreds of cenotes, subterranean pools of sweet, clear water. Scuba divers from around the world traveled to Chichen Itza to see the wonders of the underground caves. Along with Belize, Guatemala, and Tulum, Chichen Itza was a main city of the ancient Mayans at the height of their culture. The area's warm, humid climate enabled the jungle to grow rapidly. Over time, plant life sprouted over monuments and pyramids. Now in the village artisans sold their necklaces, bracelets, pendants, and other pieces in street stands. Their work was handcrafted with exquisite artistry using silver, gold, and onyx, a black stone known for its healing properties.

The last few months had been extremely painful for Alexia and Adam. Alexia was devastated by the loss of her father, but her inner strength, along with Adam's unconditional support, had enabled her to carry on. They'd traveled to Chichen Itza to fulfill the promise that Adam had made to Aquiles.

Although many people in different parts of the world had received their own quartzes and had learned how to pass the information infused in the stones along to others, only about a third of the entire population understood the magnitude of what was happening.

"How do you feel?" Adam asked once they'd settled into their room. Their hotel sat next to the Kukulkan Mayan pyramid.

"Okay. Just a little out of sorts from the flight."

This was the first time they'd had the chance to be alone for a while. Over the course of the previous months, they'd constantly worked in the presence of others.

"What should we do today?" Alexia asked.

"Let's go find the shaman friend of your father's."

Alexia nodded.

"We'll find him, don't worry," Adam said. "How does your quartz feel?"

"Very hot," she said as she brought both hands to her chest to touch it.

"Mine is too. Ever since we got to Chichen Itza, I've felt a burning in my chest. Alexia," he said softly, "I know it hasn't been the easiest few months. But I want you to know that I love you."

She felt a swell of emotion, and her heartbeat sped up. She looked luminously beautiful as she gave him one of her dazzling smiles, showing off her white teeth.

"I love you too, Adam."

They held hands. The light from the candles in the room illuminated four eyes wet with tears, two hearts and two souls united as one. They leaned toward each other, and their lips met in a kiss. It was a carnal, intimate, sweet, sacred kiss. She made him a better man. And he made her a better woman. That night, they consummated their spiritual unity through their bodies, moving and breathing as one.

For the first time, far away from it all, their bodies were radiant, their chakras so full of energy that the hotel room shone with an otherworldly glow, the light of their auras.

# 80

Adam was the first to wake up the next morning. Alexia was still sleeping; her tousled hair was spread across the pillow, reminding Adam of Aphrodite herself. Her nudity left him at a loss for words.

Outside their room, Chichen Itza was overrun with the faithful, crowds of tourists, and spiritual seekers who had come to celebrate the winter solstice on December 21, just as they had come in previous years.

*The Tanka will roil, the earth will awaken, and the men from the sun will arrive, the itza will awaken.*

Adam's mind stuck on the phrase while in the shower. *The itza will awaken; the time has come,* he thought, feeling uncertain. He didn't know for sure what would happen, or even if anything would happen at all. He quickly finished showering and got dressed.

He knew that Aquiles's dream, which he'd worked so hard to realize along with Adam's father, was going to be rewarded. The whole world was going to find out that the Atlantean tablet held the original secret of the first Adam.

But the Philosopher's Stone now rested in the hands of a man who was about to awaken its tremendous power.

# 81

# WASHINGTON, DC, DECEMBER 16, 2012

The secretary of defense was under tremendous pressure, and his expression showed the strain. The president of the United States sat next to him, along with Stewart Washington, his Operation M advisors Patrick Jackson and Sergei Valisnov, and twenty other high-level officers from the CIA and the armed forces.

The mood inside the White House was tense. Plans to destroy the approaching meteorite demanded the attention of the highest-ranking leaders of the government. Many of those present, including Stewart Washington, had not gotten a good night's sleep for weeks.

They had decided to work as a team. White House leadership, Secret Government representatives, NASA, the North American Aerospace Defense Command (NORAD), the National Oceanic and Atmospheric Administration (NOAA), and the Solar Dynamics Observatory (SDO) were all in constant contact. They also sent updated reports every half hour to heads of government around the world.

The president was anxious. He stepped over to a side table, poured himself a glass of water, and took an aspirin. He took off the jacket of his well-tailored blue suit, his dark-brown skin shining with sweat. He rolled up his white shirtsleeves and loosened his gray silk tie. His lean build and the determined way he carried himself alluded to the inner strength and courage that had to be tapped in such critical moments. The only good news he had gotten was that ten percent of the population had agreed to get the microchip of control implanted just beneath the skin of their right wrists. For the government it was a small yet significant first step. But just then the president had something else on his mind.

He asked his aide, "Any news from NORAD in Colorado?"

"Nothing new, sir. Just the same report we received a half hour ago."

The president's expression hardened. "What about the signals from the ACE satellite?"

"ACE has sent an update, but their latest reports have been strange, sir. It says that over the last half hour, they've been able to observe from the satellite some sunspots emerging on the sun's surface. According to their calculations, in just a few hours, the meteorite will be hit by one of our missiles."

"How fast is it going?"

"The meteorite is approaching at twenty-four thousand miles per hour. It's approximately a hundred and twenty-five miles across."

Everyone swallowed hard. If they didn't destroy the meteorite, no one would live to tell about it.

The president felt a tightening in his chest and loosened his tie even more. This would be the first time a nuclear missile had struck a meteorite. Operation M was deeply unsettling.

Every action undertaken by the Defense Department was carried out with rigid precision. Every task required the utmost concentration. Several experts and staff members came and went, talking in clipped tones on their phones, carrying reports. The president and his government's top-ranking leaders were the visible faces at the helm of the operation. Stewart Washington stepped back, watching how the president issued orders and worked with his team.

"I want reports every fifteen minutes now, not every thirty," the president said. "Have they seen the extraterrestrial spaceships again?"

"No, Mr. President, nothing other than the sightings reported around the world a few months ago."

The secretary of defense nodded in agreement.

"And the media?"

"It's unsettled, sir. Everything's being reported, not just what we say."

Stewart Washington glanced over at the Wizard Valisnov. The whole plan had come out of his head, but now he was sidelined. In the months that had passed since the Wizard presented his plan, it had become clear that they didn't really have any option other than destroying the meteorite.

The president walked over to the picture of Abraham Lincoln hanging on the wall.

"And what's the public's mood?"

"They're terrified and confused, sir. Many celebrities have gone on television saying they're going to move into underground bunkers, and those who can afford it have built their own bunkers."

It seemed as if events were transpiring at a faster and faster rate. They seemed to be on the cusp of the biggest tragedy yet. The waiting was unbearable, and everyone looked extremely concerned. The survival of the entire world depended on their finding a solution. Their collective fate rested on a missile, reports from the satellites, ACE, the Solar and Heliospheric Observatory (SOHO), and the Atlas V, a magnificent communications satellite launch system developed by NASA. The system was capable of taking a photo every ten seconds, and it sent data back to a base in New Mexico.

# 82

dam and Alexia walked down a narrow path that led a thousand feet into the jungle. They walked around the west side of a cenote and came to a waterfall about sixty-five feet high. They saw tropical parrots, burros, bright butterflies, even a large snake wrapped around a tree branch. Life in Chichen Itza was intense, fertile, and powerful. A heightened energy filled the air.

They reached the shaman's house in less than fifteen minutes. The atmosphere was wondrously tranquil. Children played, some women worked on weavings, and others laughed and smiled in the shade under the trees. There were no signs of modern technology anywhere.

"Hello," Adam said. "I'm looking for Master Evans. Is he here?"

"Follow me, my friend," said a slightly built man dressed all in white as he led them inside the house and into a big room.

The large house gave off a special, mysterious, almost electric energy. The magnetism in the air was palpable, like a very fine coating of dust.

There were over a dozen people in the room in meditative poses, sitting comfortably and dressed in white. Just outside was a lush, sun-dappled courtyard garden blooming with flowers and tropical plants. A fountain ran with crystalline water, emitting a relaxing, soothing sound.

"You'll find him in the room next to the fountain," the man said.

Adam and Alexia went down a narrow hallway lined with plants. People they passed offered sincere smiles, and Alexia and Adam gratefully smiled back. Alexia was radiant, holding Adam's hand.

When they entered the room, they saw a man with his back to them. He turned around, and Adam and Alexia felt as if they'd known him their whole lives. It was hard to figure out his age just from looking at him—he could have been sixty, maybe seventy years old. What was certain was that his body exuded vitality. He had white hair that almost reached his shoulders; bright, shining, kind eyes as black as onyx; and a slender build. His tone of voice was calm yet strong, reverberating like an echo. He was dressed in white, with a woven gold belt at his waist.

"Master Evans?" Adams asked.

The man nodded with a smile.

"You must be Alexia and Adam."

They smiled back.

"Welcome," he said, his gaze resting just over their heads.

Adam was surprised that he didn't look them in the eye.

The shaman smiled, revealing white, straight teeth.

"Do you have the Atlantean stone?" Adam asked directly.

"The Philosopher's Stone is made of love and wisdom. Energy and consciousness."

The man spoke in code. It seemed as if he were just awakening from a state of deep meditation.

"I understand," Alexia said. "What do you think we should do? What do you think is going to happen?"

"A mutation."

"Exactly how should we do it?" Adam asked.

"To embark on the path back to our glorious true nature, we must delve more deeply into the cauldrons of divine alchemy, through the sacred fire of transmutation."

When Evans looked directly into Alexia's eyes, she felt as if he were peering right into her soul.

"You have a beautiful light," the shaman said softly. He was quiet for a minute before he spoke again. "What we shall do is perform an ancient Atlantean ritual."

"A ritual?" Alexia asked.

"Yes. The collective ritual will make it easier for each one of our cells to recognize solar light as fuel, something similar to a plant's photosynthesis. Our entire biochemistry and how the human body functions will be radically transformed. And," Master Evans added, "we'll be introducing the life force of the soul once again into the central nervous system and into all of our electrical synapses. That's why the sun is changing; the Father Sun is emitting a shower of light."

"But...the world is in a state of chaos," Alexia reasoned.

"Yes, like before a birth. It's important to note that it is through our feelings of calm and a sense of harmony and our states of silent, deep meditation that cosmic energy will generate an impact ideal for the manifestation. The ritual will take place two days from now. Exactly four days before December 21. The ritual will go on for three days."

"Three days of darkness?" Adam said. "What's going to happen?"

"The Love Without Name," he said gravely. "The ritual will bring over one hundred thousand people together. It will be the chance to receive the arrival of the serpent's energy, the blaze of cosmic flame that my ancestors foretold, the Fire Ritual of the Stars. It's performed every time there is a solar transformation, every twenty-six thousand years. My ancestors left written testament of it, too."

"What do you mean?" Alexia asked.

"It's in this book," Master Evans replied, pointing to a tattered copy of the Bible. "Do you want to read it?"

The shaman handed her the large volume.

Bewildered, Alexia took the book.

"Look up Revelation, in the New Testament, chapter two, verse seventeen," the Master said.

Alexia lightly licked her index finger to turn the pages.

> *To he who conquers I will give some of the hidden manna, and I will give him a white stone, with a new name written on the stone which no one knows except he who receives it.*

There was a long silence until Adam spoke.

"So the Bible mentions the Philosopher's Stone too?"

"They didn't call it that, but it is the same," Evans answered.

There was a pause again.

Alexia touched the quartz on her necklace.

Master Evans smiled the enigmatic smile of one who knows much more than he says.

# 83

# DECEMBER 16, 2012

Ninety million miles from Earth, the sun's nucleus ejected a fiery mass, catapulting it outward at a velocity never before seen. It would only take eight minutes to reach Earth. In that brief lapse of time, everyone on the planet was oblivious to what was happening deep inside the sun. An implosion of energy on the scale of a supernova had taken place, only to then explode outward in a violent, orgasmic gush.

The sun's outermost layers erupted in a dance of heat, light, and energy. An immense, white-hot mass quickly reached Earth's atmosphere. The supreme star expelled another fiery burst, followed by another, and another, each more powerful than the one before.

The satellites orbiting in space were the first to burn. In an instant, communication systems, television networks, the Internet, cellular phones, and radios were out of commission. They were completely useless.

Silence.

Death.

The first problem everyone experienced as a result of the solar storm was a sudden lack of communication. Television screens suddenly went dark, and people could not make telephone calls or send e-mails.

The stock exchange plunged, and terror quickly spread through the minds of investors and corporate leaders. They had henceforth been predominantly skeptical, far removed from belief in any kind of mystical prophecy.

For the human race, it was the start of a massive confusion totally without precedent.

For the sun it was an evolution, a new spiral within its galactic ascension, a new coronation, affirming its godlike status in the Milky Way.

A series of tragic events unfolded.

Several planes that had been in the air were suddenly without their electronic flight systems. They lost contact with the air traffic control towers. They had to be landed manually. All of the electronic control systems, radar, GPS systems, and navigational tools in planes, ships, and cars abruptly ceased functioning. Technology and electricity suddenly went dead. The one thing that the systems of modern civilization relied on the most, electricity, had disappeared.

When the solar storm reached lower levels in the atmosphere, passing through Earth's electromagnetic fields, the large-scale, centralized generators stopped working, causing massive blackouts in cities and towns around the world.

The entire planet was plunged into darkness.

Some people were trapped in elevators, subway trains, and tunnels.

Hospitals had to use their own backup generators, which allowed their systems to function only at partial capacity.

Ninety-five percent of the cities around the world experienced blackouts and a complete shutdown in communications.

In the parts of the world where it was winter, people had no heat. The cold inspired even more fear.

Traffic lights stopped working, causing collisions and traffic jams. The roads were utter mayhem. Ambulance, police, and fire engine sirens blared incessantly through the streets of all the cities. The wheelchair-bound and people who relied on walkers on high floors of skyscrapers had no way to get down the stairs and were trapped.

In the cities where night had fallen, people got a glimpse of the aurora borealis, which could normally only be seen at the poles. Now, in other parts of the world, glowing green energies danced in the night sky.

Even the most rational person felt the sun had become a furious warrior, intentionally setting out to destroy human communications. The rain of fire made it impossible to make a phone call, watch the news, listen to the radio, or send a message.

Inevitably, humanity fell into the clutches of what had dominated half the world for centuries: fear.

Many cities resembled the mythical Troy, burning like a forest made of straw.

What the scientists called a "solar maximum" was unleashing all of its power on the planet. The sun, as a magnetic star, experienced the largest solar storm in human history. Over the next hour, successive waves of giant, fiery cloud masses traveled at speeds of two thousand miles per second, charged with billions of tons of electrified gas, producing the strongest, most powerful phase of the storm.

Earth's atmosphere heated up like an oven. All of the satellites in low-flying orbit had been affected and were like crumbs of burned toast floating through space. The magnetosphere, Earth's magnetic field, was no longer a protective shield and was under attack by a solar cloud bigger than Jupiter, expelling massive clouds of gas and electricity. Other satellites suddenly became lethal missiles, succumbing to gravity and plunging to Earth at tremendous speeds. They hit the ground like arrows raining down from the sky all around the planet. It was the beginning of the end.

Neither NOAA nor the SDO had been able to warn the United States or the other countries of the storm's awesome magnitude in advance. Several directors of centralized power stations had been able to see what was happening and had turned off their generators before they could burn out. They were the only ones to have a little bit of light. The almost two thousand power stations in the United States and the vast majority throughout the rest of the world were destroyed.

The SOHO satellite had reported seeing sunspots, but nothing on such a grand scale. No human or satellite could have predicted it, and the ACE and Atlas V, which were the closest satellites to the sun, were the first to burn up.

Defense ministers all around the world watched as the sun invaded their airspace, brazenly annihilating their defense systems. There was simply nothing they could do.

The great star worshipped by so many ancient cultures behaved in such an incomprehensible way, it was impossible for the human mind to understand. No one understood how they could possibly emerge from that fiery chaos. And yet in the dark, in homes all around the world, something very strange began to happen.

The people who had received a preprogrammed fragment of Atlantean quartz crystal were amazed to see how deep within the little stone that hung from their necks, a mysterious ray of light began to glow...

# 84

That day at noon, the president of the United States had the weirdest feeling, one that seemed to grow like a virus. He felt strange, confused, under water. Before the solar storms, he'd talked with Stewart Washington and the secretary of defense to plan the next day's activities.

But now the White House was like a pot boiling over. Staffers were running all around, powerless and completely incommunicado.

"What the hell is going on!" the president shouted, on edge as he strode into the conference room.

"We haven't been able to reestablish communications," his personal secretary said, with a terrified look. "The last thing we heard was that the sun was emitting some unusual fireballs."

"What about our own generators?"

"They're not functioning, sir."

"Have you been able to get in touch with any central power stations?"

"No, sir, we haven't been able to communicate with anyone. It's a total disaster out there. We can't communicate with the police or the army...or anybody else!"

The Brain and Valisnov were there already. The secretary of defense was very pale.

"Gentlemen," the president said, "what do you think we should do? Any ideas?" His question was met with silence. "Damn it!" he yelled, losing his grip.

The Brain, on the other hand, was cool and controlled, casting a sidelong glance at Sergei Valisnov. He didn't react, looking instead like a statue that was part of the room's décor. The Secret Government's highest-ranking intelligence specialist did not have any answers.

"I see there's not a whole lot we can do," the president commented. "I just hope the missile destroys the meteorite. But what can we do to counter the sun's fury?"

No one said a word. They knew it was no use.

"There's only one thing left to do," the secretary of defense spoke up. He suggested that they retreat to the reinforced security bunker.

The sun continued to determine the fate of life on Earth.

## 85

While the civilized world collapsed, Adam and Alexia walked back to the hotel hand-in-hand, deeply impacted by what Master Evans had told them.

They walked through a stretch of jungle so dense that hardly any sunlight managed to filter down to the ground. Thick, gray clouds were gathering in the sky, dark and threatening. Tall, thick trees rose up from the damp earth. They heard shrieks and grunts from wild animals, unsettled by the unusual heat.

"Master Evans is so impressive," Alexia said.

"Yes. So knowledgeable and powerful."

"Now what do you want to do?"

Adam walked ahead to move a large branch that was blocking their path. "Let's go to the cenote to think things through before we head back to the hotel. I want to see the waterfall. I can't take this heat and humidity anymore."

"All right, I think it's not far from—"

Just then they heard the snap of a branch breaking very close to where they were, as if a large animal were approaching.

"Shhhh!" Adam placed a finger over his lips.

They both stood still, waiting. Then after a minute, they continued their walk.

"Maybe it was a monkey," Alexia said softly.

Adam didn't answer. He looked to his left and right but saw only dense vegetation all around.

"Let's hurry."

A fine mist of rain started to fall, refreshing them. They were just about to emerge from the jungle when, out of nowhere, a shadowy figure rushed from behind at Alexia, grabbed her by the hair, and pulled her backward. Adam was a few yards ahead, clearing the path, when he heard a scream that stopped him in his tracks.

"Don't move!" ordered the mysterious man who'd grabbed Alexia.

He had a long, dirty beard, wore a straw hat on his head, and held a gun in his right hand. Alexia could smell several days of rancid sweat on him. She let out a moan. Wild-eyed, the man squeezed his arm around her neck even harder.

"Don't hurt her," Adam said. "What do you want?"

"Now? Revenge…"

Adam looked intently at the man.

"Revenge? For what? I can give you money, but let her go."

The man was enraged. "You don't give me orders, you idiot!"

Now his voice sounded familiar. He didn't sound like a Mexican. Adam squinted, but he didn't recognize him.

"You still don't know who I am, Roussos?" he said, baiting him.

A lump rose in Adam's throat. He was silent. Alexia's heart began to gallop in her chest. Adam tried to study the man more intently, but the rain, falling more steadily now, made it hard to see.

"I don't know you," he said.

"Stop playing games! Now, where's the stone?"

"The stone?" he stalled, still trying figure out how he might have known this man. "We don't have it."

"Where is it?" the man shouted angrily. "Tell me, or I'm going to blow this bitch's brains out!"

Suddenly, they both knew who that voice belonged to. It couldn't be.

It was Eduard Cassas. He looked like a disheveled beggar. He'd spent four weeks in the hospital after the earthquake in Athens, hovering between life and death. Gradually he recovered, although he'd suffered several serious contusions, fractured ribs, and a broken leg that had required surgery. His leg injury meant he would walk with a limp for the rest of his life.

# 86

# ROME, AFTERNOON OF DECEMBER 16, 2012

Cardinal Tous hadn't heard from Eduard at all. The young Spaniard had disappeared. It seemed as if he'd fallen off the face of the earth. In his dark, shadowy office, the cardinal felt helpless, like an eagle with wet wings. He thought yet again about the very last conversations he'd had with Eduard.

For days now Tous had been very worried, depressed, anxious, confused, and totally cut off from the world. The tenuous flame from a candle was the only light in the room, projecting gloomy shadows of his dejected frame over the walls.

His back ached. He felt a heavy weight, a burden, an emotional pain pulling at him. His lungs could barely open enough to let in small gasps of air. It hurt to breathe. It hurt to live. His head was a whirlwind of disjointed, random thoughts. He'd lost his incisive mind, his sharp edge. A lover, alone. A bird without a nest.

He stretched his hand out over his desk and reached for his Bible, hoping to find some solace there. At that dark time, he needed some comfort. With trembling hands he opened the book at random, and as fate would have it, the first thing he saw on the page was from the Book of John, chapter two, verse thirteen. The cardinal slowly read:

> *The Passover of the Jews was at hand, and Jesus went up to Jerusalem. In the temple he found those who were selling oxen and sheep and pigeons, and the money-changers at their business. And making a whip of cords, he drove them all, with the sheep and oxen, out of the temple, and he poured out the coins of the money-changers and overturned their tables. And he told those who sold the pigeons, "Take these things away; you shall not make my Father's house a house of trade." His disciples remembered that it was written, "Zeal for thy house will consume me." The Jews then said to him, "What sign have you to show us for doing this?" Jesus answered them, "Destroy this temple and in three days I will raise it up." The Jews then said, "It has taken forty-six years to build this temple, and will you raise it up in three days?"*

The sacred book grew heavy and fell from his hands. Guilt and anguish washed over him. Resignation. Emptiness. He'd been a modern-day merchant, conducting business in the world's temple. He had corrupted the teachings of Jesus, the last messiah of the sun. His heart could no longer contain the heavy emotions it held.

In the midst of so much uncertainty, he wondered if Wormwood, the star mentioned in the Bible, would fall upon the planet. *Where will I go when I die? Would a man like me go to heaven? Does heaven even exist?* His back against the wall, his deepest fears came bubbling to the surface.

He wept, sobbing uncontrollably. His mind went blank, and in his heart he could see and feel the little boy he had been. He heard his mother's voice calling, "Raul, it's time for dinner."

That made him feel even more vulnerable and defenseless. Through the eyes of the child he'd been, from that little corner of his soul where there was still a flicker of pure innocence, he saw and felt everything he had ruined over all the years he spent ruthlessly pursuing power and ambition.

## 87

You have thirty seconds to tell me where the stone is!" Eduard raised his gun to Alexia's head, ready to shoot.

His hands raised, Adam very slowly stepped backward off the jungle path to stand next to a tree. Now it was pouring rain, and Adam had to shout to be heard over it.

"Listen to me, Eduard, even if you did get the stone, the process of transformation is going to happen anyway."

"So why don't you just hand it over? If you don't I'll kill you both, and you won't transform into anything!" Eduard's eyes were bloodshot, and he was seething.

"We don't have the stone."

"You're lying, motherfucker!" he screamed furiously.

Adam tried to remain calm. "All right," he said, "I'll tell you where it is, but let Alexia go."

"Tell me right now! I'm sick of your tricks."

"It's in the cenote just over there," he lied.

Adam tried to come closer, and as he moved forward, he stepped on a branch, breaking it. Then a violent clap of thunder reverberated in the sky, as if the world were ending. Eduard looked up, and Alexia seized the opportunity of the distraction to try to get away. As she struggled against him, Eduard's gun went off, hitting the tree Adam had been standing under. Alexia wriggled out from under Eduard's arm and kicked him hard between the legs, right in the testicles, leaving him writhing in pain. She quickly darted away, off the path and into the jungle. Eduard aimed and fired three times at Adam, but he'd taken off running toward the cenote. The Owl looked behind him, saw no signs of Alexia, and then started running after Adam, hobbled by the excruciating pain in his groin and his fractured knee. In just a few yards the jungle path would lead into the clearing and the cenote. Adam was the first to emerge from the thickest part of the jungle, but with the water in front of him, he had nowhere to go. Eduard emerged, gasping for breath; now he had Adam in his sights.

"Take one more step and I'll split your head open with a bullet! Tell me where the stone is!" he screamed hoarsely.

Adam raised his hands over his head.

"It's over there," he said, pointing toward the far end. "It's behind the waterfall."

As Eduard gingerly stepped toward the water's edge to peer down, Adam quickly picked a rock up from the ground and threw it as hard as he could at Eduard's head. He missed. It was raining so hard it affected his aim. Eduard looked up and fired. He missed again. The noise of the gunshot was muffled by the rain and the jungle. Eduard could hardly see through the sheets of falling rain. He stepped down a small shelf of rock and lost his balance, falling onto the ground and almost tumbling down headlong into the waterfall. The odds of surviving a fall like that would have been very slim. While he was struggling to get up, Adam pounced on him. His gun was knocked away, and Adam pushed him back into the mud. They were both soaked through, and the ground was so slippery it was a challenge just to stand up.

Blind with rage, the Owl lunged at Adam. In spite of his physical disadvantages, Eduard was an expert in martial arts. The two men rolled over the drenched earth, their bodies entangled. One of Eduard's elbows sharply connected with Adam's head. Adam was stronger, but that powerful blow made him dizzy. Eduard knew exactly where to aim his strikes to produce the maximum results.

Just then, Alexia came running and saw them fighting. There wasn't much she could do, and she stood watching helplessly as the men hit each other. Eduard was lighter and rolled toward the cenote's edge. He reached out a hand and managed to get a grip on a damp root growing out of the ground. He supported his entire weight with that hand. Darting out the other hand, he grabbed hold of Adam's wrist.

"Help me to get up or you're going to fall in with me! I don't have anything left to lose."

Adam moved closer, extending his other arm toward him.

"I'll help you," he said. "Take it easy."

The rain pelted his face with large drops. The grip of their wet hands was slipping.

Adam was willing to help him. He looked down at Eduard, barely recognizable from the beard and the mask of panic he wore.

Adam pulled his free hand and as he did, Eduard, wild with panic, pulled hard toward the abyss. The two men fell over the edge toward the water, screaming, as Alexia looked on from above them, horrified.

# 88

lexia couldn't believe her eyes. From the edge of the cenote, looking down, she saw Eduard fall first. The brief seconds of the fall felt like centuries. She heard a splash as he landed in the water and disappeared beneath the surface. Thick vegetation and strong rainfall made it hard to see, but she could vaguely make out Adam's form. He landed in the water a few yards away to the right. She didn't see him break the surface. Her heart felt as if it would leap from her chest.

As he fell through the air, Adam saw his life pass before his eyes, like a movie. He'd often heard that a vision like that came right before death.

He'd never imagined he would die that way. It wasn't that he was afraid to die, but he still had so many important things left to do. He had to be with Alexia, he had to love and live, he had to meet the end of the Mayan calendar with his spirit full of light.

The fall seemed like a dream.

A primitive, ancestral dream.

He felt the thick air as it whooshed by, the rainwater on his body, and then the impact. Thoughts passed through his mind like a flaming comet's tail. He gave himself over to the

God. He did not struggle; he was not afraid. He felt only a profound acceptance of whatever would be.

After a few seconds, he rose to the surface. He gasped desperately for air. He looked all around. The rain fell furiously, a powerful, intense curtain of water. He struggled to swim to the edge, feeling disoriented. The wet mud made it hard to climb up to ground level, and he fell back twice. Slowly, painstakingly, he finally made it. He threw himself onto the grass, reveling in the pleasure of simply feeling solid ground beneath him, and then he lost consciousness.

## 89

# CHICHEN ITZA, DECEMBER 17, 2012

Adam came to in vaguely familiar surroundings. He slowly realized he was back in their hotel room. There were candles all around, lending an aura of mystery to the atmosphere.

*I must be dead.*

He cast that thought aside since he could feel the aches and pains all over his body all too vividly.

His head beginning to clear, he looked up and saw Alexia's face and a woman who looked like a doctor or a nurse standing next to her.

"Hmmmm…what happened?" he said groggily.

"Adam!" Alexia exclaimed, leaning down to kiss him.

"I hurt all over."

"The doctors have already examined you. There's nothing broken, and you didn't have a concussion."

"But…" He struggled to remember.

"You've been asleep for an entire day."

Then he remembered the fall.

"What about Eduard?"

"We haven't found any signs of his body. The police are still looking."

Adam struggled to sit up in his bed. He sipped from a glass of water. The doctor smiled at him.

"You should lie down and rest."

"Thank you," he said.

"Call me if you need anything. I'm going to find out the latest news," the doctor said to Alexia as she left the room.

After she was gone, Adam took Alexia's hand in his.

"I almost died," he reflected.

She smiled. "But you're very much alive."

"What latest news was the doctor talking about?"

Alexia looked at him directly. "The concierge just told me that all communications around the entire world have been cut off. We are completely incommunicado and without electricity. What do you think is going to happen?" she asked.

Adam looked unsettled. "I guess what's been predicted. I don't know, Alexia. Who can really know? We have to believe that the contact with the Atlantean Stone and the Ritual of Star Fire will give us…" He couldn't finish.

Adam and Alexia both felt that their fate rested in the hands of some higher force. Tragedy, or salvation? They didn't know. Nor did they know what would happen with the meteorite that was speeding toward their planet.

Alexia felt in her own flesh and blood how the earth was hurt, bleeding from its wounds, powerless in the face of the sun's impact.

Adam sat thinking quietly for several minutes. Something deep inside was telling him that everything that was happening must not be viewed simply through the prism of tragedy. It had to be something greater.

"Alexia, we can't lose faith in our fathers' research. They predicted it! This is the time of transition, the transfiguration of the earth and the sun. We knew this was coming. We can't start doubting now."

Adam's confidence was contagious, and Alexia wrapped her arms around his broad shoulders, feeling as if she were embracing the whole world.

"We believe in love," she said, her voice breaking, the quartz glowing on her chest like a fire's ember.

# 90

By the afternoon, Adam was feeling much better. He'd rested and had gotten a massage from one of the hotel's massage therapists. After a hot shower, they both headed back to the Kukulkan pyramid to meet with Master Evans.

A vast throng of people dressed entirely in white made its way toward the nine-level Mayan pyramid. There were over fifty thousand people, although double that number were expected to arrive. It was hard to walk quickly or to pass anyone, since they all moved as one single entity.

The massive group of spiritual seekers from around the world had gathered for the solstice. Some carried lit candles, and they all wore a small quartz crystal around their necks, symbolizing the link among them: unity consciousness. The quartz crystals began to emit a flash of light, and when it made contact with the lights from other quartz crystals, a stronger, more refined, elevated energy grew.

At the very top of the stepped pyramid, the diminutive Master Evans sat in a state of deep meditation. Several people formed a circle around him. After about twenty minutes of meditation, Evans opened his eyes to see the huge crowd that had gathered around the pyramid, forming a spiral of white light with their clothing and vital energy. He saw what no one else could see.

Adam and Alexia moved ahead with the crowd. The mood was one of respect, silence, and camaraderie. There was something in the air, a mystical, unifying aura of happiness and connection—something that had been lost in modern cities. Adam and Alexia felt more and more energized and connected to the group.

At that moment, three thoughts ran through Adam's mind: *Humanity will enter three days of darkness. We will face the Great Hall of Mirrors. We will meet the New Sun.*

"The time has come."

With the serene expression of a man who knows exactly what he is doing, Master Evans began descending the pyramid's stone steps. He held a box in his hand. His descent was slow, ceremonial, and measured. His young wife was at his side, her long, black hair gently blowing in the breeze.

When they finally reached the last step of the majestic Mayan pyramid, without saying a word, the people cleared a path for them, forming a circle around them that radiated outward for hundreds of yards. The sun was just about to sink below the horizon. The vision of that sea of humanity at dusk was breathtaking.

The Master saw Adam and Alexia and waved them over to join him. They smiled. They stood at either side of him, representing masculine and feminine energy.

The sky was a strange blend of colors. The sun glowed with strong yellows and oranges, mixed with shades of violet and gray. The people waited patiently and silently. There seemed to be no end to the human circle. Each person was a point of white light next to another white point, one cell next to another cell.

At Master Evans's signal, a group of musicians began to play tambors and didgeridoos, the most ancient musical instruments on the planet. The tambor symbolized the earth's heartbeat, while the didgeridoo represented the forces of the air, wind, and sky.

The ceremonial mood built in a gradual crescendo as more and more people arrived. The wisdom of the ancient sages was about to be dusted off, and unconsciousness would be cast out of a worldwide boat, floating incommunicado around the planet. Now only one kind of communication was possible: face to face, soul to soul. An uncertain future was just around the corner. No one knew exactly what was about to happen. Maybe there would be no future and no past, just the present.

After about ten minutes, the music stopped. Everyone felt the silence, full of life, a connecting bridge reaching inside of each person.

Master Evans began to speak, taking advantage of the stones' echo.

"*In Lakesh,*" he said in a strong voice, to which everyone responded in kind, a collective bolt of lightning.

He began the ritual with the traditional ancient Mayan greeting: "I am another you," meaning that everyone present was one and the same.

"Today we will begin the Star Fire Ritual. This is a critical moment for our survival and evolution. We are a unified force." He spoke slowly, his tone of voice conveying peace. "We are many bodies, many energies, many souls for one common intention."

Time had been speeding up and would continue to do so as the critical moment of dimensional change approached.

When the earth's pulse reached its zenith, the portal would open, establishing a frequency one octave higher, beginning another stage of creation and a new reality.

Evans looked out toward the horizon. He took a breath before continuing.

"The first step in our change may seem like chaos to you because the previous model of being has to dissolve itself before the new model can manifest. While the earth completes its work of giving birth, our DNA will transform. Over three days, we will prepare for the ascension. Three days to receive the power of the galactic serpent with conscious awareness, love, and serenity. Three days for the sun to enter into its spring."

His words electrified the vast crowd.

"The first phase of the ritual will be the Dance of the Feminine and Masculine," he went on in a deeply resonant voice. "Women will cease being women, and men will cease being men, to give way to the gods in power. Each physical body will move in harmony with the solar system, in harmony with Gaia, our Mother Earth, and with the sun.

"You will feel the dance awaken the power of the serpent, the power of sacred bioenergy. The quartz crystals you wear around your necks will begin to distill the essence of you: light. It will be the authentic light of what we are, and with that we will pass through the darkness."

No one made a sound. *Three days of darkness,* Adam echoed in his mind.

"After this process," the shaman continued, "all people will find their individuality inside of them. Beyond the mind's voices. Beyond the fears. It will be an intimate, conscious, revitalizing meeting."

Their collective breathing made a soft sound, the sound of life.

"No one can escape seeing his or her face in the Great Hall of Mirrors. It is a time of going deep inside to reconnect with your essence, with the same particle of the Fountain of Life that is inside each one of us."

Evans looked up to the sky.

"We will perform this ritual to understand what the change has in store. What the ancient wiremen called the Sixth Sun, our fountain of life over the galaxy will be crowned and raised up by the Force of Creation. We are in a magical place. The seat of the earth's feminine energy, the *itza*. From here, we put our hearts and souls in the service of the Source."

*The* itza *will awaken.*

Just then, the sky was washed in deep waves of magenta, the sun sank below the horizon, and they were plunged into total darkness.

## 91

# CHICHEN ITZA, DECEMBER 18, 2012

lthough normally the sun would have risen by then, it was still night. It was almost nine o'clock in the morning, and it was still dark. The huge group had spent the night meditating and dancing. When they fell asleep, some experienced astral projections in their dreams.

Adam and Alexia had fallen asleep holding hands. Adam sat up and took in a deep breath. The air felt warm.

Around the world, many people were truly terrified. They worried about the money they had in the bank, their families, their homes, their jobs. People who were ruled by habit and who thought of life as something secure suffered. Their belief system was crumbling.

Now people sensed that life was unpredictable, evolving. Many suffered because of what the earthquakes had destroyed and because their carefully laid plans for the future had gone up in smoke. But those who suffered the most were the ones who did not have any idea how to peer into the mirror of their soul. It was hardest for those who were always just looking for a good time, who didn't take care of their bodies and buried their emotions, who were driven by social convention, who put all their faith in money and power, people who found themselves faced for the first time with something they could not buy or acquire.

Adam saw Master Evans approach from the pyramid, along with three people accompanying him. The crowd was slowly waking up.

Evans said in a gentle tone, "Now we will begin the Ritual of Star Fire. Over the next three days, search deep in your hearts and prepare yourselves for the journey ahead."

Just then, a man standing behind the Master held out something covered by a beautiful blue cloth. Evans removed the cloth to reveal what was underneath.

The crowd gasped as the Philosopher's Stone, almost three feet high, with seven angles, was placed on the ground. The Master traced a large protective circle around it about fifteen feet in diameter and drew some symbols around the stone.

"The eye of consciousness," Adam said as the Master traced it in the dirt.

Alexia nodded.

The Master continued drawing symbols.

"He's drawing the symbols from the Atlantean tablet," Alexia said.

"He's activating the quartz," Adam affirmed.

Master Evans finished drawing and looked up at the sky. He touched the tip of the stone with his right hand and said a few words in a strange language. Then, raising his arms skyward, he said:

"This is the Philosopher's Stone that has been left to us by our Atlantean ancestors. We are ready to receive its power." His voice grew more resonant as he lowered his hands around the stone, not quite touching it, as if he were feeling its vibrational field. "We shall perform the final and most important part of the Secret Ritual. Its purpose is to generate a great serpentine spiral for the first who will undergo the vibrational ascension and then transmit this enormous human sun to everyone around the earth who is prepared to receive it."

*Sheldrake's theory!* Adam thought happily. The energy these one hundred thousand people gathered would spark a chain reaction in the consciousness of people all around the world. They would re-create the hundredth monkey theory.

Master Evans slowly stepped out of the circle. The Atlantean quartz was exquisitely beautiful, transparent, crystalline, immaculate. Twelve thousand years had passed. The quartz had evolved, like all minerals and metals, purifying its interior. Now in the middle of the ritual circle, it manifested all its inherent majesty and power. It rested on the earth, in close contact with the feminine principle, with its points facing up to the sky, receiving vibrations from the masculine principle, the sun.

An antenna between two worlds.

A connecting bridge.

"I'm starting to understand more now," Adam said to Alexia, who hadn't taken her eyes off of the Philosopher's Stone.

"Alexia, listen to me," he said, gently taking her hands in his.

She turned to face him, her eyes shining.

"I think I understand the reason for these three days of darkness," he said. "Remember the passage in the Bible where Lazarus is given up for dead inside a tomb?"

"Yes," she said. "Jesus calls out to Lazarus and gives him his life back after three days. It's the resurrection of Lazarus."

"I think it's symbolic and real at the same time," he said. "Why exactly three days? It's the same as what we're going through now."

She thought this over.

"And the same thing happened in ancient Egypt," Adam continued.

"In Egypt?"

"Yes. The spiritually initiated went into the pyramids and spent three days in darkness, meditating and listening to high-frequency sounds and vibrations before achieving enlightenment. It was a kind of spiritual alchemy. And the Mayans did the same thing in dark tunnels. Do you know why?" he asked, smiling.

"To gain self-knowledge?"

"Yes, but mostly because the pineal gland was activated with darkness," Adam said. "These three days of darkness are to produce melatonin, the hormone the ancient Greeks called ambrosia, 'the nectar of supreme excellence.'"

*If your eye was one, your body would be in the light.*

The words of Jesus reverberated like a cosmic echo in Adam's mind.

"Listen," Adam said firmly, "Jesus took three days to be resurrected. Horus, Dionysius, Mitra, and other Solar Messiahs had the same death and resurrection."

"Explain."

"They all had three days of darkness to restructure their DNA."

Alexia was thoughtful, remembering her father's project.

"Adam's secret...*the secretion of DNA.*"

## 92

# WASHINGTON, DECEMBER 18, 2012

**W**e are in God's hands," the president said sadly, looking defeated, as he headed into the secure bunker with his cabinet and family.

"I'd like to be alone for a moment," he'd told everyone earlier at the meeting in the White House.

He needed solitude and a chance for quiet reflection. He went to his office, poured himself a glass of water, and turned to the one place he felt he could find God. He took an illustrated, weighty copy of the Bible, sat down at his own chair, and opened the book at random, hoping to find some words of comfort.

But he didn't. In fact, his level of anxiety only rose after reading the passage on the page in front of him, Revelation 12, the woman and the dragon:

> *And a great portent appeared in heaven, a woman clothed with the sun, with the moon under her feet, and on her head a crown of twelve stars; she was with child and she cried out in her pangs of birth, in*

*anguish for delivery. And another portent appeared*
*in heaven; behold, a great red dragon, with seven*
*heads and ten horns, and seven diadems upon his*
*heads...*

He couldn't go on. He had to stop reading; his sharply
rising sense of alarm and uncertainty made his heart race. He
still had no inkling that those words symbolized something
even more profound.

# 93

## NASA HEADQUARTERS, DECEMBER 18, 2012

Everyone at NASA was completely baffled. The astronomers operating the few telescopes that still functioned simply could not believe what was happening to the planet.

Many satellites had malfunctioned and were no longer transmitting data. Others had fallen to Earth, having failed to predict or document the nuclear activity at the sun's center, much less how the great star, and the entire planet, had been plunged into darkness.

The entire team of scientists and technical specialists at NASA was at a total loss, completely paralyzed. They didn't even have any way to contact other scientific research groups around the world. All they could do was watch and wait.

Earth's magnetic field was changing, and darkness enveloped everything. The sun looked like an enormous circle of blackest night.

A young astronomer's eyes widened as he peered through the lens of a telescope and saw the alarming proximity of the ominous meteorite, though it was still thousands of miles away. Or more accurately, what appeared to be a meteorite—a tremendous ball of light traveling at thirty thousand miles per hour and heading straight for Earth.

"Oh my God!" he exclaimed in a panic. "Sir," he said to one of his superiors, "look at this."

The NASA department head looked into the telescope.

There was a chilling silence.

"It is very strange," he said, unsettled. "By its outward characteristics, it doesn't seem to be a meteorite or a comet."

Everyone around him exchanged puzzled looks.

"Then what is it?" the young astronomer asked.

His boss had his eyes trained on the threatening object.

Silence.

"I can't say with one hundred percent certainty, but I would swear…"

His voice trailed off. The tension in the room rose even higher.

"I would swear this is not a comet or a meteorite or anything like that…since in its center…there is no mass."

In his thirty-five years of experience, the astronomer had never seen anything remotely like it. He had never imagined he would ever say what he was about to say:

"The only thing we can be sure of is that it's an extremely rare stream of photons, of pure energy and light."

At other points around the world, other astronomers could also observe that intense concentration of light and energy, from Australia to Brazil. It was enormous and headed right at them.

And they couldn't tell anyone about it.

# 94

# CHICHEN ITZA, DECEMBER 20, 2012

The first two days of the Ritual of Star Fire were spent dancing, meditating, performing individual and group exercises, and in silence. The multitude generated an immense human heat and a sea of elevated energy. Those gathered felt as if their conscious awareness was opening to a new vision. Thousands of lit candles gently illuminated the magnificent, extraordinary, beautiful ceremony.

Evans told them that many who were gathered there, representing all of the countries of the world, blending the beauty of the black, white, red, and yellow races, were actually old Atlantean souls in search of final liberation.

Adam and Alexia were radiant, bursting with vitality. They felt a heightened capacity for energetic communication. A common vibration of unity and empathy circulated between them and the larger group.

"This is the last day of the ritual's final phase," Master Evans announced. "Today we will once again experience complete freedom, the final preparation before receiving the Great Day of Glory. Today, the Atlantean Philosopher's

Stone will give off all of its power, and everyone will feel the embrace of its energy.

"Today, the two principles of life will be one. The feminine, the eternal woman-goddess who dances and creates the magnetism of the universes, will join with the man-god who nourishes life with electricity. Now is the time to cast off our animal nature and go toward love as human beings and discover the new, our deepest dimension.

"This phase of the Ritual of Fire is called the Ritual of the Kiss of the Souls. Now face each other, sitting down with your legs crossed. Hold hands and bring your chests close together so that the quartz crystals will synchronize even more," the Master instructed. "Let your third eyes connect, with your foreheads continuously touching one another. The kiss of the souls."

In a state of intense focus, people began to approach each other, most of them strangers, and to connect through the power of the chakra between the eyes. The tambors and didgeridoos once again sounded strongly. It seemed as if the earth moved beneath them from the sheer power of their collective meditation. Gradually, the multitude went into a state of ecstasy.

Adam and Alexia felt an electrical charge travel from the tops of their heads down through the rest of their bodies. Then one wave after another of sensations, impulses, and biomagnetic currents emanated through their nervous systems.

"Begin to synchronize your breathing," the shaman directed. "Inhale and exhale the life that is within you. Nourish each other through your respiration. This makes us one single entity."

In pairs, everyone began breathing slowly and deeply. The sound of their collective deep breathing resonated, ebbing and flowing like a wave of life. They continued breathing like this for over twenty minutes.

"Now place your hand over the quartz on your partner's chest."

Instantly, over one hundred thousand people ceased to feel their physical bodies. They were pure energy, communicating in silence.

Adam and Alexia were no different. They joined together in a wave of energy and consciousness. The Atlantean Stone began generating even more light, taking on the appearance of a halogen lamp thousands of watts strong. The light began to extend outward, touching the whole crowd. Suddenly an immense, single light glowed.

The mass of initiates breathed collectively, distributing the energy through their quartz crystals and their pineal glands.

Evans continued to guide them in a low voice:

"The present moment, to be aware of the eternal now."

Light! They all felt a powerful jolt of light! Pure clarity deep inside! Their faces portrayed a transforming, all-consuming ecstasy. The last traces of ego were slipping away under the brilliant light that shone upon them all.

The light of consciousness.

*Is it not written in the Law? I said: you are gods.*

That was a new invitation to apotheosis, the initiation of a common man who becomes enlightened and discovers the power of God within himself. Adam was no longer Adam, Alexia was no longer Alexia. They were new beings, they were lights moving within a physical body, they were each other and all of the others, they were one.

Adam felt an electrical current surge up from his sex to the crown of his head; Alexia, from below her pubis, vibrated with orgasmic intensity. She, an ancestral goddess, the incarnation of feminine fire, joined with Adam's energy. Their bodies completed the ritual, coming together in a heated embrace, chest to chest, as pleasure inundated all of the pores of their skin down to their very cells.

*And the serpent said to the woman: Surely you shall not die, for the Elohim know that the day you eat of him your eyes will be open and you shall be as gods, knowing good and evil.*

Through that encounter, their life energy and their spiritual and sexual energy were transformed. The journey of serpentine energy was underway. That symbolic serpent was not an enemy, it was not tempting; rather, it was pure sexual energy fully channeled through the body and the DNA.

*When you unite male and female as one, then you will enter the kingdom.*

More than an hour after the sacred ritual had concluded, they all collapsed onto the grass, and the earth cradled them in her warm embrace.

They were ready to receive whatever may come.

# 95

## DECEMBER 21, 2012

The dawn of that so-long-anticipated day brought with it a very pleasing surprise:

The sun.

The star had returned, giving off the same radiant light as always.

Around the world, the mood was expectant and disconcerted. Was it over? Would the darkness return? Many people were terrified; some had even committed suicide. Everyone anxiously awaited what would happen next.

In London, Kate, Dr. Kruger, the children, and a hundred others were gathered in a collective, receptive state. They meditated over their quartz crystals, feeling a strong current of peace and relaxation. Other meditation groups empowered their inner selves and their genetic codes.

When the sun shone on Chichen Itza, that day's dawn was a golden ray reflected in the eyes of the thousands gathered there. Everyone waited for the final outcome.

Adam and Alexia gazed with wonder at the sun's new palate of colors. They'd never seen it like that. It rose above the horizon after the third day of darkness. The earth was enter-ing the state of cosmic alignment.

Master Evans began the day raising his arms to the sky. Everyone was completing the initiation into the great myster-ies of life.

Suddenly, something very unexpected began to occur. The earth, the great big blue and green orb, began to vibrate. A vibration that grew stronger, shaking its very core.

The earth moved again, this time as if it would swal-low everything that could be found over its surface. Some of the most active volcanoes on the planet began to erupt. The earth was also about to initiate a profound change, a powerful orgasm—an explosion of power.

Silence. Tremors. Silence.

The planet was showing itself for what it was, a living thing immersed in movements of creation and destruction, with awesome convulsions. The sun sent it a beam of light, heat, and fire.

What had at first been taken for a meteorite, a comet, a rock that would destroy the earth, a planet off its course, fast approached. As it made contact with the earth's atmosphere, it opened up in a great spiral, completely wrapping around the earth, changing its skin. The entire globe was bathed in that rain of photons, light, and energy.

Just then, that blanket of light lit up in all the colors of the rainbow and vibrated. At the same time, the volcanoes' activity grew even more intense, shaking the ground. Chichen Itza vibrated too, and up high, on the rocks of the pyramid, a serpent of light and shadows formed on one of its sides.

Adam and Alexia looked at each other with endless love in their eyes.

Suddenly, a collective vibration ran through the crowd, like a magnet, pulling them toward a circle of light. It was as if a door opened. Everyone turned to see the huge portal.

It was the portal to a higher dimension.

Ascension.

There, in that group, there was a higher power. There was no more fear or anguish. They were prepared to ascend up into the unknown, into a new dimension.

The evolution of the soul.

The portal could be seen from everywhere in the world. Immense, beautiful, immaculate, profound, mysterious, alluring.

Master Evans held his right arm out toward the portal's entrance. The vast throng stretched out their hands toward the immense circle of light. People began to slowly be absorbed into the light, one at a time, fully consciously. Those who entered the portal could no longer be seen by the physical eye.

Adam and Alexia were about to go into the portal. They looked into each other's eyes just as a powerful force made the ground under Chichen Itza shake.

*And* itza *will awaken.*

As a caterpillar emerges from its cocoon transformed into a butterfly, the multitude felt reborn. And a brilliant light reflected from inside the Atlantean quartz. The ancient Philosopher's Stone shone at its brightest, and an expansive wave undulated outward to all of the initiates.

What an explosion of light!

What a sight!

Adam felt all of his limits finally falling away. Alexia felt she was a drop of water falling into the ocean, melding with it All.

*Because many are called, but few are chosen.*

People went into the portal from different points all around the world. It was as if everything vibrating at a higher frequency was literally drawn into the portal's vibration and the collective enlightenment.

The transition to a new dimension had begun.

# 96

## ROME, DECEMBER 21, 2012

Cardinal Tous could not repent enough. His tears had opened up the deep well of pain he had hidden behind his rigid mask of power. He'd taken the wrong path, and his tears were the remnants of the ego he had basked in his entire life, immersed in the all-consuming pursuit of power and ambition. He had hidden behind his priestly robes, false prestige, an institution.

He had dominated his fellow man through pain and arrogance.

And what of happiness?

And joy?

And innocence?

And loving one's self, and loving others?

He had forgotten it all. He had lost himself.

He was like so many others who had wasted the treasure of life, that magical succession of experiences of freedom and growth. He was like so many who had obsessed over a future that never arrived, or a political party, or blind fanaticism. Those lost souls would not embark on the journey.

This was not a punishment, it was simply that *they were not able* to reach the higher vibratory frequency. It could not be bought. Man's worst enemy, fear, was still holding Cardinal Tous back.

*Like attracts like,* as the old saying went. Though it was too late now, Tous painfully remembered:

*It is better to prepare yourselves, than to have the Kingdom of Heaven take you by surprise.*

He had not prepared himself spiritually. The dead rituals, the egotistical acts of charity, the empty sermons, the false façade did not count.

His ego had to evolve, like everyone else's. He had to make his own path toward the light.

His nervous system could not withstand the intensity of the rising vibrations. Like many others who vibrate in dissonance with the energy of the cosmos, his heart, nervous system, and lungs felt an excruciating pain and pressure. He exhaled his last breath, expelling his agony.

His soul embarked on a very different journey.

## 97

# TRANSITION TOWARD THE PORTAL: THE CATERPILLAR BECOMES A BUTTERFLY

The portal continued to open up like a flower of life in a movingly beautiful display. Dancing colors blended together in endless variety; the colors *were* life, the result of the original light.

Just as the Mayan calendar had foretold, the End of Time simply meant the beginning of a reality where time ceased to exist. Time was tied to three-dimensional reality and the mind, and now the mind had no limits. People could see the different layers of energy emanating from the physical body, its ethereal vibration from the new completely activated DNA.

*Homo sapiens* no longer existed.

Their time had come to an end.

And there, as the earth roiled, the enlightened ones gave birth to the new *Homo universales.*

# 98

# INSIDE THE PORTAL, A TIMELESS WORLD

Everyone radiated an iridescent beauty. Their faces gave off a glow of perpetual youth. Thousands and thousands of transformed beings gathered in a joyful celebration. No simple human emotion could hold the new state of consciousness. Many children had been among the first to ascend to the new dimension.

*Love*, Adam felt, directing his feelings toward Alexia.

*Love*, she felt, turning to face the multitude, only to find that everyone was feeling the same thing.

Everyone was in love with everyone.

It was like the sun, shining its light in all directions equally, not just toward one place.

Everyone had the same warm glow emanating from his or her very essence. There were no races, there was just *one* race, with some variations within it. They were still individuals, with consciousness, but they were all part of a great unity that vibrated in the atmosphere and inside each of them. Their bodies were surrounded by a bright mist of light particles. They emanated grandiosity, endless possibility, power, infinity.

There was an intrinsic order that everyone perceived, but they were at the beginning of a new phase, waiting for the new reality to establish itself. *Humanity* was now *universality*.

*You have an exquisite smile*, Adam said, noting that he did not have to open his mouth to speak. He transmitted his thought telepathically, with no effort at all.

Their light and energy came together in a new embrace. Then they perceived something entirely new: the internal sense.

People they knew began to approach them, vibrating at the same frequency. Kate, Kruger, and Jacinto came over, overflowing with light, and they all melded into a collective embrace.

*Alexia! Adam!* Kruger transmitted to them, *This is magical!*

They had no need for words. Their joy and telepathy were their common language. They could travel to wherever they wanted to go simply by thinking it. They began to understand new laws of consciousness.

A strong presence appeared behind them.

They all turned to face the magnetic force pulling them.

*Hello, Alexia.* With immense love, the energy behind them greeted her.

Alexia felt all of her chakras vibrate with intense happiness. The golden circle of light crowning her head grew even brighter, and she felt it raise her up.

*Papa!*

The luminous presence of Aquiles opened his arms, inviting her to join him in a hug. The two essences fused together. The love of father and daughter was now something else, an embrace of two equal beings.

Adam felt a warm presence tug at him.

Suddenly, his father, Nikos Roussos, emerged.

*Papa! You're here too!*

Nikos smiled.

*Yes, Adam. We're all here! We always have been; it's just that you couldn't see it with your eyes. Now, the dimensions are visible.*

Adam and Alexia were exultant.

Nikos and Aquiles had given them a very unexpected gift. The emotions of the two old friends erupted in brilliant light. The new law of that state of consciousness was that the light grew more powerful when it was fueled by love.

Adam emitted a vibration through his thought, and they all caught the same communication frequency, thinking simultaneously:

*There is no death!*

Adam smiled, his face resplendent. He looked around to see how so many were reuniting with loved ones from their old lives on Earth.

It was a celebration.

# 99

A strong presence surged from the horizon. A vast number of lights came into view. Thousands of circles of light filled the sky. It was like a flock of thousands of luminous birds approaching.

Adam shared a thought with everyone:

*And then they will come bearing the sign of the future, the men of the sun.*

They were oval-shaped space ships, gathered in a gigantic circle above them all. A door opened on one of them, and the people heard a sweet sound coming from within, like a woman's voice.

*This is a new reality*, it said in a beautiful vibration. *Welcome to enlightenment.*

It was a supremely beautiful feminine presence, bathed in lights and color, transmitting her vibrational thought to everyone:

*We are as happy as all of you that you were able to pass through the portal and ascend to the new dimension. You will need to be in tune with the truth and integrity of your new state of being. Your new reality will bring many surprises. Your new genetic code will grant you comprehension. This reconnection with the universe is a gift from the Life Source that has created us all.*

*We are beings from Sirius, the Pleiades, and the Orion constellation. We are your older brothers and sisters in this galaxy. We have been waiting for you to evolve for a long time in Earth years, but it was too difficult for you to understand our relationship through your former level of consciousness. We could not change the course you were on. We have always been close by, but your eyes on Earth could not see us. Now the biggest secret of all can be revealed. You are eternal beings, changing forms. Evolving beside the Life Source, or what you mistakenly called God, a belief that generated so much conflict. But now, in this dimension, you will begin to understand the universe does not exist over time. It is eternal, forever. You will progressively understand this new facet.*

The multitude was ecstatic. The voice resonated in its feminine cadence throughout the farthest reaches of the New Earth.

*The universe is a cosmic creation sustained in the consciousness of All*, she continued. *The Life Source creates through consciousness an infinite number of universes, which exist and are regenerated; for the Source, the creation, development, decay, and death of a million universes means nothing more in time than what would be the blink of an eye to you. The infinite consciousness of All is the matrix of the cosmos. In the consciousness of the Mother-Father, the children are in their home. There is no one without a father and mother in the universe. The Life Source is in everything, and in life, nothing is at rest; everything moves; everything vibrates.*

*Everything has a dual nature; everything has two poles. Everything has its opposite; everything ebbs and flows; everything ascends and descends; every cause has its effect; every effect has its cause; everything happens according to the law of the cosmos, the original order. Everything has its masculine and feminine principle; gender is manifested in all planes of existence.*

*Since you are co-creators, everything is available; the Life Source does nothing more than destroy the old and construct the new. You have emerged from a state of unconsciousness. Now you are masters and gods in communion with the light. Now you are completely free.*

After transmitting this thought, the higher dimensional beings from Sirius and Orion began to emerge from their spaceships. They were tall, luminous, and powerful.

The feminine being who had addressed them came down along with other resplendent beings. They revealed that thousands of years ago, the Life Source had charged them with planting the seeds of three-dimensional intelligent life on the planet Earth, crossing *Homo neanderthalensis* with their own advanced, higher dimensional DNA, resulting in the species that was *Homo sapiens*.

The *Homo sapiens* were the only ones who wouldn't know there was life and existence on various levels and in different dimensions. That had been the great mystery throughout their long history as a species.

Adam, Alexia, and all of the new universal humanity joyously understood the Divine Plan and the generosity of the Original Cosmic Consciousness.

After that first encounter, a door opened on the biggest spaceship of them all. A multitude of brilliant, immaculate, angelic, beautiful energies spread out like a fan. Thousands of enlightened beings formed an enormous circle. From its center, an energy even more powerful than all the others, shining extremely brightly, rose up to address them.

*The promise has been fulfilled at last*, he communicated to the throng below.

They were all awestruck by that presence: magnetism without equal, a current of universal love, a vibration of supreme pleasure. They all felt the same jolt of powerful emotion spread through the fibers of consciousness in a strong vibratory impact. An irresistible power of attraction emanated from that luminous being, holding them all in his embrace, touching the very essence of their beings.

*The last Solar Messiah is here*, the feminine being who had addressed them before communicated, with solemn veneration. *You knew him by an earthly name, although we know him by another one.*

Everyone knew who it was immediately.

It was Jesus.

# Epilogue

## The New Reality, a Universe with No Limits

L
ove was all that existed.

Its energy circulated at every moment, in many different forms. The present moment *was* Love. It wasn't a love toward someone or something, it was the intrinsic nature of the universe. A perfume that floated in the air.

Love's only objective was to grow, multiply, and reach out.

The new *Homo universales* lived to create, feel, evolve, and share on a spiritual, sexual, and loving level, connecting with one another in a warm embrace to fill each other with light. They made the act of love a work of art, a sacred event.

The true meaning of Elohim had manifested: the union of the feminine-masculine. That was the change, marking the new humanity's infancy, and it would grow and mature, so they could interact with other evolved civilizations throughout the universe.

Individuals felt like universal beings. They had no trace of ego or separatism. The new beings shared their happiness, their art, dance, intelligence, love, and the joy of knowing they were creatures created by an amazing universe with thousands and thousands of galaxies available to go to once they finished their new phase of evolution on the New Earth. Individuals used their imagination, intuition, and intention to manifest everything they wanted to create.

The sense of death completely disappeared. All beings saw with their eye of consciousness the soul leaving one body to be born into another. They maintained their connections to one another, knowing that later they would meet again as eternal souls in new bodies.

The love for the cosmos within each of them was expressed by caring for and loving everything. No one experienced any pain; it was simply not possible. Everything was connected on the spiritual level, and life was a delightful celebration.

The new beings had discovered the secret of their origins, their DNA unfurled in all of its glorious power, their connection with the Life Source that had chosen to share itself in countless forms through the original big bang. A cosmic respiratory cycle that paved the way for a new inhalation and exhalation, to replenish itself over and over again—forever.

And that was the change of the new *Homo universales*, unlocking the most tantalizing secret that had been hidden for millennia.

They discovered who they were.

They discovered where they had come from.

They discovered Adam's secret.

*And there will be signs in sun and moon and stars, and upon the earth distress of nations in perplexity at the roaring of the sea and the waves, men fainting with fear and with foreboding of what is coming on the world; for the powers of the heavens will be shaken. And then they will see the Son of man coming in a cloud with power and great glory. Now when these things begin to take place, look up and raise your heads, because your redemption is drawing near.*

—Luke 21:25–28

# How to Program a Quartz Crystal

1. Find a white quartz with **six or seven** sides, approximately three inches high.
2. Wash it with water and coarse salt, or if possible in seawater.
3. Let it rest in the sun for one day.
4. After it has been charged with solar energy for a day, find a quiet spot and sit down—in a chair or preferably in the lotus position—keeping your back straight, gazing toward the sun.
5. Hold the quartz in your hands. Close your eyes and feel its vibration. Make friends with it.
6. Hold your left hand out horizontally at the middle of your chest, and with your right hand place the quartz in your left palm.
7. Inject your idea inside of the quartz through your third eye. Establish a bridge between your thoughts in the middle of your forehead and the quartz.
8. Once you sense the thought inside the quartz, place your right hand as if it were a lid over the quartz, with both hands holding the quartz inside.
9. Hold it for several minutes. Breathe through your nose slowly and deeply, with your eyes closed. Go into a

meditative state. Bring your mind into a state of complete connection, your brain in an alpha-wave pattern.

10. Now connect where the quartz is, at the center of your chest near the fourth chakra, directly toward the center of the sun. Travel through your imagination from your heart to the sun.

11. Once you feel a pathway of light, continue on the journey from the sun's center to the center of the galaxy—a distance of twenty-seven thousand light years that you can quickly span with your imagination. As Albert Einstein said, "Logic will get you from A to B. Imagination will take you everywhere."

12. After a minute, return from the center of the galaxy to the sun.

13. After another minute, go from the sun back to the center of your heart.

14. The quartz is now in alignment with cosmic power, your heart, and the source of all things.

15. Take a moment before moving out of your position, or continue meditating.

16. Put your quartz in a peaceful place, preferably in sunlight, and carry it with you in your pocket or handbag. Avoid contact with telephones or metals. You do not have to reprogram it every day—only if you want to inject it with new thoughts. You can program as many thoughts as you like.

17. Make sure you focus on collective enlightenment the first time you program it. Everything else is extra. Start telling your friends about it. Give them a copy of this book and a new quartz, to fulfill Sheldrake's law.

18. Project collective strength each time you practice your personal meditation. Around the world, many other people will be making the same vibrational contact. In that way, people on the same wavelength attract each other.

# AFTERWORD FROM THE AUTHOR

# WHAT WE CANNOT SEE AND WHAT HAS BEEN FORGOTTEN

Our universe (if we can even call it ours) is a wondrous, beautiful, largely unknown space, immeasurable and infinite. It is infinite in the sense that we have not found any end as far as we can see, going up, down, or to the left or right of us.

It is home to billions of stars, galaxies, planets, asteroids, black holes, supernovas—a marvelous array of creations of many colors and forms. If we were to travel throughout the Milky Way, we would find two hundred billion stars. To the human eye this is gigantic, impossibly vast.

Our sun, illuminating all the planets of the solar system dancing around it, is within the Milky Way. To our eyes, the astral king is an immense focal point of energy, light, and heat, but really it's just a small star. There are stars hundreds and even thousands of times bigger.

Small or large, the sun is the source of life on Gaia, the planet we call Earth. The ancient Greeks called the earth Gea or Gaya, and considered it the goddess mother or the great goddess, the foundation of life as we know it in the third dimension.

The solar system is made up of the planets Mercury, Venus, Earth, Mars, Jupiter, Saturn, Uranus, Neptune, and up until just a few years ago, Pluto, all with the names of Roman gods. And this planetary system belongs to just *one* galaxy. There are *ten billion* galaxies like ours. It is beyond our comprehension to even fully imagine so much space and so much creation.

Everything is in motion. Everything has its cycles. There are meteor crashes, the birth and death of stars; there are so many things happening in the universe that we don't know about, and astronomers do what they can to find out. Scientists have discovered that other constellations and planets exist as far as twenty, thirty, or even one hundred million light years away. By 2007, they had identified 270 extra-solar planets, almost all larger in size than Jupiter.

We may think of the universe as this vast "out there." But what would happen if humans were like a single cell inside the body that can't see what's "outside" of it? Or like a fish that can't get out of the water to see other worlds and other realities? For example, a shark can't ever understand the broad range of life that exists outside of its own habitat. It knows nothing of palm trees, mountains, or volcanoes. There are a very few species like crabs, seals, or crocodiles who can pass from one world to another, moving between the land and the water, like going from one dimension to another. Still, a crab will never travel on its own power to the top of Mount Everest, or the Acropolis, or the pyramids in Egypt.

We could be in the same position as the crab regarding the universe and other life forms. Among the human species, over the course of our long history, there were people like crabs, seals, or crocodiles, who have had "visions" of other realities; who could be in one plane of existence and another, which for us would be like passing from the third dimension into higher dimensions. These "crab men" could project their consciousness into different realities and see just a few palm trees on the next beach over. They were wise men, prophets, seers.

The Mayans were such seers. They predicted a great change for 2012.

The Mayans were a civilization with enlightened, wise, and scientifically advanced people. They said that the universe was a living thing. And just as the human body has its process of inhaling and exhaling through the lungs' movement and the systole and diastole of the heart, the universe has cycles that we could think of similar to the respiratory cycle. With mathematical precision, they predicted many things.

The first Mayan prophecy stated that the "time of no-time" would arrive, a period of twenty years that they called a *katun*. The last twenty years of this great solar cycle of 5,125 years began in 1992 and will end in 2012. The Mayans prophesized that increasingly intense solar winds would appear. And beginning in 1992, the human race would enter into a final period of great learning and discovery.

The second prophecy affirmed that the behavior of the entire human race would quickly change after the solar eclipse of August 11, 1999; they said on this day, a ring of fire would be seen in the sky; it was an eclipse wholly without precedent in history, as the center of Earth aligned with the cosmic cross. Almost all the planets of the solar system were positioned within four signs of the zodiac, Leo, Taurus, Scorpio, and Aquarius, coinciding with the signs of the four gospels of the Bible and the four horsemen of the Apocalypse—from the Greek *Apokálypsis*, meaning "what is revealed" and which is widely misinterpreted as *destruction*. The Mayans predicted that 1999 would be the beginning of an age of rapid change necessary to renovate human society and ideologies.

The third Mayan prophecy says that a heat wave would raise Earth's temperature, causing climate, geological, and social changes on an unprecedented scale and at a dizzying pace. The Mayans said the rise in temperature would be due to a combination of various factors, including man, who, being out of sync with nature, can only generate processes of self-destruction. And another major factor was the sun, which would accelerate its activity because of an increase in its vibratory frequency, in turn raising levels of radiation and Earth's temperature.

The fourth prophecy affirms that the rise in temperature caused by man's anti-environmental behavior and the sun's increased activity would cause the polar ice caps to melt. If the sun raises its level of activity significantly higher than normal, there will be more solar winds, more solar flares, and rising levels of radiation and temperature on the planet.

As documented in the Dresden codex, every 117 rotations of Venus, the sun suffers serious changes, which appear as giant sunspots or eruptions of solar winds. They warned that every 5,125 years, even greater alterations would be seen. When this happens, man needs to be alert, for it is an omen of radical changes and destruction. (Modern-day scientists assert the sun's largest coronal mass ejections will occur during 2011 and 2012.)

The fifth Mayan prophecy says that all systems based on fear, on which our civilization has been founded, will be transformed, in the planet and in man, to give way to a new harmonious reality. Man has mistakenly believed that the universe exists only for him, that humans are the only expression of intelligent life, and as a result he acts as a predator of everything. These belief systems will crumble so man can confront himself, finally seeing the necessity of reorganizing society and continuing on a path of spiritual evolution that will lead us to an understanding of creation. At this time, virtually all of the economies of the world will be in a state of crisis. Man must go into the "great hall of mirrors" to truly see his own face.

The sixth Mayan prophecy says that over the next few years, a comet will appear whose trajectory could threaten man's very existence. The Mayans viewed comets as agents of change that would shake up existential equilibrium so that certain structures would transform, allowing the collective consciousness to evolve.

The seventh Mayan prophecy tells us of the moment when the solar system, in its cyclical revolution, emerges from the galactic night to enter into the dawn. This prophecy predicted that in the thirteen years from 1999 until 2012, the light emitted from the center of the galaxy would synchronize all living things and enable them to voluntarily undergo a process of internal transformation, opening them to new realities. It mentions that all people will have the opportunity to change and break through their limitations, acquiring a new sense: communication through thought. People who voluntarily seek out their internal state of peace, raising their energy levels and tuning their inner vibrational frequency from fear to love, will be able to receive thoughts from others and express themselves telepathically, ingraining and firmly establishing the new sense.

We are at the cusp of tremendous change.

# ABOUT THE AUTHOR

 Guillermo Ferrara is a writer and research-er of ancient civilizations and cultures. An expert in Eastern philosophy, mysti-cism, and relevant scientific and spiritual systems, Ferrara has authored nineteen books on personal growth that have been translated into German, French, Chinese, English, Greek, Romanian, and Serbian. He lectures and gives workshops around the world about brain and DNA activation, crystals, yoga, and meditation. He works as a columnist and contributor for several TV and radio programs, as well as print media, and he was the founder and editor of *Terapias Naturales*. He was once a professional basketball player in his native Argentina. Ferrara has traveled throughout Mexico, Spain, Colombia, Germany, London, Greece, Argentina, and several US cities to conduct research for *Adam's Secret*.

www.facebook.com/AdamsSecret
www.twitter.com/GuilleFerrara

## About the Translator

Diane Stockwell has translated a wide range of commercial fiction and nonfiction. She is also the owner and principal agent at Globo Libros Literary Management, a literary agency with a special emphasis on books by and for Hispanics in the United States. She lives with her husband and son in New York City.

Made in the USA
San Bernardino, CA
15 September 2013